JAY TINSIANO

Pandora Red

First published by Dark Paradigm Publishing in 2018

Second Edition

ISBN: 978-1-9997232-3-1

This book was professionally typeset on Reedsy.
Find out more at reedsy.com

Please note: This book uses British English spelling and terms. Readers who are used to American English might notice a difference in the spelling or usage of some words. For example: tyres (instead of tires), boot (instead of trunk), and trainers (instead of sneakers).

All characters are entirely fictitious and not intended to portray any real person(s), dead or alive.

Thanks

Dedicated to my late father.

With thanks to:

Jay Newton who helped guide Pandora Red from the first draft, through extensive rewrites and the final hurdle. Jay has acted as an excellent editor and head beta reader as well as playing a major role in this project.

Cate Hogan was an excellent editor as always and helped make Pandora Red a much better final book.

Matt Fletcher offered invaluable insights into, not just the technical aspects but the story as a whole.

I would also like to thank our other team of beta readers.

Newsletter

To join the Jay Tinsiano reading group head to:
www.jaytinsiano.com/newsletter

- Free Books and stories
- Previews and Sneak Peeks
- Exclusive material

"The technotronic era involves the gradual appearance of a more controlled society. Such a society would be dominated by an elite, unrestrained by traditional values. Soon it will be possible to assert almost continuous surveillance over every citizen and maintain up-to-date complete files containing even the most personal information about the citizen. These files will be subject to instantaneous retrieval by the authorities."

Zbigniew Brzezinski.

1

March 1999. GCHQ Cheltenham, England.

Sarah Edwards glanced at the wall clock, noting it was 23:17 hours. Nearly time. The plan was to get started as the shifts changed to the night staff. During late shifts, the hexagon shaped green building, flanked by prison-like towers, had the feeling of a ship silently moving through the night. There was a faded sound, like a distant roar from outside the double glazed windows of her office, a downpour of rain Sarah could see coming down in sheets from an external building light.

The main GCHQ building was planted in the sprawl of the Oakley site in Cheltenham, England, where she had been an employee for six years. As Intelligence liaison officer, Sarah had access to top secret information that would never become public, even under the official secrets act. The glass walls of her office reflected artificial light across the floor and she glanced outside into the main section once again. A few people were still milling around, their flickering screens displaying worldwide operation updates, while the central heating hummed in the background. She moved her slight figure back into the large swivel chair and tapped once again on the keyboard, logging herself out of the main network. To access and copy the information meant using another terminal on the floor above.

Sarah cast her eyes around the office for the last time. The feeling weighed heavily that after tonight, she would possibly never see her family, her friends, or anyone she cared about again. She wouldn't be able to say goodbye either, that was the most painful part of it. For the last three months, she had churned the decision over and over in her mind and kept arriving at the same conclusion.

She put on her jacket, grabbed her bag, and slipped out across the thick carpet along the corridor, caged by metal and glass partitions that seemed to go on forever. Her feet quickly ascended the metal steps at the end, the echoes adding to her anxiety as she left G block and an entire lifetime behind her. No more after work drinks with the boys. No chinwags with her friend in the service, Janet Chambers. How surreal it would all soon seem.

She could only imagine the shock of her colleagues when the news spread about what she had done. They would understand, in time. Surely they would?

In a few years, this site would be empty of its machines, the people and the families in the housing complex would all be moved to the new GCHQ location at Benhall. The new 'doughnut' shaped complex would be state of the art at the cost of hundreds of millions and Sarah knew the security would be much tighter there, another reason to act now.

A quick flash of her identity card on the wall scanner and she was allowed through to the floor above. It would only be a matter of time before her access and subsequence actions were traced back to her but by then, all shit would have hit the fan and it wouldn't matter anymore.

Even now, it wasn't too late and she could still turn back. She could leave the building as normal and continue her life, keep her friends, and stay in touch with her family. She shook that idea out of her head quickly. This was no time for second thoughts or doubt. It seemed like a dream but she steeled herself and pressed on across the carpeted floor that hosted rows of cubicles, a haphazard mix of screens that flickered in the darkness as if watching her progress. The truth must be leaked, no matter what the consequences.

She stopped at a monitor, sat down, and quickly typed in her login and encrypted password to access the main system. There seemed to be a temporary freeze on the screen and Sarah frowned while she waited.

'Access Denied' flashed at her in large letters on the monitor.

She cursed under her breath. There was no logical reason she would be denied access at this level. Sarah retyped, her fingers stumbling across the keyboard, and she hit return to see the same 'Access Denied' once more.

Come on, Sarah, keep it together!

Slowly, she re-typed, voicing the letters and numbers in her head and breathed a sigh of relief as the familiar green coded access came up. She carefully plugged in the thumb drive that had been meticulously moulded to look like a keyless entry remote for a Honda Accord Acura TL, the exact same car she owned. It had been made through a contact that she had outside of the agency. Working with those outside the law had its benefits and discretion was essential.

She immediately hit the shortcut keys to launch the Shell access command line and typed in a sequence to bypass the computer's automatic security scan of her device.

Once again, she needed to fill in her login credentials to the remote server and then the black console screen filled with a fast moving list of file names as they copied from the 'Project Oculus' folder.

These were the very same files that she had found and read with increasing alarm and exasperation over the previous months. She had not liked what she saw one bit.

"Good evening," the voice came from behind her, making her gasp out loud. Game over, before she had even started. The sounds of the footsteps grew nearer and she spun around, squinting at the night guard. He smiled at her, nodded, and walked on by. Sarah felt her heart pumping so loud, she was sure he could hear it. "Good evening," she replied.

Time slowed down, the file transfer was still reeling through its list and there was nothing Sarah could do to speed things up. There were a lot of files to copy.

She thought about her mother and father, seeing life drift by from their Brighton semi with a fine view of the sea and the pier. Had she really forsaken them? Would she really never see them again? Sarah refused to believe that. She would find a way.

She remembered first seeing the GCHQ advert in the newspaper. It was a test to find an apprentice and Sarah's mother had encouraged her to apply. Sarah had always been top of her classes, wiping the floor with everyone else and her future glittered like gold. But dark shadows loomed in the corners of her memory: the bullying. There were a few in her class who had targeted her. She could only guess it was because of her intelligence or maybe the social inadequacy.

The only thing she lived for was her studying, the knowledge that she so eagerly soaked up like a sponge and the books she buried herself in.

She passed the test, a puzzle to decode a series of seemingly random letters and then after a yearlong selection process, began her intelligence career, working in the foreign sources section and then later transferring to anti-terrorism monitoring.

It was at the 'firm' she met her first real friends. For the most part, anyway. There were a few comments from some of the male colleagues, but all in all, it was like a family. Besides, Sarah had always seen herself as a trailblazer, working hard to fight her way into a male-dominated environment.

A beep sounded and the copy was complete. She took the drive and slipped it inside her bag then typed in: *sfc /purgecache* in the command line to delete the cache and dump any record of her folder access before shutting down the workstation. She didn't want to leave unnecessary breadcrumb trails.

Sarah braced herself for getting out of the building. For obvious security reasons, no files of any kind were allowed to leave the walls of GCHQ. She knew the routine and just hoped she had thought of everything. There was a risk. There always was.

She moved quickly now, passing the endless monitors, workstations, and desks that seemed to blur past her. She rode the lift down to the ground floor, taking even, deep breaths to calm her nerves. The lift opened and she walked up to a set of double doors, passing her entry card over the scanner, which opened them with a gentle hiss.

Without hesitation, she stepped through and placed her leather handbag with the car key lob inside onto the x-ray scanner conveyor that was manned by Gilly, the elderly night security man. He smiled at Sarah and briefly glanced at the monitor that exposed the contents of her bag. It was a well-worn routine.

"It's a bit late for you, innit, love?" he asked in his thick welsh accent.

Sarah smiled weakly at him, the thumping in her chest once again seemingly growing louder with each beat as she brushed a strand of light brown hair behind her ear. "The devil's work is never done," she heard herself say.

She stepped through the frame of a large metal detector, not unlike those in airports and held her breath as she did so. Despite there being nothing incriminating on her person, the prospect of the alarm sounding haunted her. To her relief, no alarms were triggered and she stood at the end of the conveyor, waiting.

Gilly adjusted glasses on his wide face and scrutinised the monitor and shapes of items inside her bag; her purse, cosmetics, notepad, the Honda key-less entry remote...

He glanced at her for a moment, a hint of regret on his wrinkled face and sighed.

"I'm really sorry, luv, but I have to do a random check. You know how it goes."

Sarah stared at him for a second, half thinking he was joking and then realised he wasn't. She had only been subject to a couple of random checks in her whole time there and it had barely registered as a concern in her planning. Did he know something? It wasn't possible.

His face then turned into a grin, trying to make light of it. "It's your lucky night, obviously."

Sarah then managed a smile in return but it was not good news. A random check meant a more thorough search and possibly a body check. The risk factor was rising.

"It's no problem. You've got a job to do," she said evenly.

The handbag came through and the guard began to take out the items one by one, placing them on a long table. Sarah fixed her eyes on the contents of her bag as he checked; looking inside the cosmetics pouch, flipping through the notepad at her meaningless scribbles. Most of the items had been placed in there for show; the plan always being to mix everything up in the bag. There were also random items such as food receipts or a tube of mints thrown in for good measure. She wondered if the cosmetics were overkill, especially as she barely ever wore much makeup.

His hands reached for the key lob and he picked it up, spinning it around in his fingers for a moment.

"Any weekend plans?" she asked, a forced cheery ring to her voice.

The guard turned and grinned again.

"At the allotment if it's not raining but we'll be lucky, won't we? It's bound to rain, innit?"

"Almost definitely," she said, clenching her fists inside her jacket pockets.

He sighed as if regretting something and began placing the items back in the bag and handed it to her.

"Have a lovely evening now," he said. She took the bag and smiled in genuine relief. "You, too. Fingers crossed for the weather."

The rain-washed streets cast reflections from the street lamps, the echo of Sarah's footfall bouncing off the walls of red-brick houses lining the complex where the GCHQ employees had built their lives. No one was out at that hour and a quietness hung in the air like a blanket.

No more friends.

She unlocked the front door to her cosy 2-bedroom semi where she had lived for almost seven years.

No more family.

Grabbing the large holdall bag that waited in the hall, she then walked to her Honda Accord parked in the driveway and slung it into the boot. There was no point in going back to the house. Everything she could think of had been done, cleaned down, or shredded. Anything she had not wanted them to find had been taken to the landfill, five miles away. Her entire life was now in one bag.

The car weaved its way past the red brick houses and grey block buildings, away from the complex and toward Cheltenham train station.

2

Frank was running across the underground concourse, weaving over the charred bodies, victims of some kind of fire. Their dark shapes seemed to melt into the polished marble floor and the inky black liquid congealed around his feet, making it more and more difficult to run. His pursuer's heavy breathing was close behind, yet he dared not look.

The lift service hatch was just ahead, yellow and black stripes beckoning - his escape route clearly marked. And now, worse still, the arms of the dead, constrained by the dark liquid, seemed to move and reach for him, their bony blackened hands gripping at his legs and feet. Frank's heart pumped hard in his chest and it was difficult to breathe as if air was been sucked right out of his lungs.

To his horror, the service door began to slowly close with an eerie scraping sound, like the echo of train tracks in a distant tunnel.

Five feet away.

He had to get there. Kicking away the clinging hands, Frank accidently stood on a body, the sickening crunch of brittle bones sounded underfoot but he ignored it, striving on through the sticky residue.

Four feet away.

The doors ground closer together like a slowly snapping jaw.

With a leap, Frank threw himself forward with all his energy, hands clambering to hold them open so he could lever his body forward. Somehow, he found strength again and hauled himself forward over the slippery floor and into the lift. As the doors closed behind him, he caught a glimpse of the bodies of the dead crawling after him and that of his pursuer, who had now become one of them. Burnt black and red, the skin falling away from flesh. Staring right at him through sunken sockets was the unmistakeable bloodied face of Chiu Wah On, the assassin he had thrown out of a train eight years earlier.

The sheets, soaked from sweat, were wrapped tightly around him as Frank fought to free himself, breathing hard and disorientated. He knocked the side table, pushing a glass of water to the floor, which cracked and rolled, soaking the carpet and his unread books.

"Jesus," he muttered, untangling himself. The bed looked like he had been wrestling with an army of demons. Pillows were strewn over the floor, the sheet lay twisted across the mattress. He rubbed his eyes and slowed his breathing, relieved that the nightmare was over. Every now and then, it would re-appear and he wondered why. It had been so long since Hong Kong and there had been many other demons to fight afterwards.

Frank switched on the radio and padded his naked frame over to the en-suite bathroom before turning on the shower, hesitating at the door until the water had a chance to heat up.

After a quick blast and scrub, he dried himself, checked his unshaven face and dark hair in the mirror, and threw on a T-shirt and jeans. He headed down the hallway to the kitchen and opened the fridge, glancing into the bare interior. Had Maria asked him to get the shopping in? She had been talking to him when he was half asleep that morning, which was always a bad idea. Where was she anyway? Then he remembered that she had taken the boys to see a friend and then get shopping.

A dull pain throbbed in the back of his skull but he still didn't hesitate to grab the last can of beer.

It had been a difficult reunion after Hong Kong and the horrific suicide of her father. They had been sitting in a café on Amsterdam's Raadhuisstraat two months after her father's funeral, watching the rain hammer the streets and trams trundle by the window. Maria had avoided his eyes as he uttered sympathetic words and he knew they weren't getting through. They had something, hadn't they? They'd been together under the threat of death and helped each other through those terrifying weeks that neither would easily forget.

Then it had happened. The gunshot in the living room. The sight of her dad lying on the Chinese rug, the blood and brain tissue marking it like a chaotic map.

"You blame me, don't you?" he had said. "If I had never come into your life, maybe it wouldn't have turned out like that. Is that what you think?" She shook her head, brushed a hand through her curly blonde hair, but said nothing and continued to stare at the rain, or was it his reflection in the window? He couldn't be sure.

"Of course I don't blame you, Frank. I just don't know where I am right now. I'm all lost," she said without looking at him, her green eyes seemed duller than he remembered. He tried to take her hand but she moved it too soon and they sat in silence for a while as the coffee machine growled out another customer's Americano.

He gave her his new contact card, carefully placing it on the table. When she didn't acknowledge it, he stood up, scraping the chair on the stone floor.

"Just call when you're ready," he said quietly as he followed her gaze out into the rain. "If you need to," he added.

It was too soon for her to pick up any thread they'd had in Asia. That much was obvious. She needed more time but he feared losing her. The chance of never seeing her bright green eyes and freckled face again cast a shadow over his thoughts.

Frank left the café, running for the tram in the hacking downpour, convinced he would never see her again. He certainly didn't envisage that Maria would contact him only a week later with the news that would change his life forever. The news that she was pregnant.

Adventure. Breaking up the boredom. The fact that he was certain the relationship with Maria was over. There were many reasons Frank agreed to join Carl at MI6 after he had returned from Asia.

The dark truth was he had also experienced a real adrenaline buzz throwing the Chinese assassin from that train in Thailand. And with his death, knowing the killer would never try to kill him or Maria again, just put the icing on the cake. He got the job done. Dead was dead. There was no coming back from death. Except in your dreams. Frank smiled at the irony.

Death. Once you let it pervade your life, it took a hold, became 'normal', a way of dealing with things. Something changed in Frank after that killing. He had become a different beast and knew it. A beast capable of darker acts. Kill or be killed.

No more office job BS. No more being the hamster in a wheel, a wage slave just existing to work. No, he was going to grab this chance and run with it. Run bloody fast.

Adventure, excitement, travel. That was what had driven him before. Now? Now, he had responsibilities. He needed to build a safety net. A home.

Frank nursed his beer in the stark living room and flicked to the news where footage of Riot police and demonstrators clashed in Seattle. He watched impassively as police charged the line, petrol bombs stinging the air as batons pounded heads and limbs before the newsreader moved the story quickly on, his mind still wandering.

Maria did love him now, he knew that, more than words could ever describe. When she said she was pregnant, everything had changed. Then Joe had come along, and now they had Zak as well. As the news continued, Frank wondered what kind of world he had brought his children into.

3

Maria Chapman walked with the pushchair that her youngest, Zak, was dozing in. Her older son, Joe, shuffled along a few paces behind as they made their way from Barnes Bridge Station and along a passageway that led to the main road. They scurried along to the end and turned, cutting through the streets and pausing occasionally to study a folded up map. Finally, they reached the address they were looking for.

The houses were four stories high, in semi-detached blocks of two. The adjoined house Maria and Joe both stared up at was painted with a graffiti style collage. The centrepiece was a painting of an old wry tree that stretched from the ground all the way to the top, its branches reaching across the width of both houses, spreading like a spider's web on the brickwork. The end of the branches morphed into television screens, periscopes and satellite dishes.

"Why are we here?" Joe asked, still staring up at the artwork.

"Seeing an old friend," Maria replied, pressing the doorbell.

The buzzer crackled into life and a bored-sounding male voice answered.

"Hullo?"

"It's Maria. I'm here to see Rosie Connelly."

"Okay, one minute."

Maria unbuckled the belt around Zak and hauled him out of

the pushchair onto the doorstep as Joe, now fully trained in the procedure, snapped the hood back of the buggy and folded it up.

A tall girl with braided hair and piercings on her nose and ears opened the door and beamed with delight. She threw her arms around Maria. The two had met whilst travelling in India eight years before and swore to keep in touch. They had bumped into each other a week before on a tube train and made the arrangement to meet.

"It's so good to see you again," Rosie beamed. She looked down at Joe and Zak with equal delight. "And who are these lovely boys?"

Joe placed the folded up pushchair on the ground, grinned, and held out his hand. "Joe," he said.

Rosie cooed at the manners and shook his hand. "...and very well brought up, I see."

"Hmm, maybe not so much," said Maria and laughed. She picked up Zak and they all walked into the hallway. The visitors' eyes were drawn to a huge montage of photographs of various people that had been arranged onto a cork board.

"Pictures of all the people who have lived here over the years."

They all began to study the photographs as Rosie gave a running commentary on each one.

"So what is this place?" asked Maria finally.

"A big happy family. A community of like-minded people. We're very particular who lives here. The activist, John Rhodes, owns it. He lets a select few of us run the place. Have you heard of him?"

Maria nodded her head. Rhodes, a man in his early forties, was an outspoken voice against what was being seen as a rising tide of globalisation and corporate greed spanning the world. He was also behind the alternative media group, Liberatus, that produced a weekly newspaper and had recently started publishing their content online. Maria had heard him speak on the local radio and found herself agreeing with pretty much everything that he had said. Rhodes presented his arguments in an intelligent fashion, backed by facts, and had ripped his interviewer apart as they had tried to dismiss and pigeonhole him as a conspiracy nut.

"Well, he's speaking in a few days, I think. I'll give you the details. Anyway, come on in."

Rosie led them into a spacious dining room that was adjacent to the kitchen. There was a large bay window that overlooked the truss arched Barnes Bridge and Maria walked over to peer outside. The Thames, much narrower in this part of London, along with the flat greenery of the sports clubs opposite, reminded Maria of Holland.

A shabby looking young man, with dark wispy hair and a faint outline of growth on his chin, was sitting at a large oak dining table and looked up at them from behind a Toshiba laptop.

"Maria and Joe, this is Matt. He's a kind of journalist for John's newspaper."

Matt leaned back with an impish smile on his face.

"When you say 'kind of journalist', I'll take that as a big compliment then?" Maria noted a light accent but couldn't be sure where.

"You know what I mean. *The Liberatus* isn't exactly *The Guardian*. It's nothing about your journalistic credentials, which are, of course, first class."

Matt shook his head and continuing typing. "Very nicely redeemed, Rosie."

Rosie offered her guests drinks and they sat down around the table.

CHAPTER 3

"So, what are you writing?" asked Maria, bumping Zak up and down on her knee.

"We're finishing off an investigation into a major corruption by our most trusted and elected members of parliament," Matt said and looked at Rosie. "And, as a matter of fact, the mainstream papers are picking up on the story."

Rosie smiled and rested a hand on his shoulder. "So I heard. You're doing a great job, Matthew." She turned to Maria. "Come on. Let's go out into the garden while the sun's out."

Rosie led them down the hallway towards the back of the house and through a utility room at the end, where the light of the garden seemed to be flooding in.

As Maria and Joe followed her outside, they heard a shriek, where they found a boy with blonde hair around the same age as Joe with a scowl of discontent on his face. Another older boy with dark brown, matted hair was crying, holding his cheek and pointing at him.

"Troy, did you hit him? That's very naughty!" She grabbed his arm and made him apologise but it was evident he was used to being told off. Instead, he just stared at Maria and Joe quizzically. Maria bent down to comfort the other boy.

After five minutes, the commotion was forgotten and the three boys continued playing on a large wooden climbing frame.

As the mini-drama receded, the two adults sat around a large wooden table set outside and Rosie disappeared into the kitchen to fetch glasses and a bottle of Rioja.

"Troy is John Rhode's son," she said on her return. "A right handful as you can see."

"Who?"

"The blonde one. He's staying here for a while. The other one is Tom, my first."

Maria smiled and glanced at the children, as they clambered over the frame like monkeys. "So, this John Rhodes. Tell me more about him and this talk you mentioned."

4

The sound of the door slamming forced Frank out of his thoughts and a familiar rush of feet thundered up the stairs to the flat.

"Hi, Dad," Joe said before disappearing into his room. Maria shouted from the stairwell. "I need a hand here."

"Joe, help your mother, don't just disappear like that." Frank put his newspaper aside and reluctantly got up from the sofa.

"Why don't you do it? You haven't done much today," shouted Joe from his room.

"Hey, less of that! Come and help your mother now!" Frank's authoritative loud tone boomed through the hallway and soon, a reluctant footfall followed Frank as they went back down the stairs to the front door. Frank gave Maria a peck on the lips, bent down and picked up Zak from next to his mother and a pile of shopping bags.

"Hey, big man. How's the boss of the house doing today?" he cooed in the toddler's ear. Zak chortled and waved his toy fire engine at Frank. "Mr. Fire Bug been on big adventures, has he?

"Big adventure indeed," said Maria as she handed a shopping bag to a sullen looking Joe, who ran quickly back upstairs. "Three hours I spent in that supermarket. It was total chaos."

"Blimey, that doesn't sound good. Did any of that time include lounging in the café by any chance?"

Maria narrowed her eyes at Frank. "And what if it did? Don't I deserve a coffee break?"

Frank started to make his way up the stairs, holding his youngest son.

"Of course you do. But that's why it takes so bloody long."

Frank put Zak down and walked into the kitchen where his eldest son was pouring orange juice into a glass. "Did you go to Cubs today then, Joe?"

His face remained sullen. "Yeah, we did some knot tying."

"Oh, right? What kind?"

Joe glugged down the juice and then put the glass down.

"What do you care?"

Frank tensed.

"Hey, I asked you a question. The least you can do is answer your old man."

Joe's face turned into a scowl.

"I did a bowline, halter hitch, and the carrick bend." He then promptly left the kitchen, belching as Maria came in.

"Joe! Don't do that!" Maria rasped.

"Sorry."

She began stacking tins of food into the cupboard as Frank shook his head.

"What is wrong with that boy?"

"I don't know. You need to spend more time with him. Tonight's a good opportunity as I want to go to a meeting. Can you look after them this evening?"

He sighed as he grabbed a loaf from the bread tin. "This evening? Hmm, I don't know..."

"You have something special lined up?"

Frank shrugged and moved to the fridge for some ham and cheese. He didn't have anything lined up, it was just a habit of never volunteering for anything.

"What's the meeting?"

"Well, it's more of a talk. By a man, I heard on the radio. It's all about Liberty and Social freedom."

Frank rolled his eyes. "Oh, God."

"It's important stuff, Frank!"

"Suit yourself. We'll be fine. We'll watch a stack of films or something."

Maria nodded, feeling annoyed at him but saying nothing. It was about the world that their children were growing up in. What could be more important than that?

Frank rapped on Joe's bedroom door. "Joe?"

"What?"

Frank opened the door and popped his head through to see Joe sitting on his bed with his arms crossed.

"What's wrong?"

"Just bored. You never come with me to Cubs when you're home. All the other dads go. You're away all the time and when you're here, you just drink beer and do nothing."

Frank dropped his head. "I'm sorry, son. I'll try and make the time. I work really hard when I'm away and just need to relax when I'm home."

Joe stared down at the floor and said nothing.

"Hey. Your mum's out tonight. Fancy a late film night?"

Joe's face seemed to light up at this and he nodded his head.

"Great. Just don't choose that one with all the animals that talk again."

The boy smiled. "No, I'm well bored of that one."

5

Maria Chapman moved along the aisles of chairs in the busy windowless community hall and took her place alongside the other people who had come to hear John Rhodes speak. At the front, there was a raised platform that acted as a stage with a long table set back near the back wall. The audience included a wide span of ages, races, and gender, a typical selection of a London community.

An Afro-Caribbean man and a woman went and sat down at the table, as a white-headed figure adjusted a microphone.

The murmur of conversation in the hall hushed.

"Good evening, gentlemen and ladies," he said and gave the audience a warm smile and applause rose through the small hall.

He held his hand up. "Thank you for coming, everyone. Today's meeting is a forum, not just for me but everyone here. We are all affected by the marching globalisation and criminality that casts its shadow and we all need to be involved as one voice." Rhodes took a sip of water and cleared his throat in the hushed room.

"It was the science fiction writer, Philip K. Dick, who said, 'There will come a time when it isn't 'They're spying on me through my phone' anymore. Eventually, it will be 'My phone is spying on me'.'"

There were chuckles from the audience.

"Today, we are living in a society that is on a slippery slope to a modern type of totalitarianism, where the governments are using deception and manipulation to create the society they want. One that deals in the trade of perpetual death through the Industrial military complex, a society that creates wars for profit."

Rhodes put on a pair of glasses that hung around his neck on a chain and opened a sheet of paper from his pocket.

"I want to quote a speech by an American president, just several years before his assassination."

Rhodes cleared his throat before continuing.

"'We are opposed around the world by a monolithic and ruthless conspiracy that relies primarily on covert means for expanding its sphere of influence — on infiltration instead of invasion, on subversion instead of elections, on intimidation instead of free choice, on guerrillas by night instead of armies by day.'"

Rhodes took off the glasses and returned his gaze to the crowd.

"Although J.F Kennedy was speaking in 1961, and referring to the system at the time in the US, I believe we are facing the same enemy today. They have *not* gone away. Closer to home, the surveillance culture is increasingly creeping into our lives. Nearly four million CCTV's in the UK shows how far we have gone towards an Orwellian reality. The dark shadows behind government know they can't bring in mass surveillance overnight. No, that would, or at least should, ignite a revolution. Instead, they wait, boiling the frog degree by degree over time whilst slowly dismantling our civil liberties, brick by brick. Soon, they may try to engineer some terrible event; the finger pointing at a convenient foe to advance their agenda. They've done it before, countless times, and will probably do it again."

Rhodes walked up and down the stage, moulding invisible

circles with his hands.

"All around the world, there is a sense that something is not right. Growing anger and discord is rife. We live in troubled and changing times where the gap between the populations and the global controllers, whether they are governments, corporate and banking interests, or the military apparatus that serves them, grows ever wider. There is an increasing suspicion, not just here in the UK but across the western world, that democracy is an illusion and a rigged game, designed to keep us in line within a system that benefits only those controllers."

Rhodes had stopped pacing the stage. "Bush talks about the big idea of a New World Order but let us talk about the big idea of resistance against that order. What was it H.G. Wells said? 'Countless people...will hate the new world order....and will die protesting against it.'"

He waved his hand in the air to emphasise his point and then took a sip of water from the table.

"We are pawns, fodder even, in a dangerous game that is not only making us all poorer but more worryingly, controlled and surveilled. Should we lie down and accept this? Will we wake up one day and realise we have allowed something terrible to happen...that we have allowed them to get away with it?"

Rhodes started to pace the stage again, looking around the room, mixing eye contact with gestures and a steady voice, raising and varying his tone like any good orator. He let out a huge sigh.

"So what does this have to do with us? We're busy. Trying to scratch a living, pay the bills. Are we not already walking around free in a democracy? Free to do what we want, within the ever increasing laws, of course." Chuckles.

"And what is Liberatus? What can we, as ordinary people with busy lives struggling to scratch a living, do anyway? So many questions, so little time." A few murmurs of agreement from the audience.

Rhodes leaned forward, his hands clutching the back of a chair.

"My vision for Liberatus is a common cause that rejects capitalism, feudalism, and the interests that promote destructive globalisation. Instead, we look to the construction of local alternatives: an organisational philosophy based on decentralisation and autonomy. A system that is based on sustained communities, linked around the globe. A self-efficient, self-governing entity that is prepared to defend itself.

A community that is based on mutual respect, not a society where war seems to be the ongoing instrument to boost the economy. A system that is self-sustaining rather than sucking the world's resources dry like a swarm of locusts. A future that benefits all of mankind and the planet, not the current Ponzi scheme of the stock market that we've all been suckered into!

And freedom! Freedom from being watched by the Global surveillance powers that do not have our best interests at heart. That is the way we need to move forward. That is the society we must have!"

He stood straight again, holding out his arms as if reaching out to the people in the room. There was a crescendo of rapacious applause from the crowd. Others had filtered in at the back and joined in clapping with the occasional loud whistle and shout.

A beaming Rhodes gave a wave and sat back down. A woman sitting at the organisers table leaned into her microphone, clapping along with the audience.

"Thank you very much and thank you, John Rhodes," she said.

After the clapping died off, she turned to face a smartly dressed middle-aged Afro-Caribbean man on her left.

"Okay. Now I think we're going to have a question and answer session, is that right, Marcus?" The man nodded and leaned into his microphone.

"Yes, if anyone has questions, please hold up your arm and we'll take them one at a time." A sea of hands rose and the session lasted a further thirty minutes.

Following the Q and A and a call for volunteers, a small group of people made their way to talk to Rhodes. Maria felt invigorated and excited. She had not felt this inspired since she had been involved in a human rights protest group in Amsterdam.

Maria squeezed through the bodies to sign up and then she had decided to talk to Rhodes himself. She had been profoundly affected by his speech and wanted to get involved. Everything he said had resonated with her at every level of what she believed in and she wanted to be a part of it.

"Hello there, did you enjoy the meeting?"

Maria turned to the direction of the voice and found herself looking at a short, chubby man with dark brown eyes looking pointedly back at her. His black hair was shiny with grease and mounded into a cow-lick at the front.

"Oh, yes, I certainly did," she said, smiling politely. She made to move ahead through the crowd.

"Forgive me, I didn't introduce myself," came the voice again. "Nigel. Nigel Harrison."

"Oh, yes. I'm sorry. I'm Maria. I was just looking to speak to John." He shook her hand limply. "Please let me introduce you to him myself."

Maria nodded uncertainly. "Right. Thank you."

She followed the figure through the crowd.

6

David Devlin walked briskly down the GCHQ corridor at Oakley in the depths of the iconic green building that had been a landmark in Cheltenham for decades. He passed the main offices of M block, where hundreds of employees sat at their cubicles, all focused on their own tasks. His newly shined black shoes clicking on the polished surface, a leather briefcase, containing the report that had turned his day upside down, in hand. This was red alert time of the highest order. Options swirled through his mind but he tried to dismiss them to focus on the simple facts that he was about to spill at the meeting.

He reached the door at the end and swiped a card that activated a green light on the control console, followed by a click on the huge door lock. The door slid open to the operations meeting room, where other suited figures awaited his presence.

Percy Braithwaite, the MI6 director, stood tall, a striking figure who had aged well for his fifty-five years, coffee in hand as he chatted to Fiona Geisheim from the Foreign Secretary's Office. The group finally all sat down at the large boardroom table; papers and reports were placed on the table in front of them.

All eyes fell on Devlin as he sipped a glass of water and opened a report.

"We've had a breach. One of our intelligence analysts, Sarah Edwards, managed to take a significant amount of data relating to some of our surveillance projects and has since disappeared. She has almost certainly left the country. It's not clear at this stage exactly what information she has and what she intends to do with it but we're working on finding that out. We need to assemble our response as soon as possible, find this ex-employee, and decide on the course of action going forward. Firstly, I'll say that we intend to keep this as quiet as possible."

Devlin looked around the table and caught Fiona Geisheim's eye and raised his eyebrows and nodded, indicating for her to go ahead with the question she evidently wanted to ask. She was an attractive woman, in her late thirties, with blonde hair tied back into a bun. Only crow's feet around her eyes betrayed her age but the steely green pupils sparked intelligence. Devlin noted she was unmarried or didn't sport any kind of ring at least, and momentarily wondered if she was single.

"So are you suggesting we do not seek extradition?"

"It depends on where she turns up but I would suggest we avoid that route, to begin with." He gave the minister his most charming smile.

"Firstly, what kind of data are we talking about and what damage is it likely to cause? Secondly, why isn't this on the agenda for the next Joint Intelligence Committee?" she asked, the charm evidently failing.

Devlin shifted slightly in his seat and leaned back.

"Oh, it will be on the agenda, Minister, rest assured. Regarding the information copied, it's related to a joint project with the NSA, specifically Internet surveillance working in conjunction with several telecoms companies."

"Operation Oculus," injected a voice from the MI6 Director.

Devlin sighed. "Yes, Oculus. The proposed piping of all Internet data. It's a powerful commercial product, one that can intercept and monitor real-time precision targeting of any type of IP traffic including webmail, email IM chat, and VoIP. There's a lot more to it than I can go into at the moment as I'm sure you'll appreciate."

"So once this is in place, sitting in the middle of any network, it potentially has access to all of the data flowing over that network?" Fiona Geisheim asked.

Devlin nodded in agreement.

"And the consequences of this getting out?"

"There will be a shit storm, that's for sure. The liberals will scream from the rooftops and it could severely damage the current government. There's a high risk that it could be sold or fall into the hands of terrorists, or any number of rogue governments. For this reason, I would strongly argue that an extradition leading to some kind of public trial along with all the media attention would also be inappropriate. It also looks very bad for us. This is Top Secret material and we have to aggressively track down this operative," Devlin finished defiantly.

Percy Braithwaite finished his coffee and cleared his throat. "I think we're all in agreement as to what needs doing here."

Geisheim leaned forward. She hadn't finished and stared at Devlin.

"This Oculus project, I take it the Foreign Office was going to be notified at some point?"

"Yes, absolutely, Minister, a full report is being written as we speak. This is very early stages and would probably not be operational until 2004 at the earliest."

This seemed to satisfy the minister and she nodded and returned to her notes.

"This could be extremely damaging if leaked. Everything must be done to track this rogue employee down. Have you made any headway?" asked Braithwaite.

"We have a signit team on it," said Devlin.

"Maybe you need some help from our chaps, considering the seriousness of the matter, don't you think, David?"

"We can handle it," Devlin retorted.

"Really? You might need bodies on the ground and considering it's a security issue where the target is likely to end up abroad, well, that's very much our department."

Devlin bristled inside but kept a stony straight face. He had never really clicked with Percy. The man was very much an old-school Etonian. Cricket and Champers on a Sunday and a very stiff upper lip.

"I want very much want to keep this as an internal GCHQ matter," replied Devlin curtly.

"I think there needs to be a compromise on this. This calls for an emergency meeting of the Joint Intelligence Committee and I am going to recommend that a covert team is set up. A little venture between MI6 and GCHQ," said Geisheim, flashing a grin at Devlin.

Devlin leaned back in his chair, swore silently, and rapidly clicked his pen. "Are there any further questions?" When none came, it was a signal for the meeting to end and folders snapped shut, followed by the scraping of chairs.

The GCHQ Director wasn't particularly worried about the data Edwards thought she had; that was bound to leak out eventually. If it did, it would cause a lot of problems with their associates across the pond and for all the companies involved but he knew it would be a storm in a teacup compared to what else the intelligence communities were up to. No, it was the darker restricted files that she didn't even realise she possessed that had kept him awake for the past two nights.

Devlin had been recruited into GCHQ at Oxford in the days when an approach was made; usually by one of the professors in the mid-eighties. *Those ways were drawing to a close now, of course,* the director reminisced to himself with a wry smile. Recruitment was going to become a lot more open and transparent in the coming years.

He had risen through the ranks, made connections, and played the game until he found himself perched at the top of the tree. That view gave him the realisation that certain things needed to be done at high cost and that even he was a mere cog in a wheel. Devlin had learned that there was a plan, decades in the making. Almost every major world event, be it regime change, a downturn in the economy, or terrorist attack, were all notes in a grand orchestral piece.

This latest development was one note, however, that could prove most jarring.

7

Carl Paterson buttoned up his shirt in readiness as he approached the old red-brick grain warehouse that sat astride the Limehouse Cut Canal. Once a hub of activity for bringing trade goods into East London from the Thames in the 1700's, the impressive building was now converted into commercial units for media based companies. Carl had no idea why he had been summoned here but it was a long trek from 'VX', as the MI6 HQ at Vauxhall was known.

Large loading bay doors dominated the building from the street side and Carl scanned the buzzers for 'Studio 31', the anonymous sounding front company for the project he was being pulled into.

Secrecy was a priority regarding this meeting and he had been verbally warned that it was under the radar and outlined in no uncertain terms by a Senior Officer that once he had agreed to the meeting, for which he knew nothing of the agenda, it would be extremely difficult for him to back away. It was an almost impossible position but Carl was never one to shy away from challenges. He was in one hundred percent when it came to the agency. It was his life and there was nothing else. Anna, his partner, had long gone, leaving him to decide what road he wanted to go down and when this 'offer' had emerged, Carl hadn't needed long to make a decision.

Once buzzed in, Carl climbed the metal stairway to the third floor, where he was met by a large man who looked like an ape in a suit, the kind of thug who wouldn't think twice about throwing you down a disused well. He was told to wait in a reception room that was still a work in progress with step ladders and a half painted wall. On the opposite side was a framed image of a logo for Studio 31, bold and iconic.

A meeting with the Director of MI6 meant something big. What was he walking into? Carl felt anticipation, fear even, but an excitement that had driven him in this line of work. It was what fuelled his blood and made him get up in the morning.

Perhaps he was going to be deployed again in another hostile environment? It could be the Balkans theatre. The war over Kosovo had begun and was currently plastered all over the media. Or the Middle East? There had been covert operations to destabilise Saddam Hussein ever since the 1991 Gulf conflict.

"Carl. Thanks for coming, I very much appreciate it," came a voice from nowhere. Carl turned around from the picture to see Braithwaite, his light blue shirt sleeves rolled up to the elbow. Carl shook the director's outstretched hand.

"The pleasure is all mine, Mr. Braithwaite."

"Please. Call me Percy. Do you want any refreshments? Although it's not the most comfortable of surroundings at the moment, we can do coffee."

Carl indicated that he was fine and they began to walk to another room on the Canalside. The vast space was devoid of furniture, except a couple of chairs and a table at the end. The large windows streamed in rays of light that revealed dust floating in the air. Carl sensed activity behind a shut door to his right but he didn't look, instead, focusing his attention on the director.

They sat down, Braithwaite behind the makeshift desk, his grey eyes appraising Carl.

"So you've had a talk with Keller?" he asked. The director was referring to the Scottish Senior Officer who had given Carl the brief, and the warning. Keller was a figure in the agency most were wary of. The short but ferocious Scot seemed to have ears and eyes everywhere and most of Carl's colleagues referred to him as the Rottweiler.

"I did but there were few details," Carl replied.

Braithwaite smiled. "Good, otherwise, I'd have to reprimand the old dog," Carl noted the sly reference to his nickname. He obviously had a sharper ear to the ground than was realised.

Braithwaite changed the tone suddenly. "Okay, let's get down to business. What we have here is a new completely *off the record* project. This isn't mentioned in any paperwork or on any file. You will not find a mention of this anywhere, apart from conspiracy theorists, maybe." They shared a light chuckle.

"The Joint Intelligence Committee wants our two little bands to work closer together and frankly, I agree with them. There have been a few examples recently where closer co-operation would have had much more satisfying results in recent operations."

Braithwaite leaned back, his gaze pointedly fixed on Carl.

"I want you to work with Keller, who will be overseeing several operations. He's a good chap and has put together a tight working team. It's extremely important to know that this is the highest level of secrecy. You're the man to lead this, Carl. The buck stops with you. There'll be no official benefits, no pension scheme, but you will be rewarded in many ways. You want something, a brand new Mercedes? Just let Keller know. A holiday in the best hotel in the Caribbean? No problem. Officially, you'll still receive your compensation from the company, of course."

Carl brushed a hand over his jaw in thought.

"Are you saying the responsibility of this op ends with me?"

"Not just this operation, Carl. Your team, possibly one of many within Ghost 13, the name of our little team, will be under your wing, with guidance from Keller. This is the first op, one of many to come, that needs urgent attention."

"What op?"

Braithwaite chuckled. "I certainly won't be giving you the details. You'll hear soon enough, providing you agree to move forward."

It all still sounded ominous and vague to Carl. Exactly the type of carte blanche that gave Intelligence agencies the self-appointed approval to do what the hell they liked, but he had already decided.

"Is there any kind of indication of what it might involve, sir?"

Braithwaite seemed to grimace momentarily at the formal address and then smiled and nodded.

"You'll be locating a target and then putting that target under surveillance. National security is at stake. Initially, that would be all, but it needs to be a flexible op."

Carl seemed to contemplate this for a second. "Why me?"

"Discretion and a fairly good track record. There are others who would snap this up, Carl. I'll make sure you're handsomely rewarded. There is a fast ladder to higher places in this organisation that you'll be helped up, take my word for it."

Carl nodded. "Count me in."

"Welcome to Ghost 13, Carl."

The director stood up and Carl followed his lead. Both men shook hands. Carl left the building and headed back to central London, wondering what he had got himself into.

8

The sleek black S Class Mercedes moved slowly up the ramped car park levels to the top and pulled into a free space. The cityscape view of Hammersmith shimmered under a threatening dark sky and the patter of heavy raindrops began to rap on the windscreen until a downpour opened up and the city lights blurred into abstract shapes through the glass.

A white van pulled up beside the vehicle and the driver of the Mercedes nodded at the face looking back at him. The figure turned off his engine and jumped into the passenger seat of the Mercedes.

"Viktor. How nice to see you again. You're late."

Viktor nodded to the man he knew only as 'The Marquis' and slammed the door shut.

"Traffic is a bitch in this city...so why don't you sue me. Why am I here?"

The Marquis reached to the back seat for a leather pouch. "I have a job for you. Very important. High level. I trust you still have a good team?"

Viktor nodded, pulling out a pack of Russian cigarettes.

"Not in here," the man said, looking at him with mild contempt, his eyes falling on the Russians' neck tattoo of barbed wire, creeping up to his chin. Viktor shrugged and ran his hand over his neatly trimmed goatee beard as if smoothing ruffled feathers.

"So what's this important job that MI6 can't take of itself?" he asked, with a hint of mockery in his tone.

The Marquis pulled out a report from the pouch and turned to face the Russian.

"You know who I work for and you're well aware of their reach, their power, even to your country. I don't need to tell you that trust between our two parties is paramount."

Viktor grabbed the report from the man and stared at the photograph of a young woman with dark tied back hair. "Yes, yes, you don't need to lecture me on these matters," he said, irritated. "How many times I let you down? Zero. So, Operation Whisper Hunt," he said, reading the title of the report. "Who is this?"

"An employee of GCHQ. Sarah Edwards. She has disappeared with a lot of top secret information."

"What kind of information are we talking about?"

"Secret information, that's all you need to know."

Viktor flipped through the pages, scanning over Sarah Edwards' personal details, and history.

"Will there be other interested parties?" he asked.

The Marquis flicked the lever for the windscreen wipers once and for a few seconds, they had a clear view of the city.

"There is going to be a small team on the ground, the official but covert team sanctioned by the agency. I'll do my best to keep them out of your way but the most important thing is the mission. The information and the woman are the two things you need in your sights at all times. She cannot live through this, do you understand me?"

Viktor turned back to the photograph of Sarah Edwards. "Yes. Big shame. She's very attractive."

"I will be in touch when we have more information on where she might be."

"This other team you're sending, how many? What is their capability?" Viktor asked, concerned.

"For now, I can tell you that their squad will be three men and possibly a local contact. Two of them are ex-special forces and a surveillance officer. I'll get you more details."

"Where is the woman?"

"She could be anywhere, we just don't know yet. Now, what is your price?"

"A ballpark? Five hundred thousand dollars per man by transfer before and then the same amount after completion. I need four or five men."

"That seems a bit excessive to track and deal with a woman, Mr. Kozel."

Viktor laughed. "And the covert team that you mentioned. They might get in my way and I'll need weapons, transport, and communications equipment. This is not cheap."

The Marquis sighed and handed him a phone from his inside jacket pocket. "Three hundred thousand. Now, take this and I will be in touch with further details. Assemble your team, Mr. Kozel, and be ready."

9

Maria typed in the key code on the door and quickly climbed the steps to the small, cramped office of Liberatus News on Soho Square, where she had been working for just shy of a month. She had talked Rhodes into allowing her to volunteer to help with the research for the stories and features that syndicated out through the paper and website. John had been impressed with Maria's structured approach to projects and he offered her a part-time job to help organise the activist newspaper. For the last few weeks, she had worked tirelessly on re-organising their structure and workflow to help refine the process of news research and gathering.

Their main benefactor was more than generous, yet no one knew who it was, not even Rhodes, or so he said. This had made Maria uneasy and she felt that it may come back to haunt them but without that funding, they would be in deep trouble. So she had set about finding ways to build additional income streams like web advertising and sponsorship, which wasn't easy considering the group's stance towards big business.

Maria had also become privy to John Rhode's other project, an activist pressure group, which he rarely talked about but was increasingly spending more of his time on. He needed help in providing a clear mandate, which Maria had been central to bringing about: to influence the legislative branches of government and expose corruption in governments and corporations. It still needed an incredible amount of work but was a start, a stepping stone to something she hoped would become a worthwhile entity, a cause worth fighting for.

Maria beamed a smile at Jillian, the general secretary, and sat down at her desk, working through her mind what she needed to focus on today after the usual morning chaos of getting Zak to the nursery and dropping off Joe at school. She read through a list that included a myriad of phone calls and finishing the writing of some key policy documents.

"There's still some coffee in the pot but there's no milk. I'll go and get some. You want anything else?" asked Jillian, getting up from her desk.

Maria glanced up and smiled as she fired up her computer. "No, I'm fine, thanks, Jill." Her footsteps faded as Maria focused on her first task of the day.

"Good morning, Maria." She looked up to see Nigel Harrison standing in the doorway, his dark brown eyes shifting to the side before falling on her.

"Oh, morning, Nigel," she replied, glancing up at him before turning back to her screen. He was the IT guy who John had brought in to manage the servers.

"Erm...I read the early drafts of the mandate you've been working on. It's very impressive." He moved closer to her desk and she looked up again, noticing a sheen of sweat above his lip.

Maria smiled politely. "Thanks. That's very kind of you."

"John showed me. I hope you don't mind? It was because he was so pleased with your progress."

Maria smiled at him, in much the same way she did to her oldest boy. "Ah, thanks, Nigel. I really appreciate that. There's a lot more tweaking to do yet I'm pretty sure."

Harrison hovered slightly, as if reluctant to move on.

"Well, good luck with it. Speak again soon." He didn't take his eyes away from her for what seemed like an age to Maria. She smiled again, tightly this time.

"Thanks, Nigel. See you later."

"Yes, see you later." His wide frame finally moved away from her and she noticed a large sweat patch on the back of his white shirt. Maria shook her head to herself. She couldn't figure out that man. It was obvious he had some kind of 'thing' for her, like a schoolboy fancying his teacher. She had no idea how someone so child-like in nature was a technical whiz on computers.

10

Five years earlier

Frank ran as fast as he could, skipping over fallen branches as a whistling bullet flew over his head, hitting a tree in front of him and spraying splinters of bark onto the sodden ground. He swore under his breath and kept running, moving in an uneven line so as not to make himself an easy target. Clocking a ditch yards ahead of him, he made it his goal. As soon as he was near enough, he dived, his body curling into a fetal position as he rolled into the shallow, muddy water at the bottom of the trench.

He lay there for a moment, listening hard, but could hear nothing except for his own heavy breathing and the distant bark of the dog. A glimmer of relief that he was hidden from his pursuers, if only for a short time.

Got to keep moving.

He glanced both ways along the ditch, still lying in the sludge, and saw that one end curved away from the direction of his pursuers. He forced himself to manoeuvre onto all fours before crouching his body into a sprinter position and then he bolted along the trench, keeping his head down and out of sight.

A shout echoed through the woods followed by a series of barks that seemed closer all of a sudden. They were gaining on him and that dog worried him. It was only a matter of time before he was caught. All was surely lost now but he refused to give up; he would make the bastards work for it.

They must want him alive or he'd be dead by now...surely? Were they a terrorist cell? Hardened criminals? Enemy intelligence? Carl had told him bugger all and he felt a rising bitterness at this complete cock up. The targets had known he was watching them. How had this been possible?

Twelve hours earlier at 1600 hours, Frank sat with Carl Paterson in a near derelict cottage that sat isolated and hidden in the vast broadleaved woodland in New Forest.

Frank had been picked up by Carl in his Land Rover and they had headed onto the M3 from London towards Southampton. On the far side of the River Test lay the beautiful landscape of New Forest with its two hundred square miles of meandering heathland, woodland, forests, rivers, and fields.

Frank wondered if the Marchwood military port in Southampton was of any relevance. Frank had read that the port had been built in 1943 to aid the D-day invasion of Normandy and was later used as support for the British Falklands war. Whatever it was about, he guessed he'd know soon enough.

Carl Paterson and Frank Bowen had known each other since school days, when they both neglected their work, more interested in hiding out in makeshift dens smoking and drinking stolen beer. They would often scheme about how they could make a few extra quid on the streets of London.

One of their crew, Kieran, had been badly beaten into a coma by a group of older lads for no other reason than being Irish. Both boys visited the hospital every day and, as advised by the nurse, spoke into his ear about what they had been up to. It was important to talk to victims in a coma, in case they could hear or at least some of it slipped through to their subconscious.

Six weeks after the incident, Frank and Carl had turned up at the hospital and found Kieran's very upset parents standing in the entrance hall. They informed the boys that their son had lost his fight and passed away. The culprits who murdered him were never caught, leaving a simmering rage in both Frank and Carl, and the bond of friendship between them only strengthened.

At fourteen, Carl was moved to another school, and under pressure from his parents, finally applied himself to his full ability and did well. His educational journey, along with financial help from relatives, eventually landed him at Oxford University and the intelligence connections it would bring for him.

Frank had moved to London when he was five years old to be brought up by his grandfather after his parents were killed in a car crash. The move from the quiet, flat landscape of Lincolnshire to the hectic, tough London streets was a bit of a shock to the young lad but he soon took to it as he grew up, making friends, getting into football, and becoming a part of the streets. From then on, it was a move into petty crime, drinking, and dabbling in drugs, which led to an ultimatum from his grandfather: Clean up or leave.

Frank's memory was jerked back into the present as the 4x4 heaved along the forest track until a cottage appeared and both men entered the dark, abandoned shell of a building. Carl threw down a bag onto an old wooden table and pulled out a map, a flask, and two porcelain mugs. He poured tea and handed Frank one before opening out the map on the table top.

"Target is holed up at a house in this location," Carl said, pointing to a series of lines and a dot at the edge of a vast forest.

"All we need you to do is move into position on foot where you can monitor any movements from the safe house. If there are any prisoners, or if any of the targets leave by car, foot, or any other way, it must be photographed, with notes of exact times." Carl pulled out a compact prototype Nikon camera from his bag and placed it on the table top.

He then continued to lay out a various assortment of equipment on top of the map: binoculars, night glasses, a handheld VHF frequency-range tactical communications radio, a Francis Barker M88 Prismatic compass as well as army issue food packages, three Mars bars wrapped in cling film, a large flask of water, water purification tablets, and dried nuts.

Frank packed them into his backpack alongside his own gear, which included a woollen hat, gloves, and a Swiss army knife.

"No weapons?" asked Frank.

"It's a pretty safe op, mate. Just a bit of standard surveillance. We'll need you to watch the targets for forty-eight hours, so you'll be shitting in the woods I'm afraid. Just try not to leave any tracks."

Carl then pulled out a brown folder and handed Frank a report. Photographs of a woman and two men stared back at him. The woman was attractive, with glasses and dark brown hair, while the two males, one dark haired with a beard and the other with short cropped blonde hair, appeared to be in their mid-thirties. They all wore grim, murderous expressions and certainly weren't the types you'd want to get in a ruck with.

"Who are they?" Frank asked, slurping his sweet tea.

"Sorry, can't tell you," beamed Carl, grabbing the report from Frank before tossing it into his bag and zipping it shut. Frank followed Carl outside from the small, sparse cottage they had marked as the rendezvous point: Codename: Alamo.

"What about civvies? This is a National Park, isn't it?"

"Not where we are. It's private land right up to the target area. If you do see anyone walking their dog, which you shouldn't, you're just a rambler." Carl climbed into the Land Rover.

"You have about four hours of daylight left, by the way," said Carl, with what Frank could swear was a smirk but wasn't quite sure. "See you back here in forty-eight hours," he said cheerily as he gunned the engine into life.

After a minute, Frank was suddenly alone, looking down the empty, mud-ridden track.

He had a few other questions, to say the least, but knew better than to bother asking. He returned inside and studied the map, plotting his route in his mind to cut down on stops. He needed to head south-west to a stream that would take him to the far side of the forest edge near a main road where the target house was. It was probably only three miles as the crow flies but he knew it wouldn't be a simple stroll. He grabbed his pack, checked he had everything, and started walking into the dense woodland.

As he made his way through the quiet, sprawling woods, he made a note to himself to bring his young son, Joe, somewhere like this. Get him away from the city and into some fresh air and closer to nature. He wished his grandad, Larry Bowen, had been around to meet Joe. They would have got on like a house on fire. Larry had always been full of stories from the war. Joe loved that stuff.

His mind wandered back to returning from Asia again, and the decision he had made to work with the 'company' as MI6 was called by its own employees.

The first step was to put himself through three months of basic army training, paid for by the company. It was something Frank had insisted on as soon as he had returned from Asia; to get 'match fit' as his trainer, Sam Keane, had said. Sam was a veteran army man, short, stocky, and tough, a through and through army man who had spent his entire adult life in the Royal Marines. His tour list was extensive: the Balkans, Oman, Iraq, and Africa.

They had spent many a weekend running up through the Brecon Beacons with a rucksack filled with bricks. "Sweat it out, lad. Then you can drink all the beer ya like!" Sam had yelled as they stumbled across the rocky terrain, the Welsh hills shimmering in the background.

He had used this fitness regime as a foundation for the other skills he wanted to add to his bow.

Many weekends included a strict series of sessions with a qualified hand to hand combat expert specialising in Combat Ju-Jitsu, old school fighting techniques originally from the Samurai era and taught to Special Forces in the First World War.

Then he had covered night manoeuvres, weapons handling, basic survival, H2H (hand to hand combat), signalling, marks-manship, all under the shadow of a strict schedule.

Frank opened his M88 compass as he lay hidden in the braken that covered the floor of the dense woodland. He checked his bearings to make sure he hadn't accidentally wandered off course and was at least going in the right direction. Looking up, he noted the dark grey clouds that moved quickly overhead and inwardly groaned as he packed away the device.

He checked the map again, which was wrapped in a clear plastic folder and traced a dotted line with his finger. The target's safe house was marked with an 'X' and sat next to a lonely road that snaked through the forest.

Frank estimated his current position on the map and figured it was another eight hundred metres or so away, as the crow flies. He put the compass and map away in his backpack, checked his Nite MX10, noting it was 18:15, and moved quickly through the trees, stopping every twenty metres to listen out for anything unusual. It was difficult with his beating heart and heavy breathing.

Hearing nothing, he moved again, weaving between the continuous tree trunks, their canopies darkening his path as thick raindrops began to patter into the hard ground ahead. The woodland thinned out quickly, and he was soon back out in the open and moving upwards to a ridge that would hopefully look down onto the target.

Frank crouched down as he came into sight of the ridge top and crawled the last few feet before peering over the edge down onto the rolling valley below. The rain hacked down at an angle onto his face, which made it virtually impossible to see anything clearly. He took out his field glasses and scanned the area and could only see the grey landscape of fields and woodlands. Then as he moved his glasses down to the bottom of the rocky hill in front of him, he caught a glimpse of a rooftop, partly hidden by a cluster of trees. That was it: the target house.

He continued to crawl along the ridge to get a better view as the rain hardened, coming in waves, soaking his canvas fatigues.

"What the hell am I doing here?" he muttered aloud. But he already knew the answer: It was the woman in his life and their son, Joe. He was trying his hardest to shield them from the hardship and poverty that he himself had grown up with. When he was single, it hadn't mattered to him so much, not being a materialistic type, but suddenly having a family to think about had spun an entirely different angle on things. He couldn't afford to be the old, selfish Frank anymore.

After ten minutes of crawling, he had a good view of the house and peered once again through his binoculars. The cottage was old, grey stone that had made it hard to see, with two outhouses facing into a courtyard at the rear that looked across an open field. It didn't look like anyone was home; there were no discernible lights and no vehicles around the property.

Frank fished for his handheld communications radio and held it close to his mouth.

"Charlie-two-zero Alpha...This is Echo Sierra five niner. Radio check, over."

Silence.

"Charlie-two-zero Alpha...This is Echo Sierra five niner. Can you respond, over?"

Still, there was no answer. Frank checked the radio settings once again and went through the same routine. When that failed, he put out a general call:

"Charlie Charlie...anyone there, over?"

Still, silence. It was as if the radio was missing a vital component.

"Useless piece of shit," he muttered and put it back in the backpack.

The light began to fade quickly, sinking the cold landscape into darkness. Frank swapped his binoculars for night vision monoculars and continued to watch the house through a green haze. Five minutes later, a passing bright light caused Frank to put down his field glasses and watch as the car headlights drew closer, dipping out of view occasionally before a dark Ford Transit van turned into the front drive of the house.

The van stood stationary for what seemed like an age before the engine and lights died and the house and surroundings fell back into darkness. Frank returned to his night visions and watched three figures exit the vehicle, all dressed in black fatigues and beanie hats that made any ID impossible, although one of them was definitely a female. They opened the rear doors, temporarily hidden from Frank's sight, and reappeared carrying large metal boxes that they heaved into the house. One of the figures lingered for a moment, walked around the van, glanced up the road and then chirped the locks with their remote keys before following the others. A window lit up with a slither of light on the nearest side of the house, but the curtains were already drawn.

After twenty minutes, nothing else happened and Frank placed the monoculars into his backpack and edged down the ridge a few feet before rummaging around for a chocolate bar that was wrapped in cling film. He ate gratefully and silently cursed the cold wetness of his surroundings. His feet ached from the trekking and he longed for the sweet tea he had had earlier but flasks were strictly forbidden in case the steam gave away his position. Sipping water instead, Frank wrapped a waterproof poncho around his shoulders to fend off the elements, although it seemed futile.

The rain pattered against the material, like distant drumbeats, ebbing and flowing into his consciousness. An hour passed and the noise of the downpour faded into blackness.

A distant bark snapped Frank's eyes open like an alarm. Shit! He had fallen asleep.

The steady light of an approaching dawn spread across the sky. The rain had stopped and it looked clear. Had he heard a bark? Or was he dreaming? He quickly crawled up to the ridge and slowly peeked over the edge. His heart felt like it skipped a beat, followed by a nervous trill in his stomach as he raised the binoculars for a closer look.

Two figures, dressed in the same black fatigues they had arrived in, armed with rifles slung over their shoulders, stood in the yard. The taller one held a German shepherd dog on a leash as it paced impatiently in circles. They both seemed to be talking and simultaneously glanced in Frank's direction. Instinctively Frank lowered his head. They couldn't possibly see him, could they? He was well hidden, or so he thought. He took another look and saw the black figures walking quickly out of the yard in Frank's direction, across the small field that ended at the foot of the hill at the top of which Frank was positioned.

There was no time to mull over why or how he had been blown. It was time to move–fast.

Frank grabbed his backpack and poncho, rolling it up as he ran towards the line of trees where he had come eight hours before. As his feet pounded the ground, taking him across the clearing back to the main woodland, Frank turned over his options.

Head back to the Alamo? Or go an entirely different direction and hope he could lie low and wait it out? The dog was a problem. It would track him, yard for yard, and he didn't fancy tackling a huge German shepherd, let alone his masters, who looked armed and dangerous.

He decided to head for Alamo, with a possible detour to confuse his pursuers if he could, but the question was then what? Carl wasn't due to rendezvous with him for another forty hours.

Keep calm, Frank. And keep moving.

Once back in the shielded woodland, he stopped and hurriedly took out his binoculars to scan the area he had just covered. Movement in the far tree line. A bark. They were definitely coming after him.

He continued to run across the sodden ground, his boots grinding wet leaves and bracken into the mud as he headed north. The important thing was not to get lost. He just had to find somewhere to hole up until he could think of something. A cold sweat soaked his shirt to his back and all he could think was what a great scent that would leave for that bloody dog.

Suddenly, a crack whistled over his head and hit the tree in front of him. Five minutes later, Frank was lying in the ditch he had spotted and dived into, thinking in staccato, *Move, run. Get to Alamo. Ambush them? How?*

He ran along the ditch, head down, and then, at last, it turned away from his pursuers, well out of sight. After a few metres, the ditch levelled out back into the wood and Frank heard a running stream ahead, where a fallen tree lay across forming a bridge. He scrambled over, almost losing his footing on the uneven track before jumping onto the other side. Landing awkwardly he felt a twinge in his ankle and cursed his luck.

Frank limped on, looking behind him, and upon seeing no one directly on his tail, threw his bag down and slumped down next to it on the wet ground. He rummaged around in the backpack and gulped down the cool water that felt like ecstasy in his throat and then retrieved the Swiss army knife and put it safely into his side cargo trouser pocket where he could get to it easily. Not that it would be any use against guns.

There was no time to check directions; he would have to wing it. Then, an idea. There was a tree before the stream that he reckoned could easily be climbed. If he tracked back the exact same direction and hid in the tree, maybe it would confuse the dog and they would at least get beyond the stream. Just maybe he had a chance. It was the only idea he could come up with. Limping onward, he would be caught, there was no doubt now. He had to move quickly though, otherwise, he'd run right into them.

Frank manoeuvred back through the water next to the fallen tree this time and climbed the bank back to the path he had come. He moved slowly, pausing every now and then in case they were close. He spotted the tree with low branches and hauled himself up, ignoring the shooting pain in his ankle, levering his body higher and higher upwards toward the sheltered crown. He reached a point where he was sure he couldn't be spotted easily from the ground and stopped. It was still a long shot but the only one he had. A cool breeze swept through the canopies, which felt so good against his face. He took more water and then waited.

After what seemed like an age, but was only ten minutes, Frank heard a sound, followed by another. Footfall in the dead leaves on the ground. He strained to listen. No dog? Just one of them. The sound grew closer below him and then he spotted one of the pursuers moving cautiously through the wood, his weapon slung over his back.

Frank looked behind the figure, trying the spot the dog handler but there was no sign. They must have split up? Why? Maybe the other guy thought they could head him off and encircle him somehow. It was likely they knew the woods better than him and anticipated that Frank was heading to one of the main roads. It made sense.

The figure clad in black fatigues moved slowly under Frank's tree, looking around in every direction. Frank dared not breathe. His heart thumped away in his ear like an African drumbeat. He held the Swiss army knife in his grip, inside his jacket pocket, if only for comfort. The man stopped suddenly and Frank imagined he had seen something on the ground.

Shit.

Had he dropped something from his backpack? It was game over if he had and a vision came to him of the pursuer looking slowly up, setting his stare onto Frank.

But after a quick look around, the man casually walked up to a fallen dead tree trunk and proceeded to take a piss against the dark moss covered bark. Frank scanned around the woodland again, looking for the other guy, but there was still no sign. It would have been a perfect ambush situation if he was nearer the ground, but he was too far up the tree and there was no way he could get down there in time without making a noise. Frank cursed to himself. He guessed his life was on the line, but maybe they just wanted to get information out of him. Whoever the hell they were.

Frank watched as the figure below zipped up and proceeded towards the stream. Once just out of sight, he gingerly eased himself down the tree, branch by branch, checking the coast was clear, winching with pain every time pressure was applied to his right foot.

The sane option was to head in the opposite direction and put as wide a gap between him and the other guy as possible. Find another way back to Alamo. Get the hell out of there.

But the hunters were determined to find him, whatever their reason, which Frank was becoming increasingly convinced was to shoot him dead. They had plenty of places to hide his body in this vast, unpopulated area. The thought of leaving Maria and his boy gnawed at his stomach, making him feel nauseous and cold.

No, he had to go on the offensive. The man was on his own without the dog and therefore easier to take on. Every fibre of his body screamed at him to keep running. Instead, Frank turned and walked towards the stream.

Frank stayed well out of sight as he, once again, heard the flowing water just ahead through the dark trees. He just caught sight of the figure reaching the far side, before disappearing into the wood opposite. Dark clouds moved overhead; it would rain again. He followed the same route and waded through the shallow water and then crawled on his stomach up to the grassy bank, slowly peering over the edge.

There was no sign of his adversary. He kept low as he moved to the tree line, thankful for the noise of the stream that covered his footfall. As he slowly walked into the wood, he froze as a dead piece of branch cracked under his boot, sounding way too loud to his sensitive ears. Frank quickly moved behind a wide girthed pine that hid his entire body and listened hard, his heart pounding in his chest. There was a ditch by the tree and he contemplated moving down into it for a second as his hand rummaged around in his cargo trouser pocket for the Swiss army knife.

Suddenly, there was a movement to his left side and a rush of pain hit his jaw that felt like a freight train. Frank managed to keep on his feet but only because his body hit the tree trunk as a dark figure appeared in front of him.

He must have doubled back!

Frank lunged, attempting a quick jab with his fist but the man swivelled himself out of the way and elbowed Frank's ribs, blowing the wind out of him as he fell, hitting the ground hard. The figure stood over him, blue eyes surveying him closely. A thin smile emerged. But he stood too close. With all his strength, Frank scissor-kicked his legs, forcing his opponent to the ground with a bump.

He didn't stay still, throwing himself onto Frank to take advantage of his weak position. He pulled back his right arm to start striking. A sudden buck of Frank's hips put him off balance and Frank blocked his hit, counter-attacking with a knife hand strike, a blow with the side of his outer hand.

The man's eyes opened wide as he struggled for air, gagging

and choking. He tried to grab Frank's throat, attempting to close off his windpipe with his free hand. Frank shoved him off and rolled away down the slope that morphed into a ditch below them. He quickly got to his feet as the blonde thug pulled himself up, and for a moment, the only sound was of both men breathing heavily into the crisp air.

A roaring laugh followed by a series of barks caused them both to turn around.

"Enough rolling around in the mud, boys," came the mocking tone from the second bearded man who stood with one hand holding up his weapon and the other holding back the growling German shepherd as it strained at the leash.

Frank dropped his head in defeat. It was definitely over now.

He was blindfolded by one of the men and could almost feel their triumph and then they led him back towards the stream.

11

The blindfold came off and Frank found himself staring into the eyes of his friend and operations leader, Carl Paterson. It didn't make any sense. He then realised he was inside the same cottage where he had started from. The shaven blonde thug leaned against the wooden table where Carl and Frank had talked earlier and returned Frank's stare with a smug grin.

"Hello, Frank," Carl smiled uneasily. Frank looked at him and then at the two men in half surprise, half contempt. Carl slapped his hands down on his knees and stood up.

"You did well. Not great, but well. I'm sorry for the unorthodox methods but we needed to see how you performed under, well, difficult circumstances, shall we say," he paused but the only response was a deafening silence and the surprise in Frank's eyes that was quickly turning to anger.

"You left some tracks. Where were they, Steve?"

The blonde man nodded. "Up by the hill. It made a good starting point for the mutt." He winked at Frank.

"But nothing serious, right?" said Carl, more of a statement than a question. He turned back to Frank, smiling weakly. "You avoided capture longer than some, that's for sure."

Frank's eyes seemed to darken as he spoke. "You bastard, Carl." The man winced.

"I thought I'd never see my kid again!" He pulled momentarily at the rope binding him to the chair and then lunged his body forward, head down, with all the force he could muster towards Carl, who, already sensing the attack, side-lined his body out of harm's way. The side of the chair clipped Carl's shin, making him shout out in pain. Frank, with the chair bound to his back, lunged halfway across the room before hitting the floorboards hard with a sickening crack.

"For God's sake, Frank, I'm not the bloody enemy here!" Carl rubbed his shin and then shrugged off the dark-haired man who had jumped up at the commotion, holding onto him protectively.

"Get him up," he ordered the two men. Frank spat blood from his mouth onto the floor as he was hauled back upright. A nasty yellow bruise slowly darkened his cheekbone, as if in slow motion.

"Let's stop this silliness, huh, Frank?" Carl said, short of breath. "It was an exercise. One that might bloody well save your life one day." A silence followed, punctuated only by a heavy breathing from both Frank and Carl.

"Can you untie me now?" Frank asked quietly. Carl hesitated and then nodded. The ropes came off and Frank angrily yanked his arms free, still festering, although his initial rage had subsided.

"So who are they?" Frank thumbed at the two grunts.

The one with the blonde crew cut spoke first. "Thomas Greene. Served with *40 Commando*, part of *3 Commando Brigade.* Nice to meet you, Frank." He flashed Frank a grin.

The dark-bearded one didn't look at Frank, choosing to check his equipment instead, as he spoke.

"Steve Piper. Also previous service with *3 Commando Brigade* and *21st Special Air Service Regiment, A Squadron.* Now at her Majesty's leisure. That's all I'm at liberty to say, mate."

Frank merely nodded. "And what about the third person, the woman?"

"Harriet? She's probably close to home now. Back to London and back to work in the morning. Just another employee at the company. You'll like her," Carl said.

"And what about the guns? Shooting at me like a bloody dog. Was that the icing on the cake for your little exercise?" Frank said sarcastically as he held a steady stare at the two men who had hunted him like an animal.

Piper took his sharpshooter rifle from his shoulder and took out the clip.

"This is a modified replica *LL129A1 rifle*, which is standard army issue. But the bullets are rubbers and if you were hit by one of these puppies, you'd certainly be hurt, but not killed."

"Well, the punch and kicking certainly felt real."

"Yeah, sorry about that. Realism was essential," said Greene.

"As I said, we needed to see you under pressure. You did very well, Frank." Carl returned to his chair. "You need to be prepared for live ops and I know you need another contract soon. The money would be handy, right?" Carl held out his arms in a gesture imploring Frank to trust and forgive him.

Frank rubbed his face and ran his hand through his thick black hair, the anger receding as he came to terms with the situation. Carl had a point and it certainly had given him another taste of real life-threatening danger, an adrenaline rush he hadn't experienced since Hong Kong. He thought of his partner and son and the hard time they were all having financially. The bills didn't pay themselves.

"Yes, mate, a contract would be helpful," he said finally.

Carl smiled in relief and held out his hand to shake Frank's, who ignored it. "Got something strong to drink, Carl?"

Piper and Greene cleaned up the cottage, erasing any trace that they had all been there as Frank sat in the passenger seat of the Land Rover, sipping bourbon from Carl's hip flask. The harsh liquid felt good in his throat as it slipped down.

"Listen, Frank, I..."

"Don't. No need. I know what you were doing." Frank paused, gazing at the misty haze that was building in the woods around them. "I guess it worked."

"I wouldn't have put you through that, mate. Came from above. Sorry." He turned to Frank. "You going to drink all that?"

Frank smiled and handed him the flask and they watched the two men load the last of their gear into a Mercedes cruiser.

"Those boys are good," said Frank, almost reluctantly.

"Yeah. Lots of experience."

"So is there something coming up?"

"Not yet. But I'm sure there will be." Carl gave a wave to Piper and Greene as they got into their hatchback and sped off down the track. "I'm sure there will be," he said again.

12

Frank thought briefly about that exercise five years before as he stepped off the train at Hoxton station and made his way toward the rear cobbled lane towards his destination. It had been the beginning of another life. One he couldn't possibly have imagined he would end up living. Since then, he had been sent to many different locations around the globe and seen some horrors, things he never wanted to see again. Maria wanted him to quit and he couldn't blame her. There had to be an exit strategy soon but the money certainly helped ease the pain in the meantime.

He walked into the bar where Carl had suggested they meet. It was one of the new chain style pubs that seemed to be taking over anything that was slightly old or original. Frank hated them but Carl had arranged it and besides, it was near Shoreditch where Frank and his family had settled into a flat they'd bought several years earlier. The money Maria had received from her father's will after his horrific suicide had helped with the purchase, of course, but there were still hefty mortgage payments to contend with. In fact, with the galloping house prices heading ever skyward, they wouldn't have been able to buy anywhere without it.

"Frank!"

Frank turned to see Carl in a secluded corner of the pub, his round face and short red hair shrouded by bands of light streaming in from the window. It amused Frank that this ordinary looking man, a friend from his school days, had managed to get into Oxford University and gone on to join the world famous intelligence agency. It amused him but it didn't surprise him.

After the Hong Kong episode, Frank had been at a loose end and Carl had kindly promised to see if he could help him out. Old schoolmates always looked out for each other. After all, who else would?

Then just a few days ago came word of a joint set-up between MI6 and GCHQ outside of the normal apparatus: to nurture closer ties between the two organisations. Who or what was driving 'Ghost 13', Frank and Carl did not know but it opened up opportunities for both of them.

Frank had completed a security screening process years before and began his field surveillance training. There was a lot of equipment to get to grips with: encrypted radios, secure scrambler phones, recording systems such as *livebait* and *keepnet* that allowed for comparison of different signals. Learning how this equipment worked was no stroll in the park but Frank persevered. Then there were the Honeywell computer systems that kept GCHQ in step with the National Security Agency in the U.S. There were rows and rows of them in Cheltenham, providing acres of data.

Frank took to it easily, he had always been practical and clear thinking. Carl knew him better than anyone and had been pleased with his progress. After Frank had completed the technical training, it had been time for field training that involved exercises in urban environments, tracking surveillance targets in fixed locations such as offices and houses through to mobile vehicle and street surveillance. Then there was the combat training, which Frank hadn't needed any persuading to do after his experience in Asia.

"Traffic give you hell?" Carl smiled broadly as if hoping that it had.

They shook hands and Frank planted himself into the grotesque patterned lilac seat that adorned every other chair and sofa in the establishment like a sickness.

"Not really. I took the train. That mine?" Frank said, gesturing to the pint of Guinness sat on the table.

"No, I thought I'd get as many in before I had to speak to you."

Frank sighed and took a long swig of the black stuff. It tasted good.

"So, how are Maria and the kids doing?"

"Fine, thanks for asking, Carl." Frank leaned back and looked around at the lunchtime crowd, a mix of pie-faced career alcoholics and old frizzy-haired dolly birds laughing loudly at some crude joke. A businessman sat far away from them, gulping down his lunch as if to get the hell out of there as fast as possible, for which Frank didn't blame him whatsoever.

"Couldn't you have chosen somewhere better than here?" asked Frank, turning back to Carl, who was already fishing around in his briefcase.

"I'm sorry, Frank. Got a four o'clock nearby that I cannot be late for. But it's all good for you, mate."

He slung a stapled sheet of papers onto the table and leaned forward, lowering his voice as he spoke. Frank picked up the papers and saw it was a contract.

"This one is a live operation that will start anytime soon. By that, I mean it could be twenty-four hours, so get yourself ready. I don't know too many details but it might be long haul."

Frank cast Carl a glance. "It's not one of your tricks again, is it? I'm not up for that."

Carl shook his head. "Absolutely not."

"So where is it?"

"Sorry, I have no idea but you'll be briefed at the last minute as usual."

Frank smiled thinly. Pie-face was telling another joke at the bar and the atmosphere suddenly seemed to grate on him.

"Anything else you can tell me? Will I have company? How hostile is the location?"

Carl gulped down the last third of his pint with astonishing speed.

"Ahh, all I can say is it's probably the biggest operation you've done to date."

"How do you know I'll do it, Carl?" said Frank, frowning as he tossed the contract back on the table.

Carl stood up and grabbed his briefcase and jacket off his chair before carefully sliding the papers back towards Frank.

"Because money makes the world go round. I'll see you soon, Frank."

Frank moved into the shadow of his lock-up garage and bent down, pulling up the edge of a thick rug that covered the centre of the space. He levered up the edge of the floor vinyl underneath and began to pull it up.

A year or so earlier, he had laid the flooring himself so as to stash certain items. Not foolproof by any means, but perhaps safe from the average thief. The passport that had cost him a fair penny was underneath the vinyl and wrapped in plastic.

Years earlier, Frank had made the decision to get a passport that was his very own, known to no one else, except for Jake Hale, of course. Jake was his friend from way back who operated in darker waters, creating all kinds of fake documents for shady underworld figures. The agency would give him a so-called 'legend', of course, including all the documents that make up an identity. But this was for his own insurance policy; personal use.

Frank knew his employers would be giving him a cover passport as they did for every job but he had made the decision from the beginning to have a back-up that was known to no one.

After five minutes, Frank had pocketed the passport, re-laid the vinyl flooring, and was heading through the calm night.

13

Studio 31 had new occupants and was now fully equipped. Despite the sunshine outside, the large warehouse windows were shuttered tight and artificial lights lit the rooms.

Dan Griffin, or Griff as he was known, sat at the flickering monitors, the blue light forming reflected squares on his thick-rimmed glasses. He tapped onto the keyboard and a roll of data flowed down on the Honeywell computer screen, running through a list of flight manifests.

Griff had been Frank's guide during his training on getting to know and use the surveillance equipment and they had clicked. His intelligence, when it came to computers and networks, had helped him get snapped up by the company after he graduated in Computer Science. The only child of a Tunisian father and an English mother. Frank guessed he was barely out of his early twenties.

"This is a waste of time if we don't know what name she's travelling under. You want a drink?"

"No, thanks," said Frank, looking at the mess around Dan's desk. There were two large screens on Griff's desk and a pile of hard disk drives with numerous wires forming a spaghetti junction that flowed down under the floor, along with thick data cabling.

The young IT analyst rolled on his chair over to a fridge nearby and took out a can of cola. Frank noticed it was stacked with them as he leaned back in his chair with his hands behind his head. On a large board at the end of the bare bricked room, there was a world map with a few photographs of Sarah Edwards and a few scribbled notes. It painfully lacked any real progress.

"What would she have done? Had a false passport made, assumed an identity and then she would have disappeared...somewhere?" Frank was talking more to himself than anyone else.

Carl came into the operations room with a coffee and sat down in his space, near the wallboard and picked up the telephone to dial his superior, the Rottweiler. He heard the brusque Scottish accent grunt at the other end.

"Mr. Keller? It's Carl Paterson. I need access to Echelon to see if there's any matching on some voice data we have."

"Aye, well, I see what I can do. That's casting a grand net, don't you think?"

"It's the only net I have right now," Carl replied.

"Okay, well, send over the packets and I'll get the process started for ya, Carl."

"Thanks, Mr. Keller."

Echelon, set up by the five eyes alliance of the UK, U.S., Australia, Canada, and New Zealand was a signals intelligence (SIGINT) collection and analysis global network that intercepted private and commercial communications on behalf of the western powers. The surveillance powers of this vast network of spy stations that were capable of eavesdropping on telephones, faxes, and computers were becoming more and more central to the operations of the agency.

It would take hours, more likely days, for any results to the voice sample of Sarah Edwards' voice for matches to come back, if there were any at all.

Griff turned to Frank. His eyebrows rose slightly, looking pleased with himself.

"Hey, I managed to get a high score in Warworld. Took over that neighbouring town and grabbed all their resources. Just have to get my armies up to scratch and I can push west." Griff fired up one of his other screens to reveal the bird's eye view of the game and tiny figures moving around the landscape.

Frank shook his head. "I don't know where you get the time to play that crap. Last I looked, my village had been ransacked and I was down to two knights, one infantry unit, and a wood mill."

In the lunch breaks, Griff persuaded a reluctant Frank to take up a 'Massively Multi-player Online Role-Playing Game' or MMORPG. The object of the game, as Griff had explained, was to build your kingdom, establish a castle, build up your army, and conquer territory.

"Sounds like hours of fun. Do I get to destroy yours?" Frank had said, his face deadpan.

"You can try."

Dan showed him a pop-up box in the bottom tray of the game controls and then started typing. The message popped up on the laptop screen Frank had opened on the desk: "Your mama is so big, her ass don't fit in the Grand Canyon."

"Great, right, Frank? I can taunt you directly from anywhere. It's all about using strategy skills. You grow food, mine gold and metals, and consolidate your city. Then train and expand your armies and prepare to be destroyed, my friend," Griff grinned. "I host it on my own server so it's just me and my trusted mates playing," he had added enthusiastically.

Finally, Frank had relented, logged in on another terminal, and allowed Griff to give him the full training walkthrough.

"Hmm, and what do I get if I win?"

"No prizes, I'm afraid, it's just a laugh. Top players are shown on the board."

Frank had thought it a complete waste of time but had a go at building up his avatar and empire just to keep the geek happy. He struggled to make any headway against the other factions and it was turning into a disaster for Frank's online empire.

And now, sitting in Studio 31, Frank and Griff typed comments to each other on the games comm system, in-between snippets of conversation.

"Where would you go, Griff?" Frank typed.

"Anywhere away from you, brother."

Frank turned to him and spoke. "Be serious..."

"Okay, serious...She has a plan, right? She's got to be selling it. To who? Who's going to be in the market for buying our secret shit? Russians, Chinese..."

"Yes, all the usual suspects. North Korea, rogue terrorist groups. I know."

Carl stood up from his desk and walked over to them with a sheet of paper. "This is a list of aliases she has used over the years when on company business abroad."

Griff took the paper. There were three names.

"Only three?"

"She was never a field agent so she didn't need too many aliases. However, to protect our people, we always give them the option."

"Okay, I'll run them through the manifests. Highly unlikely she'd use any of these though," Griff muttered as he began typing.

"I know, I know," Carl replied as he walked back to his desk.

Frank stood up suddenly and threw on his jacket. "I'm taking off, I'll catch you later.

"Where you going?" Griff asked suspiciously.

"To see a little bird."

14

Frank drove his black Saab 900 from the Limehouse Cut and slowly made his way along the A1203 before heading to the South side of the Thames through the Rotherhithe Tunnel. After another thirty minutes, he finally arrived at his destination and parked in a housing estate in Elephant and Castle. He walked along a concrete underpass and up the exterior steps to the fourth level before moving along to the end flat. The door was a steel monster, with a thin slit for an ill-disguised look out. Frank banged on the door and almost immediately, a pair of eyes peered out at him. The door creaked open and Frank stood looking up at the tall figure grinning a toothless smile.

"Hey, Frankie boy. How ya doin'?"

"Yeah, I'm good, thanks, Jake."

Jake Hale was over six foot, half-caste with a closely shaven head and stood in the doorway donning a red tracksuit. Ushering Frank into a gloomy corridor with a jerk of his head, he slammed the heavy door behind them, and they walked into a living room where a young Oriental guy was slumped on a sofa playing a 'shoot 'em up' video game. He threw a nonchalant nod at Frank and continued firing at a group of soldiers running through some war-torn streets.

The flat was sparsely furnished with decoration that was straight out the 1970s but it was obviously not a home. There was a pile of boxes along one wall and cut out paper, film, and cuttings strewn all over the bare floorboards.

Frank sat down at a table by the window that had panoramic views of South London as Jake went into the adjourning kitchen and returned with a bottle of Jack Daniels and two glasses.

"So what are you after, not another passport already?" he asked.

"I wanted to ask you something," Frank said.

Jake sat down and poured out the drinks. "Ask away, mate. Just as long as it's not about my sex life...you don't want to know about that."

"Really? Pretty wild, is it?"

"Ha...no. It's non-existent, mate."

Frank laughed. "My heart bleeds."

He reached into the inside pocket of his leather jacket and pulled out a photocopied sheet with the image of Sarah Edwards alone on the page and flung it onto the table top.

Jake glanced at it and then at Frank.

"I do have a girlfriend, mate, despite the sex life being crap."

Frank let out a snigger and shook his head in mock sympathy.

"No, I'm not matchmaking. I just need a name. Do you recognise her? Did you do a passport for her? It would be really helpful to me, mate. I'll be eternally grateful."

Jake shook his head and then pushed a glass of bourbon towards Frank. "Have you not heard of client confidentiality, bruv? It's when you don't go around blabbing out all the personal details of the people who pay you."

"Yeah, yeah...but I'll make it worth your while, Jake. Trust me, I will."

"You're offering your body? My missus might be giving me the cold shoulder at the moment but I'd rather keep wanking and crying, thanks."

Frank shook his head and laughed. "Please c'mon, Jake. It's just a name. Two words you have to utter. If it makes any difference, the word is she has betrayed this country."

Jake leaned his head slightly to the side and stared at Frank with concern. "She betrayed our queen?" The tone was sarcastic.

Frank nodded. "Full traitoress, mate. No holds barred."

"Shit."

Jake stood up slowly and grabbed the photograph of Edwards.

"Well, I'll give you a name for old time's sake but not for the queen." He turned to his associate, who was giving his enemies full lead.

"Mark, you remember this one? She came in for a passport a few months ago. Remember the alias she used?"

Mark looked up from the sofa and glanced at the picture.

"Hmmm, yeah, I remember her. The name?" He paused his video game and stood up, taking the paper from Jake for a closer look.

"Emily Jenkins." He handed back the paper and sat back down straight away.

Frank was standing by Jake, both men staring at the young man. "Are you sure?" asked Frank.

"As eggs." The game music kicked back on and the rapid firing of an M42 machine gun resumed.

Jake turned to Frank. "He's good at names. That's the name you want."

Frank nodded.

"Is that helpful?"

"Immensely helpful, thanks, mate."

15

Rain hammered the wet tarmac, blown almost horizontal from a sharp easterly wind as Frank grabbed his bag from the back seat of his battered Saab. Across the other end of the car park, Frank could see the huge warehouse doors ajar and three figures moving around inside the bay area. He locked up the car and sprinted across the concrete cul de sac as the roar of a Boeing 777 engine cut through the darkness overhead, descending to the Gatwick airport strip metres away.

The cargo area lay just east of Brockley Wood on the outskirts of the vast International airport. Frank had been summoned for 1100 hours and had made good time. As he approached, he saw Carl Paterson with his unmistakable sandy hair, wearing a white trench coat wave at him, with two burly figures he assumed were part of his team.

He had no choice but to keep Maria out of the loop, as usual. It was made crystal clear that he would be royally fucked if he told a single soul anything about his work. The certainty of spending the rest of his days cleaning toilets at Her Majesty's pleasure kept him on track. Close family were allowed to know that it was intelligence-related and nothing more. The contract was watertight. She had understood but in recent years had not wanted him to do this kind of work; it didn't sit well with her. "Get a normal job. You don't have to do this," she had said.

"Besides, you can't trust those bastards. The agencies and the government are carrying out their own screwed up agenda and certainly not to help us mere mortals."

Maybe she was right but the mortgage rates for the flat were still a struggle and he fully intended that his family would want for nothing in the years ahead.

"Frank. Great night for travelling, huh?" Frank shook Carl's outstretched hand and then noticed the other two men, who stood, staring at him. One of them, with a blonde crew cut, winked and blew a mock kiss.

"Oh, bloody great," said Frank, unable to mask his annoyance. "You didn't tell me I'd be going on an op with them, Carl." He jabbed a thumb towards the two men.

One of the men, sporting a black Mohawk and beard, dressed in khaki trousers and black jacket, jerked his head at Frank. "Nice to see you again, too, Mr. Bowen."

"You remember Piper and Greene then," Carl said, deadpan. "Look, I know you didn't get off to the best start but these guys are good. You'll be glad of that security, I'm sure," said Carl warily.

"Forget it! Count me out," Frank suddenly turned back to head for the doors.

"Hey, mate." Tom Greene appeared in front of him and had a hand on his chest, blocking his path and started pushing him back.

Frank remembered that thin smile now.

In one swift movement, he turned his body slightly and dragged Greene's arm forward, using his momentum to get behind Greene. Suddenly, he had his arm around the man's neck in a rear naked strangle, with his palm over his other bicep, gripping hard. Greene grabbed at Frank's forearm that held him like a vice and began pushing his chin down in an attempt to get air.

Frank knew he just needed to hold the position for ten seconds or so as he cut off blood flow from his heart to brain and the man would be unconscious.

"Frank!" Carl barked. The other man with the beard, moved closer, carefully assessing the situation.

Frank threw Greene forward, away from him, and stepped back, ready for a counter-attack but the blonde man just turned to face him, caressing his throat. His stone straight face morphed into his smile again as he stared at Frank. "Nice move."

"I've been practicing."

"Can we stop this macho bullshit?" Carl was already between them, turning from one man to the other. "Frank. A word."

Carl led Frank to a stack of crates, out of earshot from Piper and Greene.

"Look, I know you've have bad blood about that day but these are good men. They're professionals and they'll look out for you in the field. You have my word on that."

"Just making my mark, Carl. They won't respect me otherwise."

A brief glimpse of realisation passed Carl's face and he gently patted Frank's arm. "So you'll go? This is an important operation, probably the biggest one you're ever going to get a swing at."

Frank sighed and glanced at the two men.

"I hope I don't regret this."

"You won't. Now, let's do this."

They walked over to where Piper and Greene were waiting by an upturned crate that had doubled as a coffee table. Frank held his hand out to Greene as a peace offering.

Greene paused, glanced at Carl before shaking his hand, and

then Frank walked up to Piper and shook his hand as well.

"Good. Now we're all best friends again, can we get on with the briefing?" said Carl, pulling out a batch of reports from his case and handing them around. The men looked down at a photograph of a dark-haired woman in her early 30s along with a description, work history, and family details.

"We've got a target at large having taken a batch of top secret information that is a major breach of National Security. For this operation, she has been codenamed: Pandora, because she is potentially going to release a shitload of secrets from the box. Thanks to Frank here, we know she is travelling under the name of 'Emily Jenkins'. Our intelligence is telling us she went to Panama. Your job is to find her, place her under surveillance, and keep an eye out to see who she meets or talks to. She has to be selling the information to someone, we need to know who. If someone turns up, the next step will be to apprehend Pandora and the contact and haul them back to Blighty."

Carl looked up at the men. "Any questions?"

"So when do we get paid?" asked Greene, spinning a knife around repeatedly in his palm.

"Any other questions?"

16

Nigel Harrison dabbed his brow with a well-used handkerchief, quietly cursing the hot weather. He hated the sunshine and would do his utmost to avoid going out in its leery glare. The cool comfort of a darkened room and a flickering screen were more his idea of passing the time, whether it was for work or leisure. But this bloody office had big, wide windows and the fans simply moved the air around. Air conditioning was a luxury and unfortunately did not feature in the older buildings. Britain had never been equipped for heat waves and this one was in its second week. Rising temperatures always seemed to add to his anxiety, the feeling of being suffocated by the air itself.

He checked the office server status and idly typed in a config command to locate slowness in the network, his fingers skipping over the keyboard with ease but his mind was elsewhere. Guilt welled in his gut; the feeling that had grown for the previous few weeks was all down to what he was about to do.

A year earlier, Nigel had sat in the Golden Lion in Islington high street, nursing an overpriced pint, his eyes never leaving the front entrance. Thirsty punters came and went but the man he was meeting was late, or maybe he wasn't coming at all?

Part of him felt relief if this was the case. It was a normal enough request, a possible job opportunity through the University bulletin board followed by a short telephone conversation and the arranged drink. Something to do with civil rights or a political movement campaigning for radical change.

He had caught some of what the guy had said but he had been concentrating so hard on not saying the wrong thing that the details became a blur. An element of his own persona that he hated. Any situation that was out of his comfort zone and routine was enough to spark the anxiety. It was bloody annoying and Nigel vowed to overcome it. He was determined to force himself to make a go of whatever this chap was offering rather than slink back to the safety of home and the alluring glow of his computer screen. He yearned to be connected with a crowd, to be part of something exciting and it sounded like this John Rhodes might be offering it.

Nigel was amazed at how he had survived university. Being a social outcast had given him no choice but to focus one hundred percent on his studies, which paid off with a distinction in his IT and Computer Science degree.

A stout man with white hair, a short-sleeved pale shirt with a laptop bag over his shoulder entered the bar and looked around, his gaze settling on Nigel, who nervously held up a hand. The man came over and slung the bag down onto an empty chair.

"Nigel, hello. I'm really sorry I'm late."

"Oh, no problem at all, Mr. Rhodes."

Nigel quickly stood up, knocking the last of his pint onto the table surface. He cursed to himself, picked up the glass, and then held out his hand.

"Please call me John. Another drink, Nigel?"

"Oh, no, thanks. I can't drink too much."

Rhodes was soon back from the bar with an ale and eased himself into a dark wood chair. The pub crowd ebbed and flowed until it quietened down into a scene of low murmur and clinking glasses. Rhodes leaned forward as he spoke, his eyes sparkled with youthful enthusiasm as he explained his vision and the legacy that he was determined to build.

Nigel felt drawn to the man; he couldn't help but share his excitement as he explained the vision behind Liberatus, the idea of breaking from state dependency and moving to a more self-sufficient society.

"The news media group is one part," he explained. "For society to change, we need to inform the populace about what is going on—the mainstream media certainly isn't. We connect the dots for them and when they realise they have been lied to and deceived by those who purport to work in our best interests, support and action will follow."

Two and a half hours later, both men shook hands and Nigel Harrison agreed to help them build and run their computer systems for the newsgroup. The role was to take advantage of the growing popularity of the Internet and the communication opportunities that it offered as well as build an I.T. infrastructure for their operations. It was a challenge but a great opportunity and Nigel had needed very little persuasion.

Nigel glanced once again at the clock on the wall. Most had left the office, only Maria remained at the far end, her nose buried in a report. He longed for her to leave, which was not a feeling he was used to. At any other time, he would have killed to have this opportunity to be alone with her in the office. But not now. He needed to speak to John but couldn't afford for anyone to accidentally overhear his questions.

He fondled the plastic coffee cup, the remaining liquid having long lost any warmth and toyed with the idea of making another one as if to signal to her that he was going nowhere. And what if John left before? It needed to be now! They had been demanding information and making threats and he needed to give them something, anything. Nigel checked the company calendar again on his screen. It was still there in John's purple highlighted calendar, an appointment with a member of parliament for Braintree, but it didn't say where it was or who it was with?

Just as his anxiety seemed to peak to another level, Maria began to make the telltale signs of leaving, to his relief. She rustled papers together, locked them in a drawer, and then grabbed her bag, looking across at Nigel. She gave him a quick wave which he gladly returned.

"See you tomorrow."

"Yes, tomorrow it is," he returned, but they were just hollow words. He felt empty. He felt he was betraying himself.

"Don't work too late," she said, and then she was gone.

Nigel paused for a moment and then got up, walked over to John's office door, and rapped quietly on it with his knuckles, his head bowed slightly as he listened for a response.

"Hello?"

Pushing the door ajar, Nigel popped his head round to see John's expectant look from behind his monitor. His white hair seemed to catch the light of a lamp behind him, reminding Nigel of a saint from one of those paintings in a church.

"I'm sorry to disturb you, John. I'm just on my way home but wanted to update you. The server thing...," he paused deliberately and Rhodes waved him in.

"Come on in, Nigel." He stood up and stretched and reached for his mug, draining the last dregs of stewed tea.

Nigel moved into the room, clutching a batch of papers.

"There was a lot of resistance and slowness on some of the

servers. Seems to be running okay now but I'll keep an eye on it." It was no lie that the servers had indeed been struggling. Because of John's insistence on keeping everything in-house and the demand on the website from an increasing number of visitors, it was a common problem.

John Rhodes nodded and returned his mug to the crowded desk. Papers were piled high on either side of his monitor and Nigel noticed some had found their way onto the floor. He had an urge to point out this unnatural order of things but he held his tongue.

"We'll get the extra power you need soon, Nigel. It's top of my list."

"Will you be in tomorrow?" Nigel asked as nonchalantly as he could muster. He needed the confirmation. A calendar entry could be changed or postponed and in that circumstance was rarely ever updated.

John looked around his desk as if noticing the mess for the first time.

"Erm, no, not tomorrow. I've got a meeting with an MP from Westminster, might be a useful contact to have. An old friend from years ago. That kind of thing."

Nigel shuffled his feet, his hands tightly gripping the papers he held. He could feel the sweat staining them but didn't dare look.

"And will you be coming in here first or straight there?" he asked. "It's just in case there are any issues."

John was looking around for something on his desk now, playing the patient boss.

"No...Oh, sorry, yes. I have to come here first and then off to the meeting late afternoon. But just speak to Marcus if anything comes up with the servers." He glanced up at Nigel with a questioning expression as if to ask if he needed anything else.

"Great, thanks, John. See you in the morning then," said Nigel.

There was a wave of relief as he turned to leave. Hopefully, it would be enough to satisfy them and keep them off his back.

17

John Rhodes stood up and stretched his arms, the aching bones reminding him he had not left his desk since lunch.

He thought about the meeting and hoped it would open some doors, or at the very least, Leo might become an asset. The more contacts he made at government level, the more leverage he hoped Liberatus could pull when it came to their aims. Of course, he still caught up with some of the boys from his MI6 days but they never really told him anything. It was as if a distance was being created between them. Rhodes understood though. They knew he was writing a book, one that would open several cans of worms about the agency, and certainly couldn't associate with him anymore. John Rhodes gathered his laptop and made his way out of the office and into the buzzing hub of Soho.

Nigel Harrison lingered outside the red telephone box for a moment and then stepped inside. He barely noticed the stench of tobacco and piss that hung in the confined space and dialled the number he had memorised. After a few seconds, the ringtone kicked in and it seemed his heart beat louder inside his chest.

It had all started several months before after Nigel had set up the web server and things were beginning to feel good. He was being useful at last and the feeling of using his knowledge and skills for the cause made him feel valued and important, not to mention actually enjoying the job. Then the email came from a dead mailbox. He couldn't track it, despite his skills, but it didn't matter. The images were of young children, both male and female, no older than ten years old, stripped naked or semi-naked. The email simply read:

We found these on your computer, Nigel.

Then these were followed by much worse images. Children performing sexual acts, on grown men, obviously under duress – their faces were hidden from the camera. Clearly visible on a muscular arm was a London football club badge that was based barely a mile away. The frightened faces of the kids told their own sick story. Nigel had never seen anything like it and it made him physically shake. Some prankster? Someone who hated him?

After that, he clearly heard clicks on his phone line at home. There were also calls but on the rare occasion, he answered, there was just silence. The phone calls kept coming and Nigel, long since having stopped taking them, would just hide under the duvet in his bedroom, covering his ears, sometimes even shouting as if to drown out the tormentors. Eventually, he ripped out the phone line; something he hadn't wanted to do as his phone was an important link with his mother.

Then, one evening when walking home from the office, as he turned into a quiet side street near his flat, he noticed an unmarked black van parked ahead and sensed a presence behind him. He looked back and was physically assaulted with a fist to the face that threw him backwards onto the pavement. Hands grabbed him under his arms and a hood covered his head. Nigel tried to cry out but a hand covered his mouth and then he felt himself being bundled into the back of the van. He screamed under the stifling material, wondering how long he had to live. Why did they want him? Who were they? A swirl of questions dancing on his sick leaden fear so heavily, he pissed himself.

"You dirty fucking bastard," a gruff voice said.

They drove for around twenty minutes, although to Nigel, it seemed like a lifetime, with no end in sight. Blood seeped from his mouth and nose, making it almost impossible to breathe under the hood so that he had to gasp for air through his mouth. The buzzing in his head from the punch was only matched by the clasping grip of fear. It reached the point when he just wanted them to get it over with. To kill him and be done with it.

The van slowed down and seemed to take a sharp turn and then the vehicle stopped and the engine died. The sound of the back doors opening and then a steady commanding voice, which sounded slightly muffled and Nigel had to concentrate to hear the words.

"Nigel. We know who you are, where you live, what you do. Everything you do, we know about. Nod your head to show you understand me."

Nigel did as he was told, vigorously.

"The pictures of the kids," the voice continued. "They can be given to the police at any time and will be traced back to you, make no mistake."

Nigel suddenly felt his skin go ice cold, the sheen of sweat on his skin had soaked his entire shirt, and his trousers were still damp after his other accident. This was all connected to the pictures of the children? He had assumed it was a bully from years back who had tracked him down. This was obviously a lot more serious. Then he felt a kind of strange relief. They weren't going to kill him after all. Maybe there was a way out?

The voice started again.

"You will end up in prison, and either become some bitch for a nasty group of blokes inside, or you will be beaten to a pulp on a regular basis. They don't like kiddy fiddlers inside, Nigel. You will not be protected, believe me."

There was a sigh. "Or we will kill you right here."

Nigel's stomach turned.

"There is a third option though, Nigel. One where you can make all this go away."

Now Nigel clutched the phone, ready to give them the information that they had asked for: John Rhodes' major movements and appointments. They had also wanted technical information on the servers and after that, they kept coming back for more.

A low voice on the other end of the line asked for a reference number.

"HN3162," he said carefully.

A click followed and then another ring tone before a male voice answered.

"What is it?"

"Erm. Jonah is going to be travelling by car tomorrow morning. From the Soho square office to Braintree in Essex for a meeting," Nigel said.

"What time is he leaving?" asked the voice, almost a whisper now.

"About 10:30, I think, maybe a bit later."

"A meeting with who?"

"I...I don't know."

The line instantly disconnected.

18

The day was another glorious one and John Rhodes was glad he had driven down to Braintree if it only meant getting out of the city for a few hours. Leo Smith, an adviser to the parliamentary committee of MPs, wanted to meet away from any prying eyes, which John understood perfectly. The two men had known each other since university and Rhodes had recently reached out with a phone call.

He pulled his Audi A4 into a narrow road that ended at Bocking Blackwater woods that dominated the south side of Blackwater River. There was a lone silver Jaguar parked in a small enclave, set against the trees behind. Smith got out of the car to greet him, dressed in a casual chequered shirt that looked somehow out of place on him. He was a tall lean man with little hair, baldness having taken a firm grip.

"Beautiful day, eh?" John said. Smith nodded, smiled thinly, and both men shook hands.

"Shall we take a walk?" Smith gestured to the woodland path.

"Lead on," John said.

Both men disappeared under the canopy of the woods, where it was considerably cooler. The chirping of birds darting from tree to tree seemed to intensify.

"I used to play here as a child, many years ago now," Smith started. He appeared more relaxed than he had been at the car.

"Know this place like the back of my hand. Just like the area and the constituents here. They know me very well, which is why I'm always re-elected," he said with pride.

John nodded in agreement. "You're a respected man, Leo. Long may it continue."

Smith seemed to find that amusing and snorted a laugh.

"Seems like I've been playing this game for quite a while now; there's a point when you really do start looking forward to retiring."

"Hey, you're a long way from that! There's plenty more for you to do, I'm sure. In fact, that's why I wanted to see you."

"Oh?" There was alertness in his voice.

"Liberatus needs your help. We need eyes and ears in Parliament and possibly a mouthpiece."

"Listen, John, I know we go back a long way, which is why I agreed to meet, but there are things I can and cannot do. I understand what you're doing, but you're still an activist, John. I can't be seen associating with activism. Your paper has caused quite a stir. It gets a fair few backs up, shall we say."

"Who said anything about public association? I'm not asking for some joint press conference," said John.

Leo Smith stopped walking and looked at his companion.

"What is it you're asking exactly?"

John sighed. It had taken a lot to come here and do this. He needed allies in the establishment, otherwise, the inevitable conflict between the people and the elite governments might only go one way. He needed an information source.

"Do you believe in true freedom and liberty, Leo? Bullshit aside, do you think the populace has the right to freedom of speech, the right to make their own decisions for their own lives?"

Leo frowned as they began walking again.

"Yes, of course,"

"But if there was a major threat to that, and I mean an advanced, planned threat on a global scale, would that concern you in any way?"

"What are you getting at?"

John paused.

"Did you ever hear of a Major General Smedley D. Butler from the States, before the second world war? He was America's most decorated soldier, apparently."

Leo shook his head. He had not.

"Well, having helped pacify various countries in the service of corporations, Mexico, Honduras, he was approached by a group of powerful men, I'm talking high-level corporate CEOs and bankers who planned to overthrow Roosevelt and install a fascist government. But Butler was fed up with fighting for capitalist interests and blew the whistle on the plot in front of the congressional committee in 1934."

"Interesting story, John, but I still don't..."

John stopped, halting their stroll again.

"I'm not asking you to sacrifice your career or put your head above the parapet. Just to keep your ears to the ground, and keep me abreast of any information we can use."

"A sordid mole for your newspaper?" said Leo with a wry smile.

John shook his head. "No, more like a supporter of true liberty, that's under threat without anyone knowing it is."

Further down the path, a squirrel watched them approach and then made off around the base of an old oak tree. They were approaching a break in the trees, a view of rolling fields that stretched to the farthest point on the horizon.

"So, what am I looking for? Fascists?" Leo said, with more than a hint of sarcasm.

John gave him a look.

"They wouldn't call it that now. But, yes, a cross-over of corporate power and government structure is pretty much fascism in my book," stated John.

Leo paused and thought for a moment. "There is a multitude of corruption and scandal on a continuous basis at Westminster. There are secrets everywhere but if I don't know what I'm looking for, how can I help?"

They both faced the fields, admiring the view of middle England with the blue sky opening up overhead and not a cloud in sight.

"I believe there is a coup being planned in this country. It will start with mass surveillance, for which I am confident I will have evidence of very soon, and then they'll create a situation, a problem which only they can fix. Problem, reaction, solution. It may not happen soon, or even in the next ten years, but it will happen and my mission is to be prepared."

Leo turned to him. "Some might say you're being paranoid. We have a fully functioning democracy, the country is booming, it's the good times." John could sense he was playing devil's advocate now, perhaps as a way to think it through. The politician paused. "There is a shadow behind us all. You know it, I know it, and so does anyone with any kind of finger on the pulse but it's always been that way. Strings are pulled, the players play...why fight against the status quo?"

Rhodes let out a chuckle. "Why indeed?" He had already put his point across and wasn't going to flog a dead horse.

"For our friendship, I'll help in any way I can but I want a watertight method of passing information over. It has to be completely safe from detection, otherwise, it's not going to happen."

It was dark by the time John Rhodes gunned into fifth gear onto the A120 dual carriageway toward Stansted airport, where he would join the M11 motorway back to London.

He was happy with the way the meeting had gone and figured Leo would be an extremely useful ally, with a wealth of contacts in the upper echelons of government.

The roads were quiet and he anticipated getting back in no time. A black Ford Mondeo powered past him on the lamp lit road and pulled ahead out of sight. John checked his speed, seeing a steady 60 miles per hour; he estimated the car must have been doing ninety-five at least and tutted out loud.

John put on the radio and pressed the button for one of his saved stations: the sound of jazz filled the car and instantly put him in a more relaxed frame of mind. He had picked up the bug from his father, Charlie Rhodes, who usually had one of the greats playing in the background: Bix Beiderbecke, Duke Ellington, Charlie Parker. That was the great thing about jazz music, his father always used to say, you can just play it in the background and get on with what you're doing. John and his family were based in Chicago before John had decided to move to England and go to university. Once an affluent family in the press and newspaper business, the Great Depression had virtually wiped them out.

After a few minutes, he rounded a curve in the road and caught a glimpse of a footbridge that went over both sides of the carriageway. Then on the deserted road, he saw the Mondeo again but it must have stopped or slowed down because he was coming up towards it very fast. Suddenly, he was being blinded by a brilliant strobe light that seemed to come from the top of the bridge and he couldn't see at all. His hands instinctively went up to protect his eyes while desperately trying to slow down by taking his foot off the accelerator. Another foot tried to depress the brake and hit it too hard. Already out of control, the car wheeled and turned. A rush of movement, as if spinning. Screeching. A bang and the light faded into blackness.

Two men clad in black fatigues made their way down the embankment to the road from the footbridge. The Mondeo screeched into reverse, backing up to the crashed Audi that had careened onto the mid-section steel divider and then flipped upside down onto the road. One of the men crouched down at the car and shone a micro torch through the cracked driver side window and saw the slumped bloodied figure of Rhodes, who hung upside down, harnessed by his seatbelt.

A radio crackled. "Traffic coming."

A distant glow from behind the bend.

"Let's go," one of the men said.

They jumped into the rear of the Mondeo and the car pulled off at high speed as if it were on a race circuit.

A blue family Ford rounded the bend in the road and slowed down at the sight of the flipped over Audi. The driver pulled into the lay-by as soon as he could.

The rear lights of a vehicle faded up ahead in the darkness.

19

As the British Airways flight from Gatwick began its descent towards Aeropuerto Internacional de Tocumen, International Airport of Panama City, the captain announced in Spanish that the temperature was a steady ninety degrees Fahrenheit with a light south easterly wind and welcomed the passengers to Panama. The city ran twenty kilometres along the Pacific coast from the famous Canal to the ruins of the Panama Viejo.

Frank glanced across at Piper, who looked every bit a tourist in his colourful shirt and slacks. The three men had not communicated or even exchanged glances on the flight. They had each assumed identities along with the corresponding passports provided by their operations head, Carl Paterson. Frank was currently Keith Feldman, an IT contractor visiting on a tourist visa. Piper and Greene had similar stories and IDs.

The name Sarah Edwards had used, Emily Jenkins, had come up eventually. At least Griff had something to work with and there was the name on the manifest for a Virgin flight to Panama, the day after she had disappeared. Frank didn't reveal to anyone how he had received the information, that would have been against his own interests. Never reveal your sources. Carl understood and it was the lead they needed.

The passengers disembarked and streamed into the arrivals terminal and towards customs. Frank enjoyed the heat against his skin, a welcome relief from the recycled air conditioning on the flight.

"State your business in Panama, Señor."

"Pleasure," replied Frank.

The olive clad immigration officer asked a few more questions and Frank stuck to the story he was told to. The grey-bearded man glanced at him and then back at his passport photo.

"Have a pleasant stay, Mr. Feldman." He handed Frank the passport.

When they were all through customs, the three men continued to keep their distance and wandered through to the small airport arrivals area. They independently arrived at the outside taxi zone and were approached by a stocky Afro-Caribbean man who blended in with the other locals by sporting a dirty football shirt, knee-length shorts, and flip-flops.

"Taxi, gentlemen? My name is Dante Brull and I could take you all into the city if you please. Central express is the only service you can trust, believe me," he said, signalling to the men that he was their contact. Piper and Greene pretended to have a discussion and made a show of inviting Frank to join them.

Frank and the other men knew Brull's appearance was deceptive. He was a powerful and well-connected individual who had connections with numerous police departments, intelligence agencies, and even drug cartels in Central and South America. From the little information they had read, they also were aware that MI6 had employed his services since the mid-80s and he was deemed a valuable asset.

The minibus moved slowly with the other traffic exiting the airport and headed south towards the Corredor Sur freeway and Panama City. Frank watched the landscape flash by; palm trees, crumbling stone buildings, and old men sat at tables, killing time.

The skyscrapers of the modern metropolis were already in view.

Twenty minutes later, the vehicle bumped up a track in the Calidonia district, views of the La Bahía de Panamá behind them. The car pulled in front of a ground floor garage of a condo, the doors automatically opening from a key fob Brull had in his hand. Looking up at the stone white building, Frank could just make out the bottom of a balcony.

Once inside the garage with the door closing behind them, they exited the vehicle and Brull led them through an interior fire door and up concrete steps into the condo living quarters. The large room they walked into was a living and dining room combination and had a pleasantly decorated finish; two leather sofas, a coffee table, a dining table in the corner. A photograph on canvas of the Panama skyline hung on the wall over an old unused fireplace.

"Anyone else have access to this property?" asked Piper.

"No, very secure. I rented the entire building," he answered.

Steve Piper sat down at the dining table, his fingers already typing into his palm phone, sending an encrypted message to Cronus, Carl Paterson's codename in London to say they had arrived. Frank put his holdall down onto the floor and wandered to the kitchen area, checking the fridge first and cupboards. It was all well stocked.

Brull put a set of keys down on the table.

"I only have two sets. I show you the alarm system."

"Did you get any weapons?"

Brull nodded and walked over to the kitchen sink. He opened up a wooden door and pulled out a briefcase and brought it back to the dining table.

"One Glock 17 for each man," Brull said as he opened it up, revealing the weapons and ammunition.

"Is that it?" Greene was standing, staring down at the contents, clearly disappointed.

"Better than a slap in the face with a wet kipper," Frank said, picking up one of the weapons and pressing the small eject button on the side to release the magazine.

"What the hell does that mean?" Greene sneered and took a pistol himself.

"It means be grateful for what you receive, mate."

After checking the condo, their weapons and their location on the map, Brull cooked up rice and pinto beans. Bare basics. There was no time for culinary cook-offs. The four men hunched around the table, scooping up their food in silence. After finishing up, they cleared the table and Piper laid out a map of Panama. The men stood sipping coffee and studied the city layout.

Piper passed a photocopied piece of paper with Pandora's details to Brull.

"This is who we're looking for. She arrived at Panama City airport three days ago, then disappeared," said Piper.

"What are we doing?" asked Frank.

"We're sitting tight and wait for Cronus and London to find other traces of Pandora," he replied.

"So basically sit on our arses while the trail gets colder?"

Piper gave Frank an exasperated look. "What are you saying, Frank?"

"Maybe we should get busy looking. Check the airport CCTV Start making enquiries at all the transport hubs, the stations. See if Brull has any..."

"Hey, Sherlock. You're talking about an unknown amount of man-hours." Thomas Greene had dismantled his Glock to check the parts and now his narrowed eyes were looking up at Frank. "Let London locate the target and then we'll take things from there. We're not getting paid to run around this shit hole."

Frank sighed as if disappointed at a child who had stolen sweets. "I'm sure we'd all love to kick back and sip piña coladas, mate, but with every minute, this woman is getting further and further away and the trail gets colder. We're the ones on the ground who can do something." He turned to Piper.

"We need to be on this now, otherwise leads go cold, and witnesses forget what they've seen. We should at least try."

Greene clicked the magazine back into the pistol with a slap of his palm.

Piper nodded and looked back at the map.

"Let's go over what we have then."

"You think she left already Panama?" Brull asked.

"I know I would have," Greene interjected.

Brull nodded sagely. "I have some resources here, a few contacts with the police and others but..."

"We want to be careful not to alert any police to the situation. We don't know who else might be looking for her," said Frank. "I suggest we split up the tasks. Ask around where she might have used transport. The bus or train station, the airport. Someone must have seen her."

Brull folded up the piece of paper with the Pandora details. "I also have underworld contacts. She may have changed passports, no?"

Greene turned to him. "Alert the bloody underworld as well? What's wrong with you?"

"Not if we have a decent cover story. She's a common thief, a missing person. Maybe she's a friend who needs help. Why don't you try using your brains?" Frank uttered the words with quiet annoyance.

Greene slammed his coffee mug on the table top and faced

Piper. "Alright! Whatever you want to do. I'd rather be hoofing around out there in the bloody heat than be stuck in here with him." He jabbed a thumb in Frank's direction.

"Good. I'll go with Brull and you two lovebirds could maybe try and get access to the airport footage?" Frank said, eager to leave.

"Yeah, we'll do that. Now, why don't you go on your merry way?" Greene hardly held the contempt from his voice.

20

Sarah Edwards glanced at her digital watch once again and drained a glass of soda water. The evening was turning to night and would, no doubt, be another restless one. She had been living in the hotel room for nearly a month now, rarely leaving the confines of her four walls or the hotel grounds as she played the waiting game.

Where was her contact? They were supposed to rendezvous with her a week ago and no messages had been sent whatsoever. This was deeply worrying. What worried her, even more, was that everything she was risking might well be for nothing.

The ceiling fan spun listlessly at low speed, barely keeping the humidity at bay but apart from complaining again, she would have to live with it.

She had chosen the small, discreet hotel long before disappearing to Cuba: the central courtyard restaurant meant she could occasionally dine away from her room and still be out of sight from the main road that linked up with the San Pedro harbour port road. There was also a secluded back exit to an alleyway, shadowed by towering tenant buildings, where a constant rotation of clothes drying hung overhead.

The plan had gone well so far and she was sure that every precaution had been taken. The assumed identity of Emily Jenkins to Panama and then she dumped that for a new one before heading to Cuba. She was determined not to underestimate the intelligence services, whether it was the British, Americans, Russians, or Chinese. She prayed the trail would die there or at least long enough for her to find permanent shelter.

She was under no illusions that any number of agencies would happily kill her for the information. It was important to be watchful, resourceful, and not trip up. That would be a costly mistake that would ensure she would become history. A tough time waited ahead of her, that much she was certain of, but it was the right course of action. This data would be the first step to exposing the lies and corruption in the establishment she had grown to despise so strongly. She felt her cause was completely justified when she had seen the details of black operations, undisclosed holding sites, and destabilisation projects on the agency files.

The thought of moving to a different hotel had crossed her mind more than once but if she did, she might lose the connection with the contact and it would all be for nothing. It had been agreed that any direct contact via telephone or email was out of the question but now she was torn with a dilemma. Send a message and risk the net falling over her head or stay put and risk them finding her anyway? Yes, moving on might be a good idea. She decided to give it a few more days.

Footsteps grew louder on the terrace walkway outside her room and Sarah tensed up for a moment until the footfall faded and only the sound of the ceiling fan remained.

Get a grip, Sarah.

She cradled the empty glass, still thirsty, and padded over to the fridge, which was empty. Just then, the lamp flickered and died leaving her in darkness. She gasped inwardly despite knowing that it must be a power cut, the third since she had arrived, but it spiked her adrenaline nevertheless. She peered out of the blinds and noticed all the rooms had been affected. That made her breathe slightly easier but she still didn't like it. She walked over to the bed and lay down, listening to the ceiling fan gradually slowing to a halt and felt the oppressive, thick air on her skin.

After what seemed like at least an hour, but was probably only 20 minutes, Sarah reached for the phone by the bed and dialled reception.

"Buenos Dias. Reception."

"Hi. I know it's difficult to say but do you know when the power will return?" she asked in Spanish.

"It's hard to say, madam. We are trying to contact the electrical system's headquarters for more information but haven't managed to get through yet. Do you want me to let you know if I hear anything?"

Sarah paused. "No, it's alright. Mucho gracias."

She replaced the telephone receiver, unaware of the homing beacon she had just planted on herself.

21

At the Ghost 13 operations room in London, Carl felt the buzzing of his mobile in his inside jacket pocket and saw a withheld number message display on the screen.

"Carl Paterson?"

"Yes?"

"This is David Devlin. You know who I am. From now on, you report to me directly. Any update, any single item of information you learn, must be reported directly to me. Do you understand?"

Carl hesitated. "Right, I thought Keller..."

"Forget Keller. Is your phone encrypted?"

"Yes."

"Good. I will give you a phone number to call me on. Any updates on the Pandora situation must be relayed to me directly," he said, the tone deadly serious.

"Okay, will do," Carl said curtly, bristling at the tone.

Devlin gave him a number and then asked him to repeat it before disconnecting. Carl stared at his phone screen, frowning for a moment, and tossed the phone on top of the mound of paperwork on his desk.

He opened his drawer where a pile of chocolate bars were hidden and grabbed one, ripping off the top of the wrapping.

Carl had no idea what the Director of GCHQ was doing but he obviously had a vested interest in this operation. Perhaps his head must be on the chopping block over the leak? Either way, it didn't make much difference to Carl who he reported to. If the head honcho wanted a direct line, then the head honcho would get it.

Across the far side of the expansive space, Griff rolled his chair over to the fridge and grabbed another can of cola before returning to the slow progress bar on his screen. The voice recognition software was scanning through the Echelon satellite data from the previous few days in the Central America area, Sarah Edwards' last reported sighting.

The software was trying to match the voice of Sarah Edwards with an audio sample that GCHQ had of her voice on file from her recruitment process. Griff knew that the voice traffic was being routed to high-speed Voice Recognition computers using a program called "Oratory."

It was a literal needle in a very mountainous haystack but if there was a match, then the scan would find it. Carl's figure drifted across Griff's peripheral vision in the background as his eyelids grew heavy from the workload. Everyone had been pulling long hours since the operation launch and it had been a good twenty-six hours since he had slept.

A beep from the computer jerked Griff from his drifting stupor. The screen proclaimed a near match. Quickly reviving, he tapped a key to check the results and reveal the location. The GPS coordinates took a few seconds to adjust and then he was staring at a line of text displaying the words "Havana, Cuba".

"Carl! Think I've got something."

Carl came over to the screen and was soon joined by Harry, the communications officer. Griff opened a window of the audio and played it. A male voice came from the speaker.

"Buenos Dias. Reception."

A woman's voice: "Hi. I know it's difficult to say but do you know when the power will return?"

The male voice returned and then the line went particularly bad.

A snippet of the female voice returned.

"...Mucho gracias."

The line was crackly and intermittently, there were gaps of silence but words could be made out, sometimes clearly, sometimes not.

"Eighty-three percent. It's not a ringing endorsement," muttered Carl, looking unconvinced.

Griff turned to look at him, frowning as if he was questioning his expertise.

"It's a close enough match, considering the quality," said Griff.

"How did Echelon pick up an internal telephone transmission? Vortex can only pick up regional communications through ground-based microwave towers, right?"

Griff shrugged and adjusted his glasses. Carl was referring to a spy satellite named 'Vortex' that intercepted communications.

"Yeah, that's right. The power cut must have re-routed the transmission externally to the towers and then Vortex picked it up."

Carl nodded and then stood back up.

"Thanks, Griff. I need to run this by people upstairs."

Griff swung round in his chair to face Carl. "What for?"

Now Carl frowned and spoke slowly. "Because that's the way it is..."

Carl walked into a private room set away from the main operations space and dialled David Devlin's number.

22

Frank and Brull drove south in a black Toyota towards the older part of Panama City, Casco Viejo. Frank sat in the front, watching the streets blur by. It was a modern hub of activity, punctuated by the car horns of impatient drivers. As they headed south, the buildings became more dilapidated with boarded-up ruins, interspersed with terraced colonial gems. An urban slum, fighting to restore its once great place in the history of the city.

As they drove deeper, the spectre of poverty and crime was suddenly all around them.

"Sure you're cool with this guy?" asked Frank, as he brushed a hand across the bulk of the Glock tucked inside his jacket pocket.

"I know him for some years. It's okay. If he asks, just say you're a friend of mine looking for your girlfriend."

Frank nodded. "Yeah, makes sense."

Brull pulled up outside a two-storey condo that looked freshly painted; bright white against a turquoise blue sky and a view of Panama Bay completed the backdrop. Outside, sitting around a table playing cards, were three young men, all sporting dark shades. Their heads turned at the sight of Frank and Brull pulling up opposite.

Both men got out of the car and slowly strolled across the road towards them. One of the men stood up, his hand clearly reaching for an unseen weapon behind his belt.

Brull jerked his hand at him nonchalantly.

"We here to see Palacio. It's Dante."

Narrow eyes checked out Frank and Brull, looking them up and down.

"It's okay. Palacio knows him." said a fat man in Spanish who was at the table.

After a pat down, their pistols removed and kept aside, they were escorted into a reception room, where a short, squat man with curly black hair was slumped on a sofa, talking on an oversized satellite phone. He gestured with a plump hand for them to take a seat on the sofa opposite and continued bellowing obscenities in Spanish to the unfortunate person at the other end. Frank looked around at the clean, whitewashed interior. A piece of modern art adorned the wall behind the fat man, looking out of place in the sparse condo.

Palacio threw the phone down next to him and fixed two small eyes on the visitors. "So, what can I do for you, Brull?"

Brull pulled the print out from his inside pocket and handed it over to Palacio.

"My friend here, Mr. Feldman..." Frank nodded at the Panamanian. "Is looking for his girlfriend who went missing in this part of the world. She may have tried to leave covertly."

Piggy eyes scanned the photograph and then focused on Frank. The fat man smiled and for a moment, reminded Frank of a shark. "Are you sure she didn't find another man to satisfy her, Mr. Feldman?"

Frank made himself look irritated for a second and then grinned back, nodding his head slowly as if realising it was a joke.

"She is a loyal woman. I fear she might be in danger," he said.

The fat man's smile faded and he sighed, folded up the print and put it into his shirt pocket.

"I will make inquiries. Call me back in twenty-four hours," he said with a finality that indicated the meeting was over.

Both men got up and shook hands with Palacio before heading back to the vehicle.

"Do you think we'll get anything out of him?" he asked Brull.

"If anyone can find out, he can. He supplies assumed identities for many different groups, including some of the South American cartels."

Frank smiled. "Nice."

"You work many places, Frank?"

Frank gazed out at the tall stacked skyscrapers lining the horizon against a setting sun as they headed north.

"Not too many. The Balkans, Asia, Europe. Ever been to Europe?"

"Ahh, yes, many times. I like London, yes. But Paris and France is my favourite. I would love to retire there one day."

"France, huh? I didn't have you down as a Frenchie. Nice wine and cheese though."

"I like the pace. Very slow. And French women, too!" Brull said, laughing.

Frank smiled. "I won't argue with you about that. So, no family then?" he asked.

Brull shook his head. "No. There's no wife or children. That's on my list for one day in the future. But in our business, a quiet retirement is a distant dream. A very dangerous dream."

Frank nodded and paused. "Yeah, you could be right there, mate."

As the cityscape drifted by, Frank thought about Maria and the children. He missed them. Would he ever get more time with them? Would he even get to retirement himself? These thoughts always crept up again and again, something he usually tried hard to block out when working. Focus and discipline could be affected.

He tried to put himself in Pandora's shoes again. Where would he head to in her situation? There was any number of countries to disappear to in the region. To the north lay the central Americas: Nicaragua, Honduras and Guatemala. South America? Colombia, Ecuador, and Brazil? Across the Caribbean lay Cuba and Puerto Rico. Panama must have been a change-over point for Pandora before disappearing somewhere else. Somewhere near? But where?

Less than an hour later, Brull had dropped Frank off at the safe house and gone on some errands and now he stood in the condo, watching the endless ships and boats travel across Panama Bay in the far distance. The heavy afternoon was turning to evening and the sound of gabbling locals drifted through the balcony window

"She's not in any of these that I can see but it's a needle in a bloody haystack." Piper turned away from the screen of endless airport CCTV photos, his fists cupped together against his forehead. Greene also had his head buried in footage from the airport.

"Anything from Cronus in London?" asked Frank.

"No. If they had anything, I'm sure they'd be sending frantic messages," said Piper.

After their visit to the Panamanian gangster in Casco Viejo, Brull and Frank had dropped into a police station. They spoke to a police contact of Brull's telling the same story: a woman Mr. Feldman deeply cared about had disappeared. Could discreet inquiries be made? The die was now cast and all they could do now was scan CCTV footage, drink coffee, and moan about the heat.

23

Frank opened his laptop to check for messages and instantly received a notification from his WarWorld game from Griff. He started the game and opened the comms console window to find Griff was online.

He read the message on the screen.

"Ordered not to pass to you as not deemed reliable by Cronus. Eighty-three percent voice match. Good fit in my book. File attached. It's from Havana; a Hotel Castro. This line is secure as houses for your info."

Frank smiled at the screen. Good old Griff. This back channel via the game was proving to be invaluable. But why was Carl holding off with this information? That made little sense.

Three hours later, Frank drained the mug of bitter coffee as he stood with Piper and Greene around the dining table and a spread out map of Havana.

"I don't want to get Griff in trouble over this so don't mention Havana," Frank said.

"It's bullshit. They haven't mentioned anything about Havana. So it can't be confirmed," Piper said.

"This is a member of our team, a bloody good one, telling us that Pandora is in Havana."

"..And Cronus. Why isn't he giving us this intel?" asked Greene.

Frank shook his head. Admittedly, he was confused by that

little matter. "I don't know. He must have his reasons."

The loop of the recording continued to play in the background like a soundtrack to their thoughts. Snippets of a woman's voice none of them had heard before but someone they had to find as soon as possible.

"I'll go and request updates from London and see what they say first," Piper said and walked away to one of the back rooms.

Ten minutes later, he returned.

"Well, investigations in London are still ongoing. There's an order to make inquiries here in Panama."

"No mention of this Echelon match or Havana?" asked Frank.

Piper shook his head.

"No, no mention whatsoever."

Frank leaned over the table. "Maybe we're not being ordered but we are going to go to Havana. Our contract says "all actions deemed necessary to track down Pandora." If they're withholding information, then that's their problem, not ours."

At that moment, they heard footsteps walking slowly up from the car garage. The men shifted subtly, hands moving towards their Glocks simultaneously. The door opened and it was Brull, looking back at them in surprise, holding his hands up in mock surrender. Everyone laughed with relief.

Brull sat down at the table and accepted a coffee from Frank.

"Any news?"

"Nothing from our friends in the police," Brull said and paused. "But Palacio said a contact gave her a fake passport in the name of Helena Lopez. I had to pay him $2,000."

Piper, Greene and Frank all looked at each other with smiles on their faces for the first time since arriving.

"That's great work, Brull," said Frank. "Piper can get you reimbursement, I'm sure."

Piper slapped Brull on the shoulder, clearly pleased.

"If not, I'll pay you myself. That info is gold."

"So now we have a name and an address. What are we waiting for?" asked Frank.

"Let's call the hotel. Confirm that a Helena Lopez is booked in first," said Piper. Everyone nodded in agreement and Piper went off to make the call.

Frank wondered again on why London had not passed on the information as the flight from Panama touched down at José Martí International Airport in Havana early the following morning. Clearly, Griff had thought it was credible enough to go on. What else did they have? Apart from her new assumed name that Brull's gangster contact had found out.

After Piper had confirmed that their target was staying at the hotel, Brull had gone on ahead to Cuba to set up a safe house, so they wouldn't be messing around when they arrived. He was proving a very useful asset to the team.

Piper, Greene, and Frank hired a Jeep Grand Cherokee 4x4 and headed into Havana along the main autopista as a new day broke over the city. The safe house was a small, detached, run-down building just south of the busy enclave of Havana port in a commercial district, set behind a row of palms that ran along the main road.

They drove around the back of the building into a lane and pulled up into a carport that had stone walls on either side. Inside, the décor was spartan. Peeling walls, a table and chairs, and an American fridge. It was a far cry from the condo in Panama. The windows were shuttered and closed to keep the light out and the rooms felt cool; a slight smell of damp lingered in the air. Greene immediately switched on the ceiling fan and turned to

Brull, acknowledging a good job, without words.

"Did you manage to get us any equipment?"

"Si. It is all there as arranged," said Brull, leading them to a black box.

Piper checked the contents and took out several Glock pistols and handed one to Greene. Also inside was some of the surveillance equipment Frank would need to do his job, a selection of listening devices and wiring.

Frank leaned down and opened his suitcase. Taking out the piles of shirts, shorts, maps, and other typical tourist items, he placed the equipment inside. Then Frank shut the case and stood up.

Piper gestured to Frank with a grunt. "Okay, good luck. We'll be speaking real soon."

24

Harry tore off a piece of paper from the incoming printer feed and walked over to Carl's desk. "Message from Ghost 13."

It was the usual rows of numbers associated with the One Time Pad code.

"Okay, thanks, Harry. Leave this with me."

When Harry returned to his desk, Carl began to decode the numbers, writing out the message and cursed quietly at what he read.

CRONUS EYES ONLY: CREDIBLE INFORMATION LEADING US TO HAVANA. DETAILS TO FOLLOW. HAD TO ACT QUICKLY. WILL CONTACT AGAIN.

He fed the paper through a shredder next to his desk and leaned back in the leather chair and thought for a moment. They had exceeded their authority and he'd bet his house that Frank was behind it. The others, though good men, were just grunts. What had they found out? Perhaps they were right and the voice data match might be correct?

He quick dialled a number and soon the voice of David Devlin answered.

"It's Carl. Ghost 13 is headed to Havana, based on some credible leads. Just letting you know."

There was a pause. "Did you order them there?"

"I asked them to make inquiries. Makes sense as they're on

the ground already. They obviously found something. Together with the Echelon data, it's the closest we have to Pandora's whereabouts."

"No more surprises. I don't want any more actions without a direct order from us, Carl. We need to keep a firm grip on this."

"I understand but they do have carte blanch to do what is necessary to find Pandora," Carl said, determined to hold his ground. He was feeling that this operation was being steered too strongly away from his own hand.

"Nevertheless. Keep it tight and remind your team who pays their wages."

Carl sighed. "Right you are, sir."

25

Frank glanced through the car window at the passing streets of Havana. Everything here seemed touched by the sun; even the most broken down buildings have an air of majesty about them. A beautiful place for tourists, not so much for enemies of the state.

Brull tightened his grip on the wheel and turned to face Frank. "You ready for this, amigo?" Frank paused as if to ask himself the same question. He couldn't turn back now. The question remained unanswered and hung in the air as the Toyota headed along the coastal road of San Pedro, the expanse of the wide blue sea on their right. Hued shapes of cranes and ships stood silently in the distance as they passed a group of tourists and locals boarding a ferry at one of the terminals.

Frank reviewed his documentation once again. Tourist ID, passport, and driver's license, all in the name of Keith Feldman. It was more than enough to solidify the truthfulness of his false identity. Thanks to Brull, they now had Pandora's hotel and room number. She would be lying low, waiting for whatever her next move was. That was the big question they all asked themselves. What was her next move?

Brull pulled the vehicle up on the kerb and pointed one finger up the busy street. "The hotel is just there on the corner. Best that you get out here and walk."

Frank nodded. "Thanks, mate. I'll be seeing you."

He got out of the car and walked up the road with his suitcase. Brull's Toyota roared by and turned at the junction ahead. Frank checked into the hotel as he might into a winter resort, filled with optimism for a much-enjoyed visit to Havana and infecting the receptionist with his jokes.

A young bellboy escorted Frank to his room, who asked the usual questions of any tourist. What was England like? What football team did he support? He tipped him five dollars and walked into the stark room, whitewashed with a simple picture of the Havana cityscape adorning the wall. Frank could only imagine the target's room was similar, maybe even an exact duplicate.

His imagined best-case scenario had him sneaking in under the cover of darkness but it was more likely he'd have to take any opportunity. Frank opened the suitcase and contemplated the fact that Pandora rarely left her room, according to Brull's sources. Bugging her room in that respect was tricky but if she was to eat, she had no choice but to leave, even for a brief moment. And if all the rooms are as similar as he hoped, a ten-minute window was all that would be needed.

Frank peered vigilantly from the glass window through two shutters. She had probably already had breakfast but chances were, she'd leave again before long. As the hands on Bowen's Nite MX10 watch drifted by, his attentiveness to the outside world only escalated.

Frank stared through the window across at Sarah Edward's room on the fourth level opposite. The rooms were arranged around an inner courtyard that housed the outside section of the quiet restaurant below; parasols sporting the Havana Club logo spread out, sheltering the guests from the sunlight.

Suddenly, he had a visual on Edwards, scurrying from her room. The trembling in her fingers and finicky gestures told him all he needed to know about her state of mind. She looked scared. Frank shut the blinds a little tighter, just enough to watch her work at the lock with the key. She struggled with it, eventually exclaiming something unintelligible, and walked away frustrated. He watched her descend the steps and quickly moved out through his door. She was headed to the bar area. Now was the time.

Frank moved quickly, picking the lock expertly before slipping into her room with his small bag of gear. He looked around. Anywhere that was already covered up by furniture deserved a bug. He slipped listening devices behind the painting on the wall and behind the headstand on the bed. Next, he moved to the en-suite bathroom and found a gap behind the cabinet. It was trickier to get this one in place but it needed to be there, in case she made calls from in there on a mobile.

Frank double-checked that nothing looked out of place and carefully peeked through the blinds to check whether the coast was clear. On the opposite side, down a level, a cleaning woman hovered outside a room before disappearing inside, dragging a cart behind her. As soon as the door closed again, Frank walked casually out back to his room around the walkway.

Once inside, Frank dragged the desk and manoeuvred the chair to face the door and set up the Honeywell laptop. He didn't want any hotel staff seeing the screen. It was time to check the equipment and he began the pinging process, making sure each bug was active. After seeing all was in order, Frank felt a wave of relief that he didn't have to go back to her room to fix anything. He listened in for a while, adjusting the volume slightly on the recording software; the laptop screen displayed a flat audio line, telling him that was no noise in her room until a slam of the door on her return caused a spike on the screen. Everything seemed to be up and running smoothly.

She seemed so young. What had motivated her to do what she was doing? Did this nervous, stressed woman realise what she was getting into exactly? She must have her reasons for throwing herself into the abyss and must surely know her life would never be the same again? The information she held. It must be about the money; selling it to the highest bidder and then she must have some kind of exit plan.

Frank checked the fridge and was relieved to find some alcoholic miniatures and grabbed a couple of rums and a can of cola. He poured the contents into a glass and took a glug. It felt good.

Nothing much happened until she called room service for tea and a snack around 11:20 AM. For the first time, the voice confirmed that this was really her. There was no doubt in his mind that it was the same woman. Frank felt a wave of triumph, not to mention relief.

He padded across the marble tiled floor to turn up the ceiling fan, cursing the humidity, then looked through the window blind from where he could see the coming and going of the occasional guest and waiter in the courtyard restaurant below. Nothing seemed unusual or out of place. A couple of hours passed.

Again, Frank wondered at her motivation. She must have known she was risking everything. Known that she would not be able to contact her family, her friends. Probably never see them again. And then he thought of Maria and the boys and realised he couldn't wait to see them again. Every harsh word he had ever said to them now seemed cruel, uncalled for. Distance had grown between himself and his family and he had allowed it to happen.

26

Viktor Kozel, or Alexei Demenok as his passport named him, smiled. The payment had been made. It amazed him how digits could transcend space itself from one secret bank account to another. Another step towards retirement from the game, a game that had become old.

But Kozel had no regrets. He had lived his life the way it had been dealt to him. It began in the Russian army and then he helped with the muscle end of the KGB, making sure prisoners talked when they had to. He was an expert in various torture methods but had always yearned to make good money. Dabbling in arms smuggling to criminal elements, two years before the Soviet Union collapsed, got him into trouble and he was thrown into a high-security prison near the Siberian city of Krasnoyarsk.

A twist of fate came and Kozel met and became friends with Vyacheslav Ivankov, a high level and 'made Vor' or thief, marked by the eight-pointed star tattoos on each of his shoulders with the single eye in the centre. It was in the grim, red-bricked prison that Kozel himself got his gang tattoos, the barbed wire covering his neck and throat just one of them.

By 1991, the top thieves of the Soviet Union planned for a post-communist Russia and when the time came, they were ready to pounce on and feed off the state infrastructure. Ivankov and Kozel were released, helped by the corruption of the day, and walked into a violence fuelled mafia war that looked like something out of 1930s Chicago. Russia became the most violent country on earth during that time. *Great days.*

The Russian disconnected the satellite phone and walked back down to the lower basement of the unused factory, where old machinery stood like rusting hulks from a by-gone age. Faded Russian writing engraved onto the metal pointed to better times for the Cuban republic when Soviet goods flowed freely into the country. They made Kozel feel at home although he was glad to be out of the sub-zero temperatures of Moscow and hoped for more contracts like this one.

His men were in the process of unpacking the equipment that had been brought into the country in unmarked crates. Several computers, cables, and a power generator had been the first to be set up and now Yuri Tarasenko, a tough Ukrainian with a blonde crew cut and angular features, was checking the weapons from another crate.

"How is our package?" Viktor boomed. His companion grinned wolfishly, holding up the formidable Bizon sub-machine gun, a weapon chambered for the standard Russian 9×18mm Makarov pistol cartridge that was also capable of firing high-impulse armour-piercing rounds.

"Looking very good. Everything is here."

Viktor looked down along the table that held the range of weapons, occasionally picking one up to check the clips. The Marquis had delivered as promised and genuinely impressed by the strings he must have pulled to get this order.

"These ones will need cleaning again," he said, gesturing to the culprit machine guns and shooting a glare at his giant employee, Leonid Dustkin. Viktor had employed the big man ever since his foray into crime after the good old KGB days had come to an end.

Leonid nodded his bald head slowly. "No problem, Viktor."

Suddenly, Viktor slapped the big man around the face, as quick as a viper strike, leaving the man stunned. Dustkin felt his scarred cheek with one massive hand, fear in his eyes as he looked down at his boots. The other two men glanced over but continued their work, keeping their heads down.

"No names. How many times do I have to say?"

Leonid Duskin stroked his cheek and nodded, looking like a scolded cat. "Of course. No real names...Alexei!"

"That's better. Now clean up these guns." He then turned to the other two men. "We must be more careful!" With that, the short stocky Russian walked along the basement floor, his boots echoing through the huge space, up to an open metal laptop placed on a workbench. It was attached to a printer that kicked into life and a series of numbers printed out on a sheet of highly flammable nitrocellulose paper.

Viktor studied it for a moment and translated the numbers into letters from his issued codebook or one-time pad, carefully re-checking each number until he had a series of indistinguishable letters. He translated the ciphertext and an address of a hotel in Havana revealed itself, followed by a warning:

ROGUE TEAM IN PLAY. MARQUIS

27

"Havana Club, por favor."

The barman poured the golden rum into a crystal glass and placed it on the dark wooden bar in front of Frank.

"Gracias."

The barman moved away, leaving Frank gazing at the Che Guevara iconic image in a frame on the wall. He thought about the life story of this Argentinian revolutionary who had become a hero to the Cuban people. His meeting with Castro and subsequent involvement in the revolution before travelling to ignite further revolution abroad; firstly in Congo-Kinshasa and then in Bolivia, both ventures ending unsuccessfully. The latter especially as he was captured and executed by CIA backed Bolivian government troops. He wondered about Sarah again. Did she really realise what she was involved in?

Just then, Frank's mobile buzzed in his pocket. It was Brull.

"Frank. I have a very reliable source saying that there is a Russian group in Havana looking for Pandora. They are dangerous and they may know about the hotel."

"Do you know who they are?" Frank was watching the view through the sliding doors that led out into the inside courtyard.

"No, I do not know."

"They might be the buyers," Frank said.

"That is a possibility but my contact said there was a consignment of arms delivered just outside Havana...Why would they need so much weapons?" Brull asked.

There was a pause.

"You're right. That sounds more like a snatch squad."

Can you get the target out of there? Get her here? Sorry to ask this of you, Frank."

"What do I say to her?"

Just then, the line disconnected and Frank looked at the screen and cursed. Suddenly, the situation seemed to have escalated. His gaze drifted to the other hotel guests as they chatted and drank expressos under the parasols in the courtyard. A Caucasian woman wearing sunglasses with tied back black hair moved through the tables in his direction. Frank glanced away and then back again, realisation turning in his mind. She came up to the bar, standing just a few feet away and removed her sunglasses. It was Pandora, or Sarah Edwards, looking for bar service.

They caught each other's eye and Frank, not knowing in that moment what else to do, nodded an acknowledgement. He cursed himself silently. There was a sudden glimpse of suspicion and defiance in her eyes and Frank stopped himself short of saying anything at that moment as his mind raced. How should he deal with this? Play it right, otherwise, he'd lose her and the moment would be gone.

She ordered sparkling water to be delivered to her room and complained that her room phone was not working properly. It was all a big inconvenience and could they do something about it? There was a promise to look into it as soon as possible by the barman, who then moved off to get her order.

"Do you speak English?" Frank heard himself say.

She looked at him again, her eyes full of sudden fear, the defiance gone.

"Que?"

Frank asked again in Spanish.

"No, por favor discúlpeme," she replied and started to walk off.

Frank couldn't let her go. He might not get another chance.

"Your water. Don't you want it?" She stopped and turned around, checking him out with clear suspicion.

Then Frank slowly stood up from the bar stool. "Sarah, I really need to talk to you."

28

"I think you are in immediate danger. Either from kidnapping or death or probably both."

Sarah studied Frank, her brown eyes searching his for clues. She wasn't sure whether to be scared, angry, or what, but she was wary. Was this some kind of trap? Her gut instinct said no but she had to be careful. The stakes were too high.

Sarah laughed easily, as if from nowhere.

"Who are you exactly?"

Frank leaned forward, closer to her, his voice quietening.

"That doesn't matter. I was hired by a British intelligence agency to bug your room and monitor your movements. I wasn't privy to what you did in detail exactly. But there are a group of Russians looking for you. They know you are at this hotel."

"Which agency are you with?" she asked.

"Does it matter? Take a wild guess."

"I'm just trying to ascertain the facts. You could be anyone."

Something caught his eye. Through the double doors, he had a view of the reception area and beyond that, the main street. He frowned and stood up to move closer for a better look and confirm what he thought he saw. A large man with a bald head was talking to the receptionist; he turned his head momentarily and caught sight of Frank. Frank could see up to the upper levels and the staircase, where another man dressed in a suit was rapping his fist on one of the doors. Frank instantly knew the Russians were here.

"We have to leave now." He turned back to Sarah, who was looking at him, a mixture of fear and confusion in her eyes. He grabbed her arm and began to lead her to the back of the bar.

"What are you doing?"

He maneuvered her around so she was facing the sliding doors along with the sight of a seven-foot bald thug striding towards them through the patio garden. The situation persuaded her to follow his lead.

They ran through a half-empty restaurant and rushed towards a metal door that led into the kitchens. Two Cuban chefs looked up at them in surprise and started gesturing to them to get out. One stepped towards Frank as if to block his path but received a shove that threw him against a fridge door. Pulling Sarah by the hand, they both pushed through. The other chef stopped, held his hands up and stood back, clearly not wanting any trouble. Just as they reached the back exit door, there was a loud "thunk" sound against the wall, less than a metre away from Frank. A gunshot!

The sound of plates smashing onto the tiled floor exploded behind them. They burst out of the exit door and Frank slammed it shut behind them before grabbing Sarah's hand again. Running hard down an alleyway, they both saw the main road that ran along the front of the hotel ahead.

Turning left on the main road, they ran past crumbling store-fronts, darting around people as they strolled at a casual pace. There was a skeleton structure of rusty scaffolding sprawled over the pavement that forced them onto the road. Frank stole a glance behind him and saw the man come out of the alleyway onto the road. He looked around and spotting them, gave chase.

A chorus of angry car horns blared and then they darted back under a line of arched pillars that kept them out of sight from their pursuer. An intersection ahead gave them options. From his brief analysis of the city map, Frank knew the best place to lose the Russian was in the narrow alleyways and cobbled streets of Old Havana.

Turning to Sarah, who was a few paces behind, he shouted, "Left here. You okay?"

Sarah nodded but looked out of breath already.

Passing under the long shadows of colonial buildings and a line of still palms, they ran, zig-zagging around a large woman selling fruit from a cart. Busy sounds of chatter and traffic increased until they reached the busier narrow streets, where tourists were taking a stroll, looking for somewhere to eat or admiring the architecture.

Heading into the Plaza de San Francisco, out of sight from the tail, passing under the arched canopies of the 17th-century buildings, they kept close to the stone wall. The murmur of afternoon diners drifted across the square. A sudden sound of flapping wings broke as a flock of pigeons scattered, and the Basilica bell tower chimed. The distance to the next exit road was too far. Their pursuer would turn the corner and see them without a doubt.

The sound of feet running behind them echoed across the Plaza.

Turning at another street, they headed back in the same direction they had come. Rapid salsa beats drifted from a few streets away and Frank wished that he was with Maria, sipping tequilas and snacking on tapas, instead of running from this bastard. He stopped and beckoned to Sarah to duck into a large doorway adorned with crumbling pillars.

They breathed heavily and Frank gestured for Sarah to crouch down behind him. If he came past, Frank could ambush him from their position.

The street was almost empty apart from a scavenging dog, ripping apart a bin sack, and the distant cry of a child. Harsh shadows from the surrounding buildings diced up the cobbled road but no footfall seemed to follow, that Frank could hear. They waited several minutes then moved silently down the avenue.

They walked in silence and then Frank hailed a taxi and they slumped into the back seats of an old, spacious 1950's Pontiac.

"Ave de Mexico Cristina," he said to the driver, who nodded and pulled out into the road with a crunch of the gears.

"Was that FSB?" Sarah asked quietly after a pause. She was referring to the Russian intelligence service, re-moulded from the old KGB.

"I don't know, probably," he said, glancing through the rear window.

"And what's your name?"

"Frank."

"MI6?"

"Something like that."

"So this is a trap and you're reeling me in?"

Frank shook his head. "That would've been a good plan. Wish I thought of that."

Sarah laughed with a heavy tone of sarcasm. "So, where are you taking me, Mr. MI6?"

"Away from the Russians."

"How did you find me?"

Frank let out a chuckle. "I can't go giving away those kinds of secrets, Sarah."

She paused and watched the city blur past for a while. "Do you want to know why I'm doing what I'm doing, Frank?"

"I can guess, but go ahead."

She told Frank about Operation Oculus. The tentacles of the globalist surveillance plan of all online activity, the massive piping of data. Stage one of something even Orwell could not envisage. The entire western world will be watched and monitored.

"Not only is it totally illegal, but it will also set a precedent for what will come."

"Why come to Cuba? Why not straight to Moscow?"

He saw cold anger in her eyes.

"Are you saying this is about trading secrets? Selling the information? You are so far off the mark!"

Frank kind of shrugged, as if to say 'How the hell would I know?' Sarah stared out of the window and seemed to let her anger dissipate.

"Going to Moscow would be like going into lion's den, there's no way of knowing what would happen or where I would end up. This is not about being some kind of traitor or double agent, Frank. It's about exposing what's going on in our agencies."

"Look, I'm in no position to argue the rights and wrongs of what our governments are up to," said Frank.

"This goes above governments, way beyond."

"What do you mean, above governments?" Frank's eyes focused on her. Sarah sighed.

"The shadow behind the governments, the Cabal. A power that no ordinary citizen has any idea of."

Frank snorted with derision and leaned back in his seat, barely able to hide his scepticism. "What? Like a conspiracy? You sound like my partner."

"Do you really think they haven't penetrated organisations

like MI6 or the CIA? That those organisations aren't knowingly or otherwise carrying out a hidden agenda?"

Frank shook his head. "All I know is I work with good people, mostly. We're protecting our interests, the interests of the UK."

"What are those interests? Really? You really think they give a shit about you? That they would think twice about throwing you overboard to protect their interests? That's their agenda; to compartmentalise, so no one can see the big picture or suss out what all the other moving parts are doing!"

Frank smiled to himself. She really did remind him of Maria. But she had a point there. Trust was a rare commodity.

"They will use everything in their power to discredit anyone who opposes them," she continued. "They'll label me as a terrorist or a conspirator, probably already have. And they'll probably come after you, too, Frank, when they find out you've helped me."

29

Frank knocked in three rapid beats on the red door to the safe house and waited.

"How can I help?" It was a reply from behind the door in Spanish.

"It's me, Feldman," he replied, using his alias name.

Several locks were unbolted until the door opened a fraction and Piper stood holding a gun pointed towards him. He glared at him and then looked at Sarah before gesturing for them both to enter.

"Come on, get off the street."

Piper re-bolted the door and turned around, putting the safety back on his weapon. They stood alone in the small front room where the blinds on the two front windows were shut tight and a lamp in the corner cast a dim glow.

Piper looked at Sarah and grinned.

"So you're the cause of all the trouble?"

She looked at him with a frown, clearly not willing to join in with any banter.

"So anymore on this Russian crew?" Frank asked.

Piper shook his head. "I'm going to radio it in. This is a change of situation."

He began to turn and walk towards the rear of the house.

Suddenly, at that moment, glass on both front windows simultaneously shattered in a hail of machine gun fire. Frank, Sarah, and Piper instinctively hurled themselves to the ground. The gunfire continued relentlessly, peppering chunks of plaster out of the opposite wall, glass fragments spraying in every direction.

After a few seconds, there was a pause in the sudden explosion of violence that had been unleashed.

Piper shouted towards the back of the house. "Green, Brull! Incoming at the front!"

They heard Green shout from the back room. "You got a weapon?"

"Yep, a pistol. How's the car looking?"

"All good so far, seems clear," shouted Greene.

The gunfire started again, hammering into the walls and it seemed to shake the whole building.

The shooting stopped again. "They'll be getting ready to storm in soon," said Piper. He gave Frank his Glock and pulled an exact same model from his belt.

"Were you followed?"

"God, no. We lost someone in a Plaza."

Piper shook his head, "They must have followed you. Doesn't matter now. We have to get out of here and find another safe house and call this in."

Frank could already hear Greene attempting to contact Cronus, Carl Paterson, their controller in London.

"Forget it," shouted Piper. "Check the back and the car. We need to roll."

Piper turned to Frank. "Come on, let's give these bastards some kind of response."

Frank turned to Sarah, who was crouched in a fetal position, her arms around her head. "Stay here."

They crawled along the floor and cocked their pistols, leaning against the wall under the window.

"You take a look, I'll cover," Piper said. Frank nodded. Piper held his weapon up, pointing it outwards and blasted off a couple of rounds. As he did so, Frank quickly peeked through the window and then fell back down in a crouch.

"I saw an MPV. Four men from what I can see. They have heavy armour."

"All clear," shouted Greene from the rear door.

"It could be a trap," said Frank. "Why would they not cover the rear of the house?"

"We can't stay here. They'll burn us out or worse. We just have to take our chances."

"What about the equipment?" Frank shouted over another volley of bullets that peppered the back wall, showering clouds of plaster dust across the room.

"Nothing we can do. Get the girl out of here!"

Frank gestured to Sarah and crawled on their hands and knees into a wide hall that led to a back room and the rear of the property. Piper stayed in the front.

Brull knelt by the back door, holding up his Glock pistol at the ready. Greene was backing up the Land Rover to the door and Brull quickly opened the rear tailgate, throwing in a black canvas bag before jumping into the back seat.

Gunfire erupted once again, quickly followed by a shuddering blast at the front door that could only be a grenade. Frank held his ears as the loud ringing jolted through his head. Dust belched throughout the entire downstairs floor. Then Piper appeared in the hallway, coughing and holding his mouth, manoeuvring on his hands and knees.

Frank saw Piper talking to him but no words came through, only a shrill tone in his ears. He gestured towards the car and pushed Frank toward it before turning back to face the front rooms, his weapon aimed in front of him. Frank, pistol still in hand, moved towards the vehicle and saw Greene at the wheel, his face turning back towards him, waving his hand. What was he trying to tell him? Frank wondered if he had forgotten something and then he realised in a microsecond Greene was trying to stop him from coming nearer the vehicle.

Then his face caved in; a spray of red lashed out from Greene's head, which lolled to the side, lifeless within a single moment. The shock awakened Frank's senses as he heard the shot, dull but precise and caught a glimpse of the shooter, crouched behind the far wall, his weapon swinging round towards him.

Instinctively ducking, Frank dropped to one knee, firing off a volley of shots towards the culprit from the rear door of the house. Crouching, he eased behind the Land Rover, out of view, breathing hard. He checked his pistol chamber. Shit. Low on ammo and the clips were in the bags in the vehicle. There was one shot left.

Sarah and Piper were crouching in the doorway, watching him intently. He held a hand up to them, indicating he was okay.

He needed to get the vehicle started and ready to get the hell out of there. He carefully re-opened the driver door as far as it would go until touching the stone wall behind him and Greene's body slumped against it, heavy and lifeless. A waft of sickly blood hit his throat as he pulled at the body slowly and carefully, inch by inch through the gap until Green was horizontal on the dusty ground. Frank tried not to look at the hole in his head where the spraying blood had ceased and brain matter covered his shirt.

Piper gestured at driving with his hands to Frank, who nodded and then crawled aside the driver's seat, positioning himself; ready to jump in. He kept aim at the far wall through the passenger window as an eerie quietness fell, punctuated by the sound of dogs barking in the distant street alleys at the avalanche of noise that entered their lazy world. Frank saw a head quickly pop up from behind the wall to check the situation, perhaps thinking they were dead or wounded. He adjusted his aim a few centimetres to the right and calmly pulled the trigger; squeezing as if at a duck shoot. The head suddenly fell back behind the wall without a sound.

Piper saw Frank's shot hit the target and realising it was a chance, shouted and grabbed Sarah's hand. "Go! Go!"

Sarah dived into the rear, next to a terrified Brull and Piper dived into the front passenger seat. Frank jumped in and fired up the engine, which turned lazily and refused to fire as if it wanted to hang around and watch their deaths.

The sweat on Frank's palms smeared the steering wheel like grease. A huge bang threw a shock wave from behind them, quickly followed by another. To Frank, they sounded like stun grenades, designed to produce a blinding flash of light and extremely loud noise. Frank tried again and the engine revved. In his peripheral vision, another head appeared over the wall and a hail of bullets smacked into the passenger side of the vehicle.

The Jeep almost leapfrogged out of the yard and Frank span the wheel hard to the right onto the back lane, away from their pursuers, a huge cloud of dust following in their wake. Piper was groaning in pain.

"Shit!"

"What is it? You hit?"

Piper nodded, sweat pouring from his nose and chin.

"I'm good," he said. But Frank knew he was lying.

30

Frank jerked hard on the wheel, turning up onto the sidewalk. The whistling sound of bullets cutting through the air had long fallen behind them, but the tension of the moment hung thick within the vehicle, mixed in with the scent of blood pooling through Piper's shirt.

In the rear mirror, Frank spotted the black MPV's headlights with a cloud of dust in its wake, speeding to catch them. As the vehicle reached an intersection of the Paseo de Marti, he turned a sharp right onto it and pressed harder on the gas, heading south. As their vehicle easily cruised past the occasional old 1950's Buick or Russian made Lada, a distant screech told Frank their pursuers were only a block behind.

Frank killed the car lights and looked hard for a way off the main road, which was now feeling increasingly exposed. The MPV lights were behind them, gaining fast. Just ahead, Frank spotted the taillights of a large truck and overtook, before ducking in front of it, out of sight of the Russians. The truck driver flashed his lights at them but Frank ignored it.

"Keep heading north. We head to 'El Tunel'," Brull said. He was referring to "El Tunel de la Habana" that connected each side of Havana Port under the sea, a major feat of Cuban engineering and pride for the Cubans after it had been completed in 1958.

Frank glanced at Piper, who did not look good at all and was barely conscious, blood pooling through his shirt. Right now, there was little they could do for him.

"Brull. See if that Med Kit is in the black bag. We need to stem the bleeding!"

"After the tunnel, I know a place we can hide for a bit," said Brull, as he leaned back, grabbing the bag. He began to rife around inside and pulled out a medical box.

Just then, another dark MPV swerved onto the road a few metres behind them, causing an echoing screech that made them all jump in their seats.

It raced forward, drawing up beside them along the left-hand side. The windows were tinted black, no faces visible behind the glass. Suddenly, the pursuing vehicle rammed violently into the side of the Jeep, against Frank's door. They all were thrown hard against their seatbelts.

"Where the hell did that come from?" Sarah shouted.

"Shit...they have two cars. Must have been trying to head us off...hold on."

Frank spotted a right turn, changed down the gears, depressing the brake pedal slightly before swinging the wheel hard. The Jeep skidded and fishtailed across the asphalt and then Frank floored the accelerator hard, causing a cloud of smoke to appear behind them before they shot down the side street. A few evening strollers turned their heads and stared at them in alarm. Frank raised his eyes to the mirror and saw their pursuers had overshot the turning. There was a glimpse of the vehicle reversing into view.

Brull leaned forward with a bandage and began helping Piper to get it on his wound, who groaned in pain.

"Hold it tight...stop the bleeding," Brull urged.

Frank veered at the first left so they were heading in parallel with the Paseo de Marti towards the entrance of the Port.

"How far now, amigo?"

"Not far...ten minutes."

The Jeep sped along the largely empty roads and up ahead, they caught sight of the shimmering moonlight reflected off the sea.

Frank moved Piper's hand back over the bandage, pressing it hard. "Hold it tight, Steve, tighter!" He managed a faint smile and did as Frank said. It was obvious to Frank that weakness was seizing control.

They headed around a large maze of a roundabout that circled around the Parque Martires del 71 that led to the tunnel entrance. The headlights from the MPV appeared behind them on a curve for a moment, gaining on them fast as they went under a number of flyovers before hitting the harsh yellow light of the tunnel. It was a narrow, two-lane road with a white tiled wall that separated them from the opposite side.

"Policía!"

Brull pointed to the white Lada ahead of them.

It was too late. Frank would have to shoot past them and they'd soon have cops on their trail as well.

Well, if it was going to happen anyway...

"Hold on. Got an idea, gonna try to clip his wing."

Before anyone else could object Frank had sped alongside the police car so his front left fender was parallel to their rear wheel. He slammed the police car, sending it spinning on the asphalt, control clearly lost. As it barrelled in a 180-degree motion, Frank slowed to avoid broadsiding it and then slipped on past the Lada. Once again, he floored the accelerator to pick up speed.

Frank checked his wing mirror and noted with satisfaction that it had come to a standstill across the two lanes, blocking the path for the Russian pursuers. They wouldn't be stuck there for long though.

It was another neat little trick he'd learned from Sam Keane, his trainer, called the 'pursuit intervention technique' used to stop a vehicle pursuit. At speeds over seventy mph, it would only have needed a tap on the opposing car's fender but he had needed to slow down to match the police car's speed. As it was, he had to use much more force and a scraping sound told him he must have damaged the Jeep's wheel arch.

"We'll have police looking for us now. We need to get there quick..." muttered Brull, a hint of annoyance in his voice.

"I know, I know," Frank replied, his eyes fixed on the rearview mirror.

They came out of the tunnel under blue archways and sped up the carriageway, which curved around to the right. As they came around the bend, Frank saw a line of toll booths ahead. He breathed out and tensed, preparing to smash through them.

"Don't worry, they are empty at this time," said Brull. Frank nodded and gave a sigh of relief. "Good."

The Jeep sped past the unmanned booths and continued east along the carriageway.

"Next right," said Brull.

"Piper? How are you doing?"

In the faint yellow of the street lights that flew by, Piper's face was looking paler by the second.

"Fine," Piper moaned from the passenger seat, head bobbing and hand resting lightly over his gut. "Hurts like hell."

"I bet it does," said Frank. "We're gonna get you patched up as soon as we can, mate, okay?" Piper mumbled an acknowledgement.

"Brull, tell me where the hell we're going?"

Brull gave instructions and within seconds, they were hurtling down a side road.

"Another left," Brull commanded.

The Jeep swerved into another side road and Frank picked up speed again.

"We'll need medical help. Know any doctors, Brull?"

"Yes, there is someone. I will call now."

Brull fished around for his phone.

"What about the hospital?" asked Sarah.

"First place those guys will look, I imagine. They didn't exactly look like they wanted to negotiate."

Frank turned to Piper again and pressed his hand to keep the pressure on.

Gradually, the environment became less industrial and increasingly populated by dilapidated structures. Roads were emptied of any meaningful populace. They had entered a place where the reins had been returned to nature, but not enough that the buildings were entirely out of use. Many still belonged to family stores or were still used as industrial storage facilities, the latter of which provided the perfect cover for covert operations.

Brull gave detailed instructions on the roundabout, discreet roads leading up to the building, a worn out, tannish building with limestone-crusted windows and a hand-painted "no vacancy" sign. Four doors led, presumably, into the large storage blocks.

"Drive around," Brull instructed, pointing towards the upcoming street. Around on the other side, the building more resembled a traditional store with a single, metal door.

Frank eased onto the brakes and brought the Jeep to a halt in front of the building.

"Stay here." Brull hopped out of the back and turned back to Frank. "Get him out. Hurry!"

Frank doubled over to the passenger side and helped his comrade out and towards the building door, assisted by Sarah.

"Brull, can you grab that Med Kit?"

"Si, Si. I'll get it," he replied and opened the vehicle back door to retrieve it. He then moved quickly to open the building door and followed them inside, closing it securely behind them before running ahead to clear the surface of a metal gurney. All three hauled the now near unconscious Piper on top of it.

Frank carefully pried Piper's bloodied hands away from the wound in the side of his stomach and ripped his shirt open to a sea of dark blood.

Brull ripped bandages and prepared a patch. He met Frank's eyes and nodded, the sweat glistening on both men as Piper groaned.

"Stay with us, mate," said Frank urgently. He could barely keep the fear out of his voice.

Brull pressed the dressing over the wound and carefully wrapped a strip of bandage over his stomach and around his back, pulling it tight with each wrap.

"Okay, that'll have to do for now," Brull nodded and Frank pinned it through.

"I'll go look out for that doctor."

Frank nodded. "Stay hidden though." Brull jogged to the front doorway and stepped outside.

Piper stared glassy-eyed at Frank and moved his lips but no sound came out.

Frank leaned closer. "Say again, mate?"

"Pro...protocol. You have to call this in..." He gasped for air, struggling to speak.

Frank leaned even closer so their faces were inches apart. Piper's eyes closed.

"Piper?"

Frank slapped his face and the dark eyes opened again.

"A doctor's on the way. We're gonna fix you up, mate, okay?"

Piper managed a smile. "You think so? I think I'm out this time...Frank...I.."

His eyes stared straight ahead, staring past Frank at nothing.

"Piper?" Frank felt his pulse and feeling nothing, checked his heartbeat. It confirmed his worst fear.

Frank slammed his hand down on the table in anger and turned away.

"Shit!"

He booted an old tin can on the floor. A flood of anger raced through him. He could have saved him. Maybe they could have pulled in somewhere along the way, hidden, and tried to make a better job on the wound.

Sarah came over and rested a hand on his shoulder as if knowing his thoughts.

"You did all you could, Frank. We were chased all the way."

The door opened and Brull stepped inside, looking expectantly at Frank and Sarah, his eyes moving to Piper's still form on the table.

"How is your amigo?"

Frank slumped down onto the concrete floor and leaned against the bare brick wall, staring straight ahead. A sudden rush of anxiety coursed through his veins, the feeling of being in over his head cast a deep shadow over his thoughts. He saw the faces of Maria, Joe, and Zak for a second in his mind. One mistake and he'd never see them again. A sick feeling overwhelmed his stomach.

"Dead. You might have to cancel your doctor," he said finally.

Brull cursed in Spanish and went over to Piper's body, needing to confirm the news with his own eyes.

They hadn't deserved to die; despite his differences with them, he respected their professionalism. Professionals with a lot of experience had been ruthlessly taken out and outwitted. But by whom? And why?

He took the Glock, quickly released the magazine, and then slammed it back in. He repeated the action four times as if testing himself. He knew he would need to take more lives to survive this.

"You got a cigarette?"

Brull nodded and threw Frank his pack and lighter. It had been 3 years since he'd lugged on one. *It had been a bad day though,* he thought as he sparked the lighter and inhaled. *A very bad day.*

"What's the next move, Frank?"

Frank threw back the cigarette pack, followed by the lighter and Brull pulled one out for himself.

"I dunno. Get out of the country. Sarah, I'm afraid you'll have to come with me. It's way too dangerous here."

"And you don't think it's dangerous back home? I'll be thrown in prison, or worse!"

Frank shook his head. "Just bear with me. I need to communicate with home, somehow." He looked at his mobile phone and thought for a moment.

"Damn. My laptop is at the hotel."

Brull inhaled sharply. "They will definitely be watching it."

"Who do you think "they" are?"

Brull shrugged as he exhaled grey smoke. "Your guess as good as mine," he said quietly.

Frank started to dial a number on his mobile. "I'm calling Carl. Fuck protocol."

He paced around the space, listening hard, and then cut the call and tried again. After several attempts, he put the phone back in his pocket.

"Impossible to get a connection. We'll need a phone box. You can cancel the doctor but can you arrange to get his body to a morgue?...And there's Greene at the safe house, too."

Brull nodded, flicking ash onto the floor.

Frank walked over to Piper's still corpse on top of the table and began to go through his pockets, making sure there was nothing incriminating. He paused and looked at his still face, now at peace.

"I hate leaving him here."

31

Carl made his way up the metal stairs and keyed in a combination at the main door of Studio 31. It was just before 11pm and had been quiet on the roads, so he had arrived quickly after his pager alert. He stepped into the main reception and moved into a corridor before stopping at one of the steel doors. He typed in another sequence of numbers onto the pad before they hissed open and Carl stepped through.

Harry, the comms operator, looked up from his screen and grunted a greeting. He had been there all night and looked it. There was a pile of plastic cups and cans littered all over the table and the remnants of continuous grazing including crisp packets, wrappings, and screwed up burger foil.

"Jesus Christ, Harry, this place looks like a bomb hit it," said Carl, glancing around with an unimpressed glare.

"Sorry, boss. I'll clean it up. It was another quiet one. There's still been no word from Ghost 13."

Carl contemplated this for a second. The team in Cuba; Frank, the others. An operation that David Devlin had taken a personal interest in. He wasn't going to be happy with this latest report.

"Nothing at all? Is the surveillance feed still active? Anything going on there?"

Harry shook his head. There had been no developments he said and began to play the last section of activity on the audio feed;

the sound of footsteps leaving the room.

"That was 20:23 hours Havana time. She hasn't returned since."

"That sounds to me like she's packed up and left."

"That's why I thought I'd better call you, sir."

"Yes, rightly so, Harry." Carl sat down and waved at Harry to stop the audio.

"I put a request in with Echelon for any activity in Havana in the last twelve hours, especially the police radio traffic. Should be coming through any time now," said Harry, draining a mug of coffee.

Carl was leaning over Harry's desk, frowning at his monitor. The feeling that something had gone wrong gnawed away at him, like an incoming swarm of wasps, quiet at first, growing louder. He'd worked with Piper and Greene many times and Frank on a handful of missions since his recruitment. Things may have screwed up in the past but there had never been a complete communication breakdown.

Several hours later, a beeping sound alerted both men to the encrypted file that had just appeared on the local server. Harry downloaded the file and opened it via the encryption software as was the process. The data package contained several documents and audio files. After ten minutes of scrolling through the docs, they found a report from the Policía Nacional Revolucionaria transmitters of extensive gunfire in the neighbourhood of Rodriguez Este, exactly where the team had been stationed. The report was at 1:30 am, dated several days after the team's arrival. It could not have been a coincidence.

Carl and Harry kept looking but they found no other references to the incident.

"This doesn't sound good," muttered Carl.

"What do we do?" asked Harry.

"Just keep looking through that lot and call me if you find anything more. I'll have to let upstairs know."

Carl's mind raced as he dialled the number for Devlin. Had his friend, Frank, been caught up in all that gunfire? Hard to know; hopefully he was at the hotel but it didn't seem likely. So what the hell was going on?

Just then, Carl's mobile began buzzing furiously. Another unidentified number.

"Hello?"

"Mr. Cronus...this is Mr. Feldman."

Carl stood up and began to walk to the private room. It was Frank, obviously on an unsecured line.

"Mr. Feldman? It's good to hear from you. I hope you're well? How's business over there?"

"Not so great. Mr. Pegasus and Mr. Aquila are permanently out of the deal. There seems to be a rival business in town."

Carl caught his own breath. Piper and Greene dead? His worst fear from moments earlier had manifested itself.

After a long pause, he spoke. "That's very unfortunate, Mr. Feldman. Are you able to wire or email me further information?"

For a moment, the line went bad and Carl could only hear a transatlantic hiss of noise.

"The telephone equipment is bad here. I'm unable to find or use it right now," Frank said.

Was he referring to the telephone line? No, he meant his laptop, probably lost or destroyed in what had clearly been some kind of ambush. Which was why he had to use a standard phone line. That could complicate things, especially if the Cuban authorities got hold of it. All fingers would point to British agents operating inside Cuba. It would cause an absolute shit storm.

"You'll need to get that phone back if you can. The company wouldn't be happy, especially with all those numbers on it."

"Okay, I'll try. Also, I think we need to leave the country, Mr. Cronus."

Carl paused, trying to think things out. It was getting complicated.

"Can you hang in there and see if Mr. Libre can find you a safe bed for the night? And see if you can sort out the telephone situation. What about Pandora?"

There was a pause and suddenly the line went dead.

David Devlin sipped his scotch, wrapped in a black silk dressing gown, his feet warmed in sheepskin lined leather slippers. In front of him was a perfect view of the Thames from his penthouse apartment. Behind the dark jagged shapes of the skyline, the glow of the city at night could be seen, rising and fading into the black sky. He leaned forward, opened his laptop and ran a message from Cuba, a table of six letters in seven columns of which there was a long list of rows. This data file was the input that he ran the encryption process on, generating the ciphertext output that translated the message into something he could understand.

It was a message from Kobra, leading the Russian team.

TO MARQUIS. UNKNOWN MAN AND PANDORA PURSUED WITHOUT SUCCESS. VISITED G13 +1 DOWN BUT OTHERS ESCAPED. PANDORA WITH THEM. AWAIT INSTRUCTIONS.

Devlin exhaled heavily and downed the last of his scotch before banging the crystal glass onto the coffee table.

Bloody idiots! What was he paying them for? They had lost them even after he had given them the safe house address on a silver platter.

The GCHQ Director tossed the laptop aside and then stood looking over the city of London, watching a tugboat make its way down the river. The pink dawn sky was turning to a clear blue, the seagulls circled both sides of the water eagerly scouting for food.

Interesting that one of the Ghost 13 team had helped the whistleblower though. It kept them all in the same neat package. Kept things simple. He just needed to find them.

Just then, his mobile chirped. It was Carl Paterson updating him. They had heard from one of the team who had confirmed that two were dead. Devlin already knew but acted with shock. Was there anything they could do? Pull them out was the suggestion. Perhaps. "Let me think about that," Devlin had replied. "Keep me posted on where they go and I'll look at options. Try and confirm what is happening with Pandora. Where is she?"

Carl said he would and the call ended.

Devlin felt himself breathe easier. It sounded like he could get their location soon enough and then things would be back on track. He sat back down with his laptop, logging into his MI6 profile. He tried to find any Ghost 13 files. Nothing existed. Then he remembered that Keller had been instructed to keep it off all official databases, for now at least. Probably wise considering the box of secrets Pandora had opened. The entire system and all procedures would need a massive overhaul when this whole gang fuck was over with.

Bowen. The name suddenly came into his mind. Overheard from a discussion, one that probably shouldn't have taken place but did anyway. Was it with Keller or the time he met Carl Paterson? No matter, as he remembered now. Frank Bowen. He was 'Auditor', the surveillance man.

Devlin dialled the number for Keller.

CHAPTER 31

"Keller. Tell me about Frank Bowen."

32

Brull pulled over several hundred yards away from the hotel on the opposite side to see the front entrance. The early morning sun cast sharp shadows across the street, an occasional taxi or scooter hurtled by, and birds scavenged at a heap of rubbish on the sidewalk. From their vantage point, they could see a group of men play cards on a table down a side street. A boy of around nine or ten raced a bicycle up and down past the card players.

"What are the chances of police having been here?" Frank asked. He was thinking about the chase through the kitchens and the gunshot. The hotel would surely have called the police.

Brull laughed. "It is early. There'll be no police here. But maybe in an hour, they come."

They watched as a trio of tourists came out of the hotel entrance and milled around, looking at a map. There was a couple in their 50s and a tall, heavyset, blonde man in a pale blue shirt. A member of the front desk, a young male, stepped out behind them and appeared to give them directions.

"Can we go past, slowly, and park around the side?" Frank asked.

Brull nodded and fired up the engine and the car cruised past the tourists who were glancing and nodding as the hotel man pointed down the street. The blonde man glanced at the car briefly before returning his attention back to a map.

"Was that one of them?" Sarah asked.

Brull turned into a narrow road on the same block.

Frank shook his head. "Can't be sure, I never really got a good look at any of them. Apart from the shooter behind the wall, I think he was dark-haired," said Frank.

Before heading to the hotel, they had stopped in a store for new clothes. Frank had bought another plain shirt, a Panama hat, and large shades. Sarah bought a demure sunhat, a t-shirt, and jeans. Anyone glancing at them would automatically think they were Average Joe tourists.

"Are you sure you should do this? Maybe too dangerous," stated Brull as he stopped in sight of the hotel rear entrance and switched off the engine.

Frank sighed. "I have to try and get my laptop back. It could be damaging to the company if it fell into the wrong hands. Trust me, I'd much rather leave it but I have to try."

"And if something happens to you? What do we do?" she asked.

Frank looked at Brull.

"You can go on your merry way, I guess. But we can't protect you. I take it you have a plan to disappear somewhere?"

"I had disappeared until you found me. But, yes, Frank, I can look after myself. I would like to check if there are any messages at reception though."

Frank shook his head. "Not going to happen. Too risky. Let me go in first." He turned to Brull. "Can I borrow your lighter?"

Brull nodded, looking at him quizzically but handed it over.

He stepped out of the car and walked toward the rear entrance, a metal gate that led into a small courtyard garden and a doorway, just around the corner from the kitchens. Frank inhaled and stepped inside the hotel and a long corridor with guest rooms. Turning left, away from where he knew the kitchen and bar were, Frank padded along to the front area of the hotel, his eyes scanning the walls and ceilings as he went. A maid came out of one of the rooms with towels and smiled at Frank before heading in the opposite direction. He came to another external door that led out into the inner courtyard. It was breakfast time and most of the guests were enjoying their first coffee of the day.

Frank scanned the faces looking for anything out of place; a Spanish looking couple, an elderly man in his 60s and two European looking women were left in the courtyard. There were no signs of any police. Frank continued down the corridor; ahead were double internal doors to the bar and restaurant and just before was a fire alarm on the ceiling. Frank peeked through the doors and checked the bar; only a barman cleaning tables. He closed them again and took out Brull's lighter, lit it, and held it up to the fire alarm sensor.

Within seconds, a loud wailing sound echoed through the corridors and Frank immediately rushed to the courtyard, making his way across to the metal steps that ascended the different levels. There were shouts from several hotel staff and the remaining tourists looked around in confusion, looking for guidance. Within a minute, Frank was on the fourth level and approaching his room; he glanced down and saw staff rounding up any stray guests, showing them to the exit through the reception area. Then he caught sight of the tall blonde man in the pale blue shirt who had been outside the front and was now walking towards the steps Frank had just climbed. A concierge approached him, pointing towards the front of the hotel and then got a punch in the gut for his trouble. The man crumpled to the floor.

Definitely one of the Russians.

Frank quickly unlocked his room door, went inside and looked around, his heart sinking as his eyes rested on the empty space on the table where he had left the laptop. Taken. Either by the authorities, the hotel staff, or more likely the Russian. The suitcase he had brought with the surveillance equipment was also gone. No use hanging around. He slipped out of the door and looked down at the lower levels and the courtyard. There was no sign of blonde guy but it wasn't easy to see from that angle. Frank walked around the opposite direction so he could see the steps better, keeping close to the wall and then he locked eyes with the Russian who was looking back up from two levels down. Shit!

He started to bolt, running fast along the terrace and then up the third flight of steps. Frank looked around mind racing. One of the rooms? He tried a few doors. Locked.

Just a metre above, he could see the edge of the terracotta tiles of the roof, under which flower pots hung on chains from the gutters. At the end of the walkway were black painted railings. He eased himself slowly onto the railing so he was standing on it, steadying himself with his hands on the roof edge. On the other side was an eighty-foot drop onto the side street. One slip and he was dead. The men were still playing cards and now seemed to be arguing.

Frank hauled his body upwards until he was bent forward on his stomach, the top half of him now on the roof. A running footfall on the metal steps got closer and from his position, he could see the Russian appear along the walkway, looking around for him and clearly puzzled by his disappearance. Frank edged forward, inch by inch on his stomach until his whole body was flat on the angled part of the roof. A piece of tile broke loose under his weight and slipped down onto the street below.

Shit! He must have heard it.

The angled side of the roof flattened out at the top and Frank eased himself onto his hands and knees, slowly moving across to the other side. Behind him, the sound of scraping from the railings. The Russian was on his tail, moving quicker without the fear of making noise.

On the high roof, the skyline of Havana made an impressive view, a blue sky overhead without a cloud in sight. Frank jogged across the flat section, past a large ventilation box that pumped out air from below, until he was on the far side of the building.

Peering over, he could see another angled section of tiled roof and the street below where Brull and Sarah waited in the car. He moved along the edge, looking for a way off.

A glimpse of a window balcony.

Glancing back, he saw the Russian's blonde head bopping up and down as he climbed up to the flat section.

Frank crouched and moved onto the tiles, crab fashion, moving slowly to where he would be above the balcony.

Running footsteps.

The Russian was at the edge of the flat further along and looked down at Frank, a wolfish grin appearing on his angled face. He turned around and eased down onto the tiles, copying Frank's crouch style and began to move towards him. Frank was easing himself over the edge, looking down at the balcony below his feet. It was a twelve-foot drop but it only stood a few metres out. The Russian was right on him. It was fight or drop time.

A boot stomp-kicked Frank's left hand and he grimaced in pain. He began to swing himself away from the building to gain momentum so he could land in the right place and not risk falling back over the balcony.

"I hope you can fly," taunted the Russian as he continued to kick and grind at this hand and fingers. Lifting his foot for a second to slam a boot down hard gave Frank the chance. Letting go, he dropped, holding his body as upright as possible. His feet slammed onto the balcony and he fell back against the railing with the impact, hands desperately grabbing the top of the metal rails to hold himself.

A tile smashed by his right foot as the soles of Russian boots appeared over the side, directly above him. Frank reached down for a plant pot and banged it against the window, cracking and weakening the glass, and then elbowed the rest with hard but directed jerks. When there was enough space, he reached in with his hand and unlocked the window and hauled it upwards. The Russian had maneuvered so he was directly above him and dropped just as Frank scrambled into the hotel room. He heard the slam of boots behind him but didn't look, running hard and fast across the room and out into the corridor. The alarm had stopped but the hallways were still empty of any guests or staff as Frank bolted down the stairwell to the ground floor. At last, he reached the rear entrance where he had first entered the hotel and ran onto the street towards the car, which Brull had sensibly turned around engine idling.

Frank jumped into the passenger seat.

"Go! Go!"

Brull did as asked and screeched off towards the main street ahead of them.

Frank turned around to see the blonde Russian sprint onto the road through the rear window. He came to a stop and spat on the ground as he watched the vehicle speed off.

Sarah was staring back at Frank, wide-eyed.

"Whose bloody idea was it to get the laptop back, huh?" Frank asked, flashing her a cheeky grin.

Sarah sighed, frowning at him.

"That'll be your great idea," she replied.

33

They drove back towards Centro Habana on Zanja, a long freeway that cut through the heart of the city taking them east to Calzada de Zapata in Vedado. There was an odd architectural mix of crumbling pillared mansions and ugly pancake stacked 1950's high rises that housed the city's population.

The vehicle headed into a labyrinth of Cuadras, neat one hundred metre blocks that made the grid layout straightforward to follow, street signs in the form of small stone blocks placed at every corner.

Brull nodded as he swung into yet another turning. "This one, it is Calle twenty."

"This place is a maze," Frank muttered as they pulled into an avenue, looking much like the others with compact, brightly painted houses nestled behind a row of palms. The car slowed and pulled over, the engine idling, as they both looked at the house Brull had specified.

"Stay here and I'll take a look," said Brull. It was quiet, barely anyone around in the midday haze. A lone dog rummaged around a group of bins, tugging at a black bag with its teeth. Brull got out of the vehicle and strolled across the dusty avenue and then disappeared into the house. After a few minutes, he returned and leaned into the passenger window.

"All clear," he said, glancing down the street.

Frank turned off the engine and then took the Glock out of his backpack. He checked it briefly and then tucked it into his belt under his shirt, then got out of the car with his backpack.

"Let's go, Sarah."

They went inside the house that had small sparsely furnished rooms with crumbling walls and the usual ill repair Frank was beginning to become accustomed to.

"It's okay, all safe here," Brull said.

"Let me look around," said Frank. He walked through to a central living area that had a large dining table and led to a hallway towards the rear. He passed a spiral staircase that led upstairs and carried on walking to a modest kitchen that had the bare basics. At the back was a small courtyard surrounded by high brick walls, and a metal table and chairs, rusting from lack of use. He then carefully moved up the staircase to see two sparsely furnished rooms. When he came back downstairs, Brull and Sarah were sitting at the table. Frank joined them and slumped down with a sigh of relief.

"So what is this place?" he asked.

"It belongs to a relative. They are away and only I have the key," said Brull.

Sarah was looking at Frank with narrowed eyes.

"I really appreciate you helping me but I'm not going back Frank," she said evenly.

Frank sighed and avoided her gaze, studying an old cross that was nailed onto the whitewashed wall instead.

"It's a bit dangerous with that gang running around out there."

"Maybe I should take my chances."

Frank looked at her with an expression of concern etched on his face.

"Why don't you wait until morning and then decide?" he asked.

"We eat and rest for now," Brull interjected.

Sarah, her face pale with exhaustion, seemed to think for a moment and reluctantly nodded.

Frank placed his palms flat down on the table top and stood up. "Good. Right now, I need to update Cronus on where we are and try and find some kind of exit to this situation. It's getting out of hand."

"I'll take you to a phone box. Maybe you can get permission to go home."

Frank nodded and thought of home. That was one place he yearned to be right now.

34

Frank was quiet as Dante Brull served up a stew that had been cooking for over an hour. He had contacted Carl Paterson in London, updated him that they were in another location, and was told to sit tight and wait. Frank had then reluctantly told him that Pandora was with him, something that hadn't gone down too well. But what the hell was he supposed to have done when another group had crashed the party? She had to be protected and if he had to choose again, he would have played it the same way. As he had grown closer to Sarah, he wondered what would become of her. She was a good person. Sure, she had an agenda but fundamentally, she wasn't that far away from his own moral compass.

Sarah poured water into mugs and laid out bowls on the wooden table and they all sat down.

"This smells really good, Dante," Sarah said after dipping a piece of bread into the stew; she was looking at Frank.

"It is if I might say. My mother showed me to cook this dish, God rest her soul. It is Potaje de Frijoles Blancos, white bean stew."

Frank didn't wait to be asked and dived right in, shovelling the stew into his mouth and the mixture of beans, beef, peppers, and cumin tasted incredible.

"So, your family. I take it your mother is no longer with us?"

asked Sarah. Brull crossed his chest and pointed upwards.

"She is in God's hands now, along with my father."

Sarah nodded solemnly and then glanced at Frank again. "Everything okay, Frank?"

He looked up from his food. "Yes. Just thinking. Wondering why they want us to stay here."

"They re-think probably. Making new plans," Brull said, shrugging.

A gust of wind slammed one of the window shutters at the rear of the small house, causing their heads to turn.

"Weather reports a hurricane coming in tonight. But nothing serious, as we should only get the tail of it, but it will still be choppy," said Brull.

Just as he was standing up to deal with the shutter, the light dimmed and then cut out completely, leaving them in darkness, apart from a faint residue of light that penetrated through the windows from outside.

"What's going on?" Sarah's voice.

"Ah, another power cut," Brull replied and he soon had a flame from his lighter to guide him. "It's happening more and more in Cuba. I get the gas lamp."

Frank stopped eating and stood up. "I don't like it...are you sure it's not just us?"

They both walked to the front and Brull glanced out through the blind.

"No, everywhere is out. Just a normal blackout. I check the fuse box."

"Are there any other ways in here besides the front and back doors?"

"Only windows."

"Let's get them all closed and bolted up tight," Frank said. "It might be an idea to have someone stay awake through the night."

Brull checked the front road, which was quiet, and closed up the window shutters outside and locked the windows. Frank headed to the rear courtyard and closed up the two windows at the back, before looking up at the high wall towering over the property at the end of the courtyard. He heard the sound of neighbours talking as they moved chairs and loose items back inside their house. The rumour of the hurricane had spread.

Brull volunteered to take the first shift on staying awake. "You will need sleep, more than me. I will wake you at four."

Frank and Sarah bedded down on roll-out mattresses in the small room upstairs while Brull cleaned up before returning to the table to sip coffee and smoke cigarettes. The wind was increasing outside as if angered and its powerful gusts slammed the cuadras. Brull fished around in a cupboard and found what he was looking for, a fresh bottle of rum to perk up his coffee.

Viktor Kozel scanned the row of casas through his night vision binoculars. The chaos of the hurricane would give his men perfect cover for the infiltration of the house. Although, it might also be a hindrance. He put down the binoculars and turned to the other three men in the back of the MPV. "twenty minutes and then we go."

There was a collective groan. The men had been cooped up in the vehicle for three hours now and were keen to get moving.

The palms on the street were alive and swaying like demented dancers, the gusts played havoc with trash bins and debris flew across the air.

"It getting worse. Maybe we should hold off," said the bald Leonid Duskin from the back of the vehicle. Tarasenko and Glukhov both turned and glared at him. They didn't want to hang back for another few hours or even minutes.

"We have one chance to get them. There was a big fuck up last time, remember? So, definitely no room for failure now!" Kozel rasped. He hated it when his crew got itchy feet and whined. Duskin dolefully clasped his huge hands together and peered back out of the window.

Kozel sighed heavily and looked at his watch. They had been there long enough. He turned to the blonde Taransenko and the smaller, wily Glukhov and nodded.

The two men slid out of the rear doors and walked as best they could in the screeching wind, heading back along the block, parallel to the street where their targets were holed up. Their figures moved slowly against the force that nature threw against them, their dark clothes flapping violently. The tall figure of Taransenko suddenly ducked as a piece of corrugated iron roof flew past him.

"This is crazy!" he shouted to his comrade. Glukhov didn't answer but gave his comrade a look of understanding. Both men bent their heads and headed for the alleyway, which gave them some respite from the storm. The noise level was quieter there and they moved quickly down the narrow rubbish-strewn alley, counting the houses behind a high brick wall until they reached the target.

Tarasenko squatted down with his back against the wall and gave Glukhov a foot up with his clasped hands, grunting at the weight. Glukhov leveraged himself up. Tarasenko then changed position to support him with his shoulders as his comrade peeked over the wall to check the situation.

The howling wind tore away at loose window shutters and there was the occasional smash or thud of objects crashing into each other.

Seeing it was all clear, Glukhov eased himself onto the top of the wall and reached down a hand to pull up his comrade. They both eased themselves down into the small courtyard on the far side and crouched in the shadows, assessing the rear door and window to the house.

The Ford MPV rocked gently, buffered by the rasping tail of the hurricane as Viktor Kozel and Leonid Duskin sat in the front, smoking. They watched the palms lined down the road swaying and bending more and more erratically and shifted uncomfortably in their leather seats.

"Getting worse, I think," mumbled Dustin. Just then, the phone in Kozel's hand vibrated.

"They're in the back. Time to move."

The two men clambered out of the vehicle. Duskin's side was receiving the full brunt of the wind and he struggled to close the door for a moment, and then threw a backpack over his shoulder. Soon, the two figures were slowly making their way down the street.

Brull was sitting at the table, having drained his second glass of neat rum, and shook his head to revive himself. It had been a long time since he had caught any sleep. The wind, coming in waves, made the whole house creak and groan, reminding Brull of an old ship. Window shutters rattled continuously, especially the door in the kitchen at the back of the house. Brull's eyelids flickered. The food, rum, and lack of sleep all catching up on him.

Some small part of his brain was alerted to a noise that cut through the howling wind and rattling shutters, a sound like a footstep, barely audible from the kitchen. He slowly swivelled his torso around to the bookshelf and his hand found the Glock, where he had left it. Brull checked the weapon and slowly stood up.

The dancing shadows from the gas lamp made Brull more anxious and then they faded into blackness as Brull paced slowly down the carpeted hallway. He had been at the house long enough to know to avoid a small table that had a large vase placed on it. The back door that had been rattling was silent now and Brull felt the rush of outside air from the kitchen, which died in a moment. A hand grabbed his mouth and he felt a knee slam into the small of his back, sending shock waves of pain throughout his body. In the flash of his final thoughts, Brull realised they were already in the house. He had failed to be ready and on guard. He had let in the enemy. Then a hunter's knife opened his throat, sending warm blood streaming down his chest and his body, held by the unseen figure, he rapidly weakened and slumped into oblivion.

Frank stood on a tube station platform under a bluish hue of light as if in a hospital or laboratory. The service lift dinged at the end of the floor, a green light announcing its arrival.

Footsteps echoed from the blackness of the tunnel against a backdrop of hissing wind. Frank stood facing the blackness, feet apart as the steps grew nearer. Then a light, no, two lights. The train was coming, distant but getting nearer. The figure appeared, walking in the middle of the tracks, the same side as the train. Frank shouted and as he did so, he saw it was Greene. Thomas Greene, his colleague in Ghost 13. The lights were brighter now, the whoosh of the wind rushed the platform.

Frank shouted to warn Greene, who hadn't seemed to have noticed the train. He just looked at Frank and then made a signal to him with his hands, as if trying to tell him something, for him to back away and move back.

"Greene! Get off the tracks...Train!"

Suddenly, Greene's head seemed to pop in a spray of red mist as if blasted from an unseen vantage point. There followed a violent banging sound as the train slammed into his body and into the station.

Frank sat up, his deep sleep ended by the banging window shutter that had worked loose in the wind. He rolled out from under the sheet on the makeshift bedroll and padded over to the window. He glanced into the darkness outside that seemed to boil with the chaos of the hurricane and pulled the shutters together and closed the latch.

"Surprised you could sleep at all with that racket," came Sarah's voice from the bed. Frank returned to the bedroll on the floor. "Yeah, must have been dog-tired. You get any shut-eye?"

"Not much. I think this is more than a tailwind."

There was a distant clank and thud from somewhere. It was hard to tell. The wind sounded like a freight train and was getting louder and more violent.

Frank looked at his watch and tutted. "4:30. Damn, Brull should have woken me." He jumped up and pulled on his jeans and shirt.

"If you feel the need to make tea, I wouldn't say no," she said. Frank could sense her smirking in the gloom.

"Sure thing, madam. Peeled grapes with that?"

"Yep."

Frank descended the stairs that circled down to the centre of the casa.

35

Only flickering shadows from the gas lamp greeted Frank as he stepped onto the tiled floor. The table was empty, apart from the overloaded ashtray and a bottle of Havana Club. Frank cursed Brull for not waking him up, but now he was suddenly concerned.

Where the hell had he gone?

And then he noticed Brull's Glock was missing from the top of the bookshelf and the chair he had sat in was pulled back as if an imprint of some earlier scene. He wasn't in the toilet as that was upstairs and he would surely have heard him. Perhaps he was checking the back courtyard?

As Frank moved across the room, he caught a glimpse of some kind of shape on the hallway floor. As he edged closer, a wisp of light from the lamp behind him revealed Brull's lifeless body, his eyes staring into the abyss. Frank froze, suddenly fully aware that he was in danger. As soon as that thought crossed his mind, an arm had him by the throat, crushing his larynx and his ability to breathe. He ground his chin down to try and give himself leverage but his vision was tunnelling, the oxygen to his brain dissipating fast.

Suddenly, the pressure lifted from his neck and he could breathe. A cold piece of familiar steel pushed against his skull, indicating the game was over.

"Do not move or you will be dead meat," whispered a gruff,

accented voice in his ear. He felt the presence of another figure nearby and then saw a figure with some kind of goggles on. Night vision goggles.

"Okay," he said. The figure in front of him removed his goggles and shone a torchlight onto his face.

Frank squinted against the blinding torch, making his irises contract suddenly. He held a hand up to shield the light.

"Where is the woman?"

Frank shook his head, wishing he had been more careful. There was light to see now and he looked down onto Brull's body. It made him feel sick inside. He had liked Brull and grown to trust him and now the poor bastard was dead.

"Did you have to kill him?"

The taller figure pushed him back into the large living room. "Just get your hands above head."

They moved back into the room and Frank stood, his hands on his head, back against the assailant.

"What do you want?" Frank asked.

He noticed the smaller of the men begin to creep up the stairwell, his pistol held out in front of him.

"Don't hurt her!" he rasped.

"Shut up," the masked figure growled and nudged a steel pistol against his cranium.

Minutes later, Sarah was standing in the middle of the room and they were both waiting, staring at the men. The taller one was the same man who had chased Frank across the rooftops at the hotel.

One of the intruder's phones buzzed and he walked to the front door and let in a stocky man with a Mohawk and a black goatee beard, dressed in a tight dark tee shirt and military fatigue trousers. The man studied Frank and Sarah for a moment before speaking to the others in what Frank recognised as Russian.

The assailant Frank had rumbled with moments earlier took out a roll of duct tape, turned Frank around, ordering him to put his hands behind his back, and wrapped the tape around his wrists. He then did the same to Sarah before taping both their mouths.

A thought came into Frank's mind. Something his old trainer, Sam Keane, had shown him. He buried the thought for now and looked over at the men. Who were they? It was the same crew that had ambushed them, he was certain of that. Russian secret service, the FSB? It seemed plausible.

Suddenly, their heads were covered with black hoods and they were led outside via the front door, where Frank felt the angry winds that continued to sweep through the city. They were pushed and bundled into the back of a vehicle and ordered to lie down and keep quiet.

Frank heard the engine start and felt the vehicle reversing fast to the end of the road and then away onto the main roads. After twenty minutes, he guessed they must be leaving the city and wondered about their fate.

36

The two burly men pushed Frank and Sarah through the warehouse door, shouting in Russian. Their hoods were taken off and Frank saw they were in a huge, dilapidated space. Lengths of rusted chains hung from pulleys on rails that crisscrossed along the entire area. Frank's eyes darted along the boarded up windows, desperately looking for clues to a possible escape route. The windows looked well secured with metal sheets bolted onto them. Only a gap in the warehouse roof, letting in the early dawn light, at least thirty feet above them offered any hope and that looked like an extreme long shot. He glanced at Sarah, who was clearly frightened and tried to give her a reassuring look whilst struggling to hold his own uncertainty at bay.

The taller blonde thug took the duct tape off their mouths and commanded Sarah to lie on a pair of wooden planks that had been set on the ground by an old piece of machinery in the centre of the warehouse. She refused and he swung and punched her in the stomach. Sarah recoiled and bent double, gasping for air.

"Hey! You bastard..." Frank lurched forward but was grabbed by his arms from behind.

The bald man with a scar pushed her down onto the planks and proceeded to tie her hands and feet with rope before tipping the planks upward so her feet were higher up than her head. The other man then placed bricks underneath to prop them up.

A sound of footsteps echoed up towards the roof space, growing louder and Frank looked and saw the man with a black goatee beard and Mohawk from earlier coming in behind them. Frank noticed he had an arrogant swagger and as he came closer, he saw the tentacles of barbed wire tattooed on his throat for the first time. He held up a closed laptop and gave Frank a little wave with it.

"Have you missed this, Mr. Bowen?"

Frank stayed tight-lipped and just stared at the Russian, who was assessing him with his dark, cold eyes.

"We could use the information on this. Your employer. MI6, isn't it?"

He broke into a wolf-like smile at his continued silence and threw the laptop across to the blonde Russian, who caught it haphazardly. He balanced it upright on the shelving of a nearby machine and folded his arms.

"So, my friends. We have searched you from head to foot as well as your hotel room and found nothing. Where are the documents?" the one with the mohawk asked.

Sarah took a deep breath, seemingly digging deep for a stronger resolve.

Viktor clicked his fingers and the scar-faced henchman walked a few metres to a bucket and pulled out a damp cloth before placing it over Sarah's face. She seemed to know what was coming and took a deep breath before it covered her.

"What are you doing?" Frank protested.

He suddenly got a sharp kick in the small of his back from the other man standing behind him, throwing Frank onto his hands and knees. He grunted in pain and spat onto the dusty concrete floor.

Viktor spoke in Russian to the large, scar-faced one, who pulled him back onto his feet. Frank stared hard at the man in front of him, who smiled and took a piece of folded paper from his pocket. He opened it up and held it in front of Frank's face.

"Take a close look. You see who this is? You recognise?"

Frank blinked at the grainy photograph on the fax, momentarily disbelieving the image in front of him. It was Maria and Joe, both blindfolded. They each held a separate side of *The Times* newspaper. Conveniently placed underneath the image was a zoom shot of the newspaper's date: November 14th. A few days ago.

A sickening feeling in Frank's stomach overwhelmed him and he closed his eyes, trying to contain the rage that overcame him.

"You fucking bastard!" he mouthed quietly.

Viktor sucked in air through his teeth and stared impassively at Frank.

"Your girlfriend and son are in our hands. Think carefully about that. They are a long way from here and their lives are now up to you. Now, tell me, where are the documents?"

Frank wondered: *Why only Joe? Had they missed baby Zak?* He must be with the babysitter or one of Maria's friends. Thank god for that at least. He glanced at Sarah on the bench, attempting to breathe through the face cloth.

"How can I be sure you'd let them go?" Frank asked bitterly.

Viktor laughed, a low guttural sound that carried through the huge, open space.

"You don't. You have no cards to play at all."

Frank said nothing, his mind a whirlwind of questions, mixed with pain and anger. How had they found them? A tracking device? Someone in Liberatus? Carl knew where they were...and who else in Ghost 13? He knew the Russian was right. His options were zero, but he still couldn't give them the answer they wanted. Only Sarah could. He glanced down at her covered face, sinking and rising quickly as the mould of her mouth in the cloth desperately tried to suck in air.

Just then, goatee took a pager from his pocket, which beeped, and stared at it for a second, frowning. He looked up at the scarred thug still holding Frank.

He rasped in Russian and Frank suddenly felt hands grab his arms, pulling him to his feet followed by another shove in the shoulder for good measure.

Viktor began striding across the floor, away from them back towards the main entrance door from where he had come.

Frank caught a glimpse of the short stocky one pulling over a hose that snaked its way back into the depths of the warehouse towards Sarah. A glugging sound welled within its tube and suddenly, a stream of water burst free. The other man switched on a radio that rested on the old machine behind them and loud pop music began to blare out.

Sarah was already struggling to breathe, her lungs crying out for air when the water hit her face. It was a matter of seconds before she felt panic well up inside her, her mouth gulping for precious air but there was none. She felt like she was suffocating, her muscles burning, contracting with every second. Just as she felt like she had reached her last possible breath, the water stopped and the cloth came off. She gulped in oxygen, her face reddened by the near-asphyxiation, and then choked as phlegm caught in her throat.

"Where are the documents?" the Russian voice asked again.

"I don't know. Please stop," she pleaded.

"You don't know? You have the documents before. Where are they?"

Sarah choked and breathed in, a nasty wheezing sound that

carried up into the roof space.

As Frank was pushed towards a door at the back of the warehouse, he turned his head to try and see what was happening.

"Let her go...she knows nothing!" he shouted, trying to buy time if nothing else.

The Russian grabbed Frank by the scruff of his neck and shoved him against a metal door, his body hitting it hard, causing a shockwave throughout his body.

He then pressed his Glock pistol hard against the side of Frank's head, causing him to freeze. The pain already replaced with a feeling of imminent death but surprisingly, he felt no fear, only concern for Sarah. His family. Frank felt his heart race hard in his chest.

"Keep your mouth shut, unless you tell me information. Understand?" the Russian growled.

Frank breathed hard through his nose, his face pushed against the door.

"Yes...I understand."

The man pulled the weapon away and shoved open the heavy door, which revealed a corridor leading to other rooms. Frank was pushed into the first room that had once been an office. Water dripped from a crack in the ceiling onto a large desk. An old filing cabinet lay flat on its side on the ground and a scattering of papers and files that had been pulled from the drawers lay discarded next to it. Frank felt another shove against his back. The Russian then grabbed his shoulder, turning Frank to face him and then punched him hard in the stomach. Frank grunted loudly in pain as he doubled up and reeled backwards.

Scarface laughed, a low, repeating staccato sound.

Getting into the spirit of the occasion, he grabbed Frank again and threw a massive right hook across his jaw. Frank fell backwards against the cabinet and crashed down onto the hard ground with a thud. A dull blackness circled, threatening his conscious state, and then the large hands grabbed him by the shirt collar and hauled him back up onto his feet. The laugh came again but muffled this time.

Frank forced himself to focus, his vision blurring. The thug was grinning ear to ear and his breath stank of stale coffee.

"You having plenty of fun, clever guy?"

Through the pain around his jaw and stomach, Frank knew one thing for certain: he had to get out of there. Not just away from this maniac but because Maria and Joe were in real danger. He had no idea how he would find them but there had to be a way.

Scarface turned his back on Frank momentarily, looking around for something. Some rope to replace the duct tape perhaps. Frank didn't care. It was the moment he had been waiting for, the little trick Sam Keane, his old trainer, had shown him years before. Without further hesitation, Frank quickly raised his bonded hands above his head. He pulled down with as much force as he could, pulling his arms apart, using all his strength, and as he did so, the duct tape broke with a snap, freeing his hands.

He lunged a thrust kick with his heel against the back of the Russian's right knee with all his force. Crumbling onto his knees, the big guy yelped in agony. Pivoting quickly, he threw a roundhouse kick at the Russian's upper arm in an attempt to make him drop the pistol. The Russian hunched up at the impact but stubbornly held on.

Continuing his momentum, Frank jumped forward, thrusting his knee into the centre of the Russian's back. The thug fell forward, hitting the ground hard with a thump and Frank immediately grabbed the hand holding the weapon, smashing it up and down, crushing his knuckles onto the concrete.

The Russian, still strong despite the blows, began pushing himself upwards with his knees and left hand, attempting to roll Frank off. Quickly realising the danger, Frank grabbed the back of his skull and smacked it hard repeatedly against the concrete floor.

The man groaned woefully and a puddle of dark red blood pooled from his nose, soaking the floor. Frank was now able to disarm the Russian, peeling each finger off the barrel of the gun. Even half unconscious, the big man didn't want to release the weapon. Frank smacked his head again for good measure and was finally able to pull it free from his clutching hand.

Frank stood up, breathing heavily, his senses of his surroundings slowly coming back to him as the adrenaline left his system. Hearing a rasp and scuffle, Frank turned, surprised to see the Russian slowly pushing himself onto all fours, mumbling and swearing in his native tongue. This guy was one mean mother.

Reaching down, Frank cupped his head and drove his knee hard into the big man's jaw with a sickening crack. Scarface hit the ground, finally out for the count.

Frank, unsteady on his feet, checked the chamber in the Glock before wiping spittle from his lips. He tucked it into his belt and went back into the corridor. He slowly opened the door to the warehouse and was met with Cuban Salsa beats from the radio. Then a shout. Sarah's voice.

"Get off me!"

What the hell were the bastards doing?

Frank slipped out the door, moving slowly behind a large piece of nearby machinery that ran parallel down the length of the warehouse. He needed to surprise them as they could easily gun him down if they saw him, even just a few feet away.

Frank kept low and glanced quickly around the edge of the rusty bulk. One of the men had his back to him but the other was on the far side of Sarah and would see him coming from this position. He doubled back and then moved towards the men from his original position.

The blonde man was pulling her jeans down and had them around her knees, taunting her as he did so.

"Priyatnogo appyetita! Enjoy it, bitch."

Frank heard her gasps and sobs, which only steeled him further for what he had to do. He let emotion evaporate off his body as he crept quickly across the wide, open space between them while being careful not to kick an empty can or stupidly trip on the numerous bricks strewn on the ground. He was scurrying now, closing the space. The pistol was aimed high in front of him; the weapons training he had received gave him the technical know-how but didn't stop his sweaty palms or his thundering heartbeat.

Ten feet away and the tinny sound of their radio increased. The smaller thug threw the cloth back over Sarah's face, while the blonde one had pulled her jeans off and was forcing her legs apart, whilst trying to undo his own trousers. Sarah kicked and struggled.

"Okay, bitch...you like Russian?"

Seven feet. Their backs to him.

Frank gripped the pistol harder, checking the safety catch was off.

Five feet.

The blonde thug said something to his associate, who followed his order and held one of her legs, attempting to restrain her. Frank noticed the other had his weapon tucked into the back of his belt. Good.

Three feet.

The man with the dark hair sensed a presence behind him and his face began to turn but before he could react, his body was pushed forward with the force of a direct head shot from Frank's weapon. The other thug turned at the sound of gunfire, hand already moving behind for his piece. Frank swung his pistol around to aim at his head and fired again. A hole ripped violently into his forehead, his facial expression held a look of surprise as his body slumped down onto the floor with his associate.

Both down. The leader would be fully alerted and there was no way to know if there were others in the building.

Frank quickly put the weapon down and removed the cloth that covered Sarah's face. She sucked in air hard, her eyes wide with shock as she focused on Frank. He quickly switched off the radio and began untying the rope as he spoke softly.

"Sarah, it's okay. Everything's alright. They're not going to hurt you anymore." Sarah nodded. Frank glanced towards the front of the warehouse. No sign of any back up yet. The rope was tight and he was wasting valuable time. Finally, he got her hand free and he moved onto the other one.

A slight noise from the far end, boots carefully creeping up metal steps. Frank looked across the floor and then, for the first time, saw the top of the stairwell leading down to some basement. A glimpse of the familiar black hair as the other Russian quickly glanced over the floor towards Frank and fired a shot that whizzed past and shattered something behind him.

Frank returned a shot. The bullet ricocheted, causing sparks on a metal wall plate and the head quickly ducked down. The sound of descending footsteps as the Russian retreated.

Frank saw that the noise had been his laptop, now lying

shattered all over the floor in pieces. Shit! He returned to grappling with the knot in the rope and got it free. He helped her get off the planks and supported her weight as she moved onto her feet.

"Can you lie low here?" he asked, hating to leave her. She nodded, relieved to have some time to recover. She glanced at the bodies on the floor. "No problem." Then she looked at him. "Please, be careful, Frank."

"I will."

Frank moved behind another hulk of machinery, his pistol aimed squarely at the stairwell.

37

Moving forward slowly, Frank kept his eyes fixed on where he had seen the Russian. His thoughts were a mix of self-preservation and keeping the last man alive for questioning. Suddenly, the Russian appeared in a flash of movement, firing a volley of shots in his direction. Frank dived to the hard floor, barrel rolled behind a crate, and returned fire.

A shout from the Russian just before bolting out of the entrance door told him he had hit the target but he instantly regretted firing. He needed him alive. There was a dull sound of a car engine gunning into action outside. Frank, rising to his feet, moved quickly towards the door, following the Russian's footsteps. He just caught a glance of a black MPV vehicle banking hard down the dusty driveway and then turning left on a road that was a few metres from the warehouse.

Frank kicked a stone on the ground in frustration.

"Shit!"

The only connection to his family's fate was now speeding off into the Cuban sunset.

He saw there was a second vehicle behind him and tried the doors. They were locked.

Frank stepped back into the warehouse.

Check that the basement is clear and get Sarah.

Standing at the top of the metal steps, he heard a creak of aged metal, like a groan from the depths of some vast submarine. He crouched down as low as he possibly could and quickly glanced below the edge of the basement ceiling. It looked clear. He descended on his hands and feet like a crab, step by step, carefully manoeuvring himself so he was ready to either fire his weapon or retreat back up the stairwell. The air was damp and musty. The dimmed light made it hard to see anything but shapes and Frank felt too exposed for his liking. He saw a crate at the bottom of the stairs and made his move, jumping three steps at a time. The hard metal shot pain into his feet like shock waves but in seconds, he was where he wanted to be, behind the cover of the huge container.

Listening hard, there was a dripping sound and the same random creaking from the back of the basement. He chanced a look, his eyes already adjusting to the low light and noticed a workbench against a partitioned wall, with new equipment stacked on top that looked out of place alongside the old rusted machine parts. Frank moved silently further into the open space towards the sound, stopping dead at intervals until he found the source, a wooden door that was catching an air flow from an air vent in the wall.

Satisfied there were no other Russians hiding, he returned back up the steps and towards the rear of the warehouse where Sarah was waiting, her body turned away from the dead bodies, her head in her hands as she sobbed quietly.

Frank bent down and put a hand on her shoulder.

"It's okay. There's no one left now, we're getting out of here really soon. I just need to check on a few things." Sarah nodded.

Frank went to the back office and checked the still unconscious Russian. He hunted around, found some rope, and tied up his ankles and wrists before coming back out into the warehouse.

"Just got to check these guys," he said as Sarah hauled herself up from the floor.

He searched the pockets and it wasn't long before he had a compact Nokia phone in his hand and was scrolling through a small list of numbers, each with a name in Russian. There was also a book of matches with a logo of a tiger on the front, a bar called 'Stripes', which Frank quickly pocketed. He rang one of the names on the phone, the number was dead. The second one rang from the pocket of the first man he had killed. A third mobile number, which had been phoned the most according to the log, named 'кобра', began ringing.

Then there was the sound of a click as it was answered and silence at the other end. Frank could hear the humming of a car engine in the background.

"How's your wound?" Frank asked, almost sounding sympathetic.

"Fuck you."

"Let's start afresh, huh, comrade?" Frank said.

"You've killed my comrades, for that, you will pay," the voice said, quiet but venomously. Frank didn't doubt for a second that he meant it.

"Sure, but that's the business we're in, isn't it, Cobra? Is that your code name?"

Frank knew little Russian but 'кобра' was one word he did know.

"You can call me your fucking death knell, Frank."

"Okay, Cobra. I want to do a deal. My family, you know who's holding them and you want the information we have."

Humouring him probably wasn't ideal after catching him with a bullet going out the door but he had to keep him talking.

"That information your employer wants, I know how to get it

now." Frank glanced at Sarah as he said it.

The voice came back. "Keep that phone, I call you back."

"Wait!"

The line went dead.

Frank held back the urge to throw the phone onto the floor in frustration but his white knuckles held firm and he dropped his head.

It was risky. They could easily trace that phone but it was the only option right now. He'd ditch it as soon as he could but now, it was the thinnest of threads to the kidnappers and his family.

They both walked down the steps to the basement, Frank, realising she was still shaken from the ordeal, comforted her with a hand on her shoulder.

Frank returned to the workbench and flipped on a lamp that hung on a string of wires and looked over a modern Cuban-made shortwave radio. He saw a Ford embossed key lob and immediately pocketed it. His foot tapped a metal bin underneath and he picked it up to check the contents. Remnants of blackened crispy paper that had been burned. Something familiar. A small triangle of white paper that had not blackened caught his eye. Distinct handwritten numerals, a clear '4' and then another number that he couldn't make out.

"What's that?" Sarah asked.

"A piece of nitrocellulose paper. It's the same communication method we use." He handed it to her.

Sarah studied it. "Yes, it's nitrocellulose alright, from a one-time code pad."

Frank began to get the distinct feeling that nothing was as it seemed when it came to his Russian friends. He assumed they were FSB, Federal Security Service of the Russian Federation, the intelligence agency re-born from the KGB but now, he wasn't so sure.

"Are you going straight back to England? Your family."

Frank nodded. "I need to find them and work out what the hell is going on."

Sarah leaned against the worktop. "Of course. Thanks for saving me from those animals, Frank."

"No problem."

"Listen, the information on the drive, the cause of all this shit, you'll need some kind of negotiating position. I heard you say it yourself on the phone. I want you to have it," she said, looking at him with renewed determination. Frank returned it with a sideways glance.

"What? After all you've just been through to keep it safe, you'd really give it to me, just like that?"

Sarah fixed Frank with a genuine stare.

"Look, this data is too important to fall into the wrong hands. As long as they think you have it, it will buy you a few precious days of keeping your family alive. You know as well as I do, your family is just a loose end waiting to be tied up, a bargaining tool to get you to do their bidding, and as soon as they are no longer of use, it's over for them. This is your only chance to save them."

Frank looked at her with admiration.

"Wow, that's good of you. Thanks, Sarah. You were pretty good at keeping its location quiet, you must have hidden it someplace well."

"It's down the coast towards Matanzas," she said, rubbing her arms, as if cold.

"How far exactly?"

"A couple of hours' drive."

Frank thought for a moment and shook his head. "How's it going to work? They'd know that copies might exist. Handing over a thumb drive isn't going to help my cause."

"No, it's encrypted. It can't be copied that easily, unless it's accessed and if it is, then a log file is created. Frank, you need that file to bring them down. We go there, get it, and you can take it back with you as long as you get it to my contacts in London who can make it public but give yourself a few days to find your family first. I can give you their details."

Frank nodded. "Right. What if they don't believe I have it?"

"They will. Get an email address and send them a screenshot, so they know you're not bluffing. I'll give you the encryption code."

Frank thought for a moment.

"Okay, let's get out of here...we can talk on the way."

38

The room was dark apart from small cracks of light around the edges of the chipboard that had been hammered against the window frame. The gloom made it hard for Maria to see but when their eyes adjusted, there was nothing to focus on anyway. A lone bed, with sheets, a blanket, and a sidelight placed on the carpeted floor was all she could make out. She held her arm around Joe and they sat on the floor, leaning against the wall.

"What do they want, Mum?" Joe's voice broke the silence.

"I really don't know, Joe, but don't worry, we'll get out of this."

"I'm not worried," he said, almost as an act of bravado for his mother. Maria couldn't help smiling in the gloom, despite their grim situation. That was typical Joe, always the brave one.

"I know you're not, but it's okay to be afraid sometimes."

"I'm not afraid!"

He pulled away from her and stood up, sighing loudly, clearly agitated. They had been in that room for at least a week and it soon dawned on them both that this was not going to be a short visit. Maria also guessed there was a high chance their lives were at risk, despite their kidnapper assuring them that this was just a bartering move.

Just then, the door unlocked and the tall man with cropped black hair appeared, the light casting his frame in darkness.

"What do you want?" Maria asked coldly.

The man took a couple of steps inside, his eyes fixed on Joe.

"Your boy. How old is he?" Maria could see that he was grinning, a wide sickening grin and in one horrifying moment, realised what he was saying.

"Joe. Come here," she said calmly but firmly, holding out her hand and gesturing for him to move. Joe did as he was told and walked over to his mother and she put her arm around him, her eyes fiery orbs that radiated hate towards the Russian.

"You fucking dare touch him," she said, her voice low and venomous.

Just then, a shout came from downstairs and the man slowly moved out of the room, locking up behind him.

Several days earlier, the morning had begun as usual. Maria's friend, Lisa, had dropped by to take Zak to nursery and Joe, who should have been at school, had complained of feeling feverish and was to stay home.

"I hope you're not just going to play your video games all day, Joe."

Joe groaned from behind his door, "Noooo."

Lisa had just left with a car full of three-year-olds and Maria genuinely felt sorry for her. She grabbed her bag and glanced at herself in the hallway full-length mirror and then the buzzer blared through the apartment for the second time that morning. It could only be Lisa. Did she leave something? Maria glanced around the kitchen and on the work surfaces to check. There was nothing she could see. She descended the stairs and opened the door, frowning at the visitor on the step.

"Hello, Maria," said Nigel Harrison.

"Nigel. What are you doing here?"

"Can I come in? It's really important." He looked scared.

Maria felt perplexed and slightly put out but something in his demeanour told her to roll with it.

"To be honest, I was on my way to the office. Can it wait?"

"No, I'm afraid not. It's John. He's dead."

Maria leaned her arm against the wall as she struggled to take in those words.

"Dead?"

"Yes. A car accident. Look, I'm sorry to have to tell you like this. That's why I came."

"Yes, of course, Nigel. I'm sorry, I didn't realise. Please come in. Shut the door behind you." she said, her shock displacing any previous irritation she felt. She turned and slowly walked back up the stairs as Nigel loitered in the doorway.

On not hearing his footfall, she turned back staring at him quizzically.

Nigel's eyes were wet as they looked up at her, almost pleading for her forgiveness, and then a shadow appeared next to him. A giant hand shoved him aside and a tall man with black short hair in a leather jacket appeared. He proceeded to point a small handgun at Maria, whose mouth fell open in shock.

"Stay there, bitch," he said, in a heavy accent. He sounded Russian.

The large man climbed the steps towards her and Maria dared not move. She would be dead in a second.

"Okay," he nodded, indicating for her to continue back into the flat and shoved her in the back.

"Nigel! Come here. Close door!" he commanded without looking back. Nigel dutifully shuffled in and Maria heard the lock click.

"Anyone else in the house? Do not lie."

Maria closed her eyes, wishing she did not have to say the words.

Maybe Joe had heard and had hidden or he could find a way out. It was possible and she couldn't think straight.

Maria stared at his beady eyes that seemed to drill into her soul. She shook her head.

"No, it's just me," she said loudly, hoping Joe would hear and get the message if he hadn't already.

The intruder glared at Nigel and jerked his head. "Go look!"

Nigel shuffled off, as ordered, towards the living room. There was a stillness in the house, just the sound of footsteps moving to the bedroom.

Maria assessed the situation, stealing glances at the intruder, wondering what the hell was going on, her stomach sick with worry. What had she done?

Nigel returned, his watery eyes glancing at Maria.

"It's clear," he said.

"Clear? You sure," the big Russian growled.

"Yes, I'm sure."

"Okay. We take this bitch and go."

Maria began to feel the relief as they headed to the apartment door. She had done it. Joe was safe and would call the police.

Then a sound, like a knock. Maria's stomach tightened.

"What was that?" the intruder boomed. He grabbed Nigel by the arm and slapped Maria across the face with the outside of his massive hand.

"I told you, bitch. Do not lie!"

Maria let out a sob and tried to grab his arm as he marched back to the bedroom.

"Please, don't hurt him!"

He kicked the door down and walked in, breathing heavily as he looked around at Joe's bedroom. Posters of a rock band adorned the walls, typical of any kid's bedroom. A large wardrobe stood in the corner. The Russian opened the doors to find nothing but hanging shirts and football kit stuffed into carrier bags at the bottom.

Maria appeared in the doorway, Nigel behind her, eyes wide with fear as she looked around. Had he got out?

"Please," she mumbled.

He turned his attention to the single bed and with one hand, uplifted it, smashing it against the wall. The wide eyes of a boy stared up at him. The intruder bent down and grabbed him by the arm, forcing him to stand up.

"Up! Bastard, up!"

Joe struggled initially and then seemed to think better of it when he saw the man's gun in his other hand.

"Don't hurt him, you fucking bastard!" Maria screamed.

He shoved Joe towards Maria, who grabbed him with both arms and pointed the pistol at them both.

"Out...out!"

Maria and Joe went into the hallway where Nigel waited. The Russian bore his dark eyes into Nigel and spoke quietly, "I deal with you later."

"What do you want? Where are you taking us?" Maria demanded.

He glared back at both Maria and Joe.

"We're going on a little trip."

39

It was mid-morning as Frank and Sarah headed out of the closed down industrial estate and onto the main Via Blanca coastal road. Soon, they were cruising along palm tree-lined fields with spectacular mountainous backdrops heading south. They had driven the Russian's black MPV to the nearest town and then spent an hour or so looking for a car garage, where they swapped it for an older, less conspicuous Chevrolet. The garage owner was delighted with the deal.

Sarah leaned against the window as they continued on the coastal road south and watched a group of school children in bright white shirts running along the road, their satchels bumping behind them. There was an endless trail of destruction from the hurricane. Roofs ripped from their joists, and trees uprooted and thrown aside like a rag doll from a bull.

"So why did you choose all the way down here to hide this thumb drive? You could have hid it anywhere."

"I gave it to someone I trust with my life. Someone I would never betray, even if it meant my death."

"You can definitely trust this person?"

"Yes, totally. I met her in my gap year when I took off around Central America for a few months. It was a low time for me but she became a good friend when I was over here before. But she has no idea what is in that key fob anyway."

Frank acknowledged with a slow nod of the head.

"Better that way," he said.

After twenty minutes of driving along the pot-holed road, Sarah directed Frank off along a maze of dusty back roads that came to an immaculate, small, single story house, painted bright blue with red tiled roof set against a line of trees. In a field beyond it, oxen grazed and the landscape seemed to stretch forever. It was one of the most tranquil scenes Frank had ever set eyes on, as if plucked straight from a picture postcard.

Frank pulled up, switched off the engine, and they both got out of the vehicle and went to the house.

A woman in her 50s with white, fuzzy hair and dark skin opened the door and shrieked with delight at her visitor crying, "Hola! Hola!" and wrapped her large arms around Sarah.

"Mi bella consorte!"

They stepped into the small modest but clean hovel and the woman gestured for them to sit at a wooden table in the centre of the main room. It was cool inside, a welcome relief from the rising temperature of the day.

"This is Frank," Sarah said and the woman smiled broadly at him. "Si, Si. Frank. Soy Vanesa."

Frank smiled and took the seat offered to him, glad of the rest. Vanesa disappeared into the back and returned with a jug of lemon water and snacks before she and Sarah caught up, chatting in Spanish. It was to this background ambience that Frank's eyes grew heavy and he was soon escorted to a more comfortable chair by Vanesa, who continually beamed at him, gesturing that she understood his tiredness.

He took the opportunity to grab some sleep, wondering how Maria and Joe were doing as he drifted off. Work out a plan and get back to England. But that was the problem, there wasn't much of a bloody plan. He had no idea where to start. Yes, there was the key fob and Sarah's suggested idea, a faint hope maybe. Keep the Russians talking...make them follow his rules but he would only have 2 or 3 days to find Maria and Joe. How the hell was he going to do that? Any more time and they would track down the information. They weren't amateurs after all.

These thoughts drifted through Frank's mind as he drifted off. Less than an hour later, a clunk of a plate woke him up and he saw food being laid out by Sarah and Vanesa. Frank sat down at the table and tucked into the rice and black beans with a healthy dose of fiery sauce.

After eating, as Vanesa cleared away the dishes, Frank took Sarah outside.

"Sarah, this is all very nice and I needed the rest but I have to get home."

Sarah flicked a wisp of dark hair behind her ear, her expression was one of understanding and a vague hint of sadness.

"Yes, of course, you do. I'm so sorry. I'll get the thumb drive." Sarah went and spoke to their host and returned, handing over the key fob that she had brought from England.

"You'll do the right thing with it, won't you?" she said.

Frank stared at her. "You're not coming with me?"

Sarah sighed. "You know I can't go back to England. Not at the moment. Maybe some sunny day," she smiled. "But I want to tell you where my parents are. If you ever get a chance, let them know I'm well and that I'm alive."

"They found you before, they'll find you again."

"Not if you do the right thing with this. Once this is out, they're not going to be interested in me anymore," Sarah said.

Frank exhaled slowly and cast a long glance across the fields.

"I hope you stay lucky, Sarah, I really do."

She laughed easily. "I think you had something to do with my luck, Frank. Without you stepping in, I'd either be dead or hooded in some godforsaken pit – instead of here," She swung an arm out and gestured at the landscape.

"By the way, you'll need some money." She pulled out a wad of notes.

"No, I can't, you'll need it."

"I have plenty. I've been planning this for months, Frank. You have no access to money, right? Not without setting off some major alarm bells," she jerked her head, emphasising her point.

Frank thanked her and took the money. As he pocketed the cash, he found the book of matches he's taken off one of the dead Russians. It was a lap-dancing bar in London, according to the inside front. Had the team been in London before Cuba?

Sarah saw Frank frowning and smiled.

"You better get going, Sherlock. Find your family. There's one other thing I want you to do for me when you get back, Frank."

After leaving Sarah at her friend's house, Frank drove the vehicle back to Havana, dumped it, and found an Internet-connected computer in a hotel near the airport and proceeded to log into WarWorld, browsing through the remnants of a destroyed empire but Frank was not logging on to play games. He searched for other players online and found Griff's username, thankfully online, and nudged him via the chat terminal.

Frank read Griff's first message: *What the hell's going on out there? I heard the team got hit.*

Yes. Ambushed by bears. Can we keep this between us?

Sure, bro, no problem.

My partner and kid have been kidnapped. Russian connection. Highly possible that they're in London. Can you make enquiries?

Shit. Sorry to hear, Frank, but where the hell do I start?

CCTV around Shoreditch. That's where we live.

Will see what I can do.

Thanks, Griff. I'll send you a detailed description of the main guy.

Frank described the Russian with the goatee, a mohawk, and the prominent neck tattoo, who was becoming a major pain in Frank's life and sent it across the network.

It's a start, thanks, replied Griff.

That's the best I can do for now. I take it you can get an image of Maria and Joe OK?

Yeah, probably.

Also, there's a bar called Stripes...can you check it out? There might be CCTV on the same road?

Wilko Bravo

OK, thanks, I owe you. Over and out.

Frank logged off and then went in search of the next flight to London. He was in luck and saw a flight that took off in 3 hours. He walked over to the British Airways desk and used the passport that his old friend, Jake Hale, had made for him and paid in cash.

After taking the tickets, he found a quiet corner and took out the phone that he had taken from the dead Russian and dialled the number again.

"I thought I tell you to wait?" the familiar voice said.

"I'm fed up of waiting. What's going on? I want my family back!" Frank tried to keep the anger at bay but he was struggling with the concept.

"Do you have the thumb drive?"

"I'm working on that – where are you going to want delivery?"

"How do I know you're not lying, Frank?"

"Give me an email and I'll send you a screenshot of the first few pages when I get it. That'll be your proof."

There was a pause.

"Okay. We want delivery in London. Probably in a few days. You wait my call or text. Don't phone this number again."

"Use text from now on, it'll be wiser," said Frank. A thought had come to him. "Voice calls could be monitored easier," he added.

It was a lie. Both text and voice calls could be picked up but Frank didn't want any UK style ring tones sounding if the Russian decided to ring him in England. It would give away his location.

The Russian paused. "I text you email, save image in drafts folder. Then we know you're serious."

The call ended. Despite not being a religious man, Frank prayed that somehow he would be able to track down and save Maria and Joe in the narrow timeframe he had. If only Griff could work his magic.

Frank dared not even begin to imagine living his life without them. If he lost them...Frank shook the possibility out of his thoughts. It would not happen. It must not happen.

40

After touching down at Heathrow, Frank went through the maze of a busy passport control, where no one looked twice at his details and soon found himself in the public area of the airport, gripping his holdall bag. He checked his Russian mobile phone and saw a text message with an obscure email address and login details.

Making his way out of the airport, he immediately began looking for an Internet café. After thirty minutes of looking, he found one, bought a coffee, and made his way to a computer at the back. He went online, logging into the WarWorld game and found Griff's avatar online as usual.

Frank began to type him a message:

Hey, G, am back in the UK. Did you find anything out for me?

There was a pause as Griff began to type and Frank watched the flashing cursor indicate a message was coming.

There might be something worth looking at. I think you should see it.

Did you tell anyone? Frank answered.

Nope, are you crazy? We need to meet with this.

Frank paused. It was entirely possible that Griff had been turned and was now ordered to keep track of Frank and reel him in. But he didn't believe that, not for one second.

Can we meet at that place where you took me for that cheap lunch when I was training?

Griff agreed to meet in two hours' time. Frank said goodbye and logged off before slipping the thumb drive out of the key fob and plugging it into the computer. A password prompt came up and Frank typed in the series of letters and numbers that Sarah had given him. The parent folder appeared on screen. He clicked through to the 'Oculus' folder and opened the document that booted up a PowerPoint programme and the title page appeared. Frank screenshot it with the 'print screen' button on the keyboard and then logged into the email, pasted the image into a new message and saved it to drafts.

He logged out again, wiped the browser cache, and grabbed the thumb drive out of the slot.

Several hours later, Frank, well out of sight, watched Griff stroll into the café. Frank had taken care to alter his appearance but he wasn't too worried. He figured anyone looking for him would be in Cuba, not London.

Griff seemed nonchalant enough. Frank could see him behind the glass, walking up to the counter to speak to a woman before sitting down at one of the tables set against the wall. Frank waited for several minutes more and looked around, both ends of the street. There was no sign that there were any suspicious vehicles or anyone looking around. He strolled across with a confident gait, moving between the cars and stepped into the café.

He passed Griff, who was too busy studying his phone to notice him and ordered a mug of tea and a bacon sandwich. Slipping into a chair opposite Griff, he put down his mug of tea, surprising the young lad, who hardly recognised the man he had helped train in technology and surveillance equipment. Frank was bearded now and wore a hat pulled over his head.

Griff adjusted his geek style specs.

"Jesus, you look like you've taken a beating out there."

"It wasn't the holiday I was expecting."

"Hmm, no, I did warn you about that crazy beach life." Griff paused and looked solemn. "I'm sorry about your team. So any more details on what happened out there?"

Frank sighed and watched the street carefully. Rain had started to patter against the window, hard and grey.

"As I said, it all went to shit. An ambush at the safe house. A Russian mob. Greene got hit and Piper died of his wounds later on. We must have been sold out somehow. Who knew about the safe house? The only ones were the agents on the ground and you boys here in London." Frank put on an air of accusation in his voice.

Griff shook his head and held up his hands. "Not me, man."

Frank continued. "I know, Griff. Just messing with you. When Brull found me and Sarah a new safe house, it somehow got compromised again. Our Russian friends turned up, murdered Brull, and then took myself and Sarah to their charming warehouse, for questioning." Frank spoke, the venom hardly hidden from his voice.

"You were with the whistleblower?"

Frank sighed. "Yes. Didn't Carl tell you?"

"And the files she took?"

"Never mind that now, did you get me any information? I need to find where the hell Maria and my kid are," Frank said, his patience at breaking point.

Griff nodded, sensing the deep concern in Frank and pulled out a large envelope from his inside jacket pocket. "I looked at a lot of C.C.T.V footage around Stripes, the gentlemen's bar. I was able to dismiss plenty of possibles from the way you described the guy but men with black goatee beards and mohawks seem to be 'in' at the moment so it was a nightmare."

Griff handed over the printouts to Frank.

"So, any possibles in here?" he asked, tearing it open and fishing out a batch of printouts.

Griff shrugged and leaned back in his chair. "You tell me, buddy. Take a look."

They were distracted momentarily by the café owner as she shouted out numbers and navigated herself around the tables, carrying cooked breakfasts, three at a time.

Frank thumbed through the various grainy photos of men matching the description coming out of the bar but they didn't immediately see any that looked like the Russian bastard he had encountered in Cuba.

Frank shook his head in frustration.

"No dice?" asked Griff.

Frank shuffled through the papers again.

"No, not..."

One of the prints was a possibility the second time he looked at it, but it was far from clear. A man in the street outside the Stripes bar, his face half turned, slightly obscured by another figure in front of him. There was a familiarity about the shape of the cheekbone. It was possible.

"When was this taken?" he asked.

"About twenty-four hours ago."

"Can you get more from this camera at around this time?"

"Well, yes, I can get the film but I'm breaking a million protocols here."

Frank stuffed the print out into his jacket pocket.

"Join the club. Just find out who he is if you can. I'll go visit this bar. Hey, Griff, thanks for this. I owe you one."

Griff nodded. "That makes me feel all warm and fuzzy inside.

I hope you realise all the sneaking around I'm still gonna have to do?"

The waitress appeared and put down a plate of fish and chips in front of Griff and a bacon sandwich cut in half in front of Frank. "There you go, loves," she said. Her mouth was arranged in a permanent droop where she probably would have had a cigarette fixed in place had it not been for the smoking ban.

Frank grabbed one half of his sandwich and took a bite as he slid a mobile phone across the table. "So we can communicate without having to go on that stupid game."

He got up to leave, finishing the sandwich in a few bites as Griff put the phone in his pocket.

"What are you calling a stupid game? Are you not eating that other half?" Griff asked, his hand already swooping towards Frank's plate.

"Go for it. I've got to go, my partner and kid are being held by a posse of maniacs, remember? See if you can get that film as soon as you can. I'm going to take a look around at that market."

Griff looked up. "And the gold, Frank? The information Pandora took? You didn't say whether you got it?"

Frank simply winked at him and then walked out of the café.

41

Less than an hour later, Frank stood sheltered under a tree from the continuous rain opposite the house where Maria's friend, Rosie lived at Barnes Bridge. The autumn golden brown leaves scattered on the ground, an impressionist picture as if taken through a blurred camera lens. A policeman stood outside, draped in a waterproof overcoat, standing stoically on guard. The kidnapping had obviously been reported and someone had the sense to make the call that maybe Frank's other family members were at risk.

He wondered what his sons would end up doing with their lives. Would he even see them grow up at all? The spectre of death had hung over him more than once in recent months and then he steeled himself. He had to survive, for their sakes at least, and he had to keep alive to get Maria and Joe free from whatever psychopathic gang were holding them.

How had it come to this? Watching from under the shelter of a tree, hoping to catch a glimpse of his youngest son. Approaching them was too risky; they may be under surveillance but he just wanted to see that Zak was okay with his own eyes. He zipped up his jacket as the rain came down in sheets as the creeping realisation that he needed help gnawed away at him. But knowing who to trust was impossible.

There was Carl who had recruited him into this mess. What was he hiding? Did he have a hand in the turning events? Frank shook that thought from his mind. He didn't believe Carl was involved in the kidnapping for a second, yet that didn't stop the growing frustration that he had not properly protected his family.

The door slowly opened and Rosie struggled with a pram down the steps, holding a child in one arm, followed by other tiny figures. He realised as she put down the child that it was Zak. There was a flood of relief as his instinct that Zak was out of harm's way was confirmed.

Just then, the Russian mobile buzzed a text message and Frank read the screen.

Are you in the UK yet?

Frank began to type:

About to leave Cuba. Problems with flights.

Frank needed to buy time, whether the Russian believed him or not. He began to walk to the tube station away from the house.

After a minute or so, another text came through.

Employer is happy to negotiate. You bring product, agree not to distribute, and your family will be safe.

Frank replied, *They'd better be...I will come after you and never stop if any harm comes to them.*

Immediately, a return text came through.

Don't threaten me, Frank. Just be ready when I tell you the meeting place. You make sure you deliver.

42

Frank came up the steps of Tottenham Court road station and walked east along Oxford Street, skirting the border of Soho.

The crowds had thinned out now that it was after lunchtime but it was still busy by any smaller city's standards. He kept his head down, hands in pockets, and hunched his shoulders in case the ever-increasing number of surveillance cameras picked him up.

After several minutes' walk, he turned left and crossed Soho square to an address he had memorised and took a step up to the newly painted black door of one of the red-bricked Georgian houses that had been converted into offices. After a short exchange of words, he was buzzed in and came into a plush reception room where he was greeted by a casually dressed receptionist who offered him a seat and a coffee.

"Mr. Brady won't be too much longer," she said, giving him a broad smile before going out to get his refreshment.

After five minutes, Frank had drained his coffee cup; the warm liquid felt good on his throat after being in the cold outside. A tall black man, dressed in a white shirt and jeans, appeared in the doorway behind the reception desk. He wore wire thin steel spectacle frames and had the demeanour of a man in charge as he cast an intrigued eye over the dishevelled visitor in front of him.

"Hello there. I'm Marcus Brady. How can I help you?"

Frank placed his cup down on the glass table and stood up to greet the man.

"I'm a friend of Sarah Edwards," he said quietly. Brady looked at him, surprised for a moment, and then nodded in acknowledgement.

"Please, come this way."

The two men sat down in Brady's office in low set chairs that were arranged around a coffee table in the middle of the room, packed with shelves of box files that seemed to bow under their weight. Above a disused fireplace, a framed print of the *Liberatus* front page adorned the wall.

"Our most recent edition," said Marcus, noticing Frank was looking at it. The headline ran: British M.P. Jailed for Perjury.

"We exposed that bastard a few weeks ago. He had been involved in high-level corruption in the government, had links to a CIA think-tank, and was involved in a Middle East arms scandal. Eventually, some of the national newspapers picked it up and one thing led to another. It's what our mission here at Liberatus is, to hound the corrupt." he smiled.

"Sounds like a worthy cause," said Frank.

"It is. John Rhodes, who was the founding father of our group, was involved in a car crash a few weeks ago. Which leads me to how Sarah Edwards fits into all of this."

Frank held up his hand. "Before we get onto Sarah, I want to talk about Maria."

"Maria?"

"Maria Chapman."

"Maria Chapman? Why, yes, she's employed as a researcher here but she stopped coming into work a while ago. I don't know why. Do you know her?"

"Maria is my partner. We have two children, Joe and Zak."

Marcus smiled broadly. "Ah yes, she talked about them a lot. How are they doing?"

Frank paused again, hoping he was doing the right thing.

"Maria and Joe have been kidnapped. I was away, on a job. That's when it happened," Frank said, studying Brady's face intently.

Brady leaned forward now, frowning with concern.

"Kidnapped? When, how?"

Frank related the story, leaving out the parts he thought he shouldn't know. The initial mission, the change of plan for Edwards, and then an unknown Russian crew crashing the party.

It didn't matter now. He just wanted his family back. He didn't give a shit about all the bullshit politics and games they played anymore. Sarah Edwards had assured him he could trust Brady and that he would be able to help find them. That's all that mattered now.

Brady leaned back in his chair, nodding his head silently at Frank's breakdown of events.

After he had finished, Frank leaned forward.

"I have something very important for you," said Frank quietly. "Something Sarah wanted you to have."

He fumbled in his inside pocket and brought out the thumb drive. He paused, holding it in his hands, and then handed it to Brady.

"You need to sit on this for three days to give me a chance to find my family. Then I'm either dead and it can be released or I succeed and it should go public anyway."

Marcus looked at him for a moment and nodded. "Sure, three days," he repeated.

Brady played with the key fob in his fingers.

"Such a small thing for so much trouble," he said. "John was supposed to go to Cuba to meet her. It had all been arranged but then, the accident..."

"He was the contact she had arranged to meet?" asked Frank.

"Yes. Unfortunately, it all went wrong." Brady said, looking at Frank, his eyes betraying a genuine sadness. "But Maria and Joe kidnapped? Jesus. Yeah, I will help you any way I can, you can count on it," he added.

Frank nodded. "Thanks, Marcus, that's very much appreciated."

He stood up and made his way to the door. "I'm afraid the bad news from Cuba is that Sarah is dead, in case you were wondering."

"Dead? What happened?"

"I don't know exactly, that's the information I got. Sorry, I can't tell you anymore. Needless to say, she would be happy that you got the information. I'll catch up with you later."

Frank left Marcus Brady staring at the door as he closed it behind him.

43

Grey clouds swirled overhead, casting a dark shadow over the city and then the rain came again in torrents. Frank kept to the side streets as best he could making his way inland from the embankment, past Covent Garden, and then north-east and to the place where the kidnapper was last sighted. It was all he had to go on and hope slipped away like rainwater that streamed down the street drains.

He found the Stripes bar and knocked hard on the door but there was no answer. Frank glanced at this watch. Probably too early. He strolled down the street, looking for somewhere to grab a coffee and found himself standing across the road from Smithfield market and remembered seeing a café in there once. Sure enough, it was still there and he bought a takeaway Americano and strolled around the stalls. Wholesale meat traders were selling their finest cuts of every type of meat and poultry in the Victorian Grade II listed-covered market building. Customers were flooding inside to purchase their supplies for restaurants and cafés across London.

It seemed to Frank that the Russians must have been based in a house around there somewhere. If they had been to the club before Cuba and the photo was the man who called himself 'Kobra' then they must have returned to the same area and re-visited the lap dancing club. It must be worth flashing the photo of the Russian around?

Frank immediately started to ask traders if they had seen him, showing them the C.C.T.V photo of Viktor Kozel. After several shook their heads, he walked over to the trader, a bald, obese man in his 40s and nodded a greeting.

"Hi, mate. What can I get ya?" he asked, barely looking up from the lamb cutlets he had been stacking on a plastic tray.

"I'm looking for this man. Have you seen him?"

The trader looked up at the photo Frank held out in front of him, then cast a suspicious eye at Frank.

"Why? Who's asking?"

Frank fixed him with a level stare; there was no time for games.

"It's really important I find him. We know he was here a few days ago. This image was captured on a camera nearby."

The trader raised his eyebrows slightly. Anyone with access to those cameras was probably worth keeping sweet.

"Well, I don't remember the man. We got shed loads of people coming through here every day. My memory's not so good anyway."

He gestured with a burly forearm at a stall opposite him. "Ask Steve, he's got a memory for faces. Eyes of a hawk and memory of an elephant, that Steve."

The ruddy-faced vendor called Steve looked closely at the kidnapper's photo as if the cogs were turning in his mind. He looked up at Frank and nodded. "Yeah, I think I saw him, mate, couldn't miss a guy like that. Russian or Slovak. Something like that."

"Anything you can remember about him? Anything at all? Which direction he went afterwards?"

The trader shook his head. "Couldn't tell you, mate. He bought produce a couple of times, that's all I can say."

Frank gave him his new mobile number. "Do me a favour, if he turns up again, discreetly send a text." Frank slipped a Fifty-pound note to him along with the number and gave the man a knowing look. The trader smiled, more eager to help as he took the note. "Sure thing, pal. I won't ask any questions."

Frank circled the market, keeping his eyes open and head down. It seemed logical that the house Maria and Joe were kept in was close by if the man had been buying food from the market. Again, it was a loose lead but it was all he had.

The following morning around 5:15, Frank's mobile buzzed and he read the message. He jumped out of bed, threw his clothes on as quickly as he could, and then drove over towards Smithfield.

Frank watched the crowds jostling and pushing to get a look at the produce on sale. Deep frustration was growing by the second. The morning calm had made way to a Saturday bustle along with a rise in noise level, which the high metal roof dispersed, making it sound like a cattle market.

The text was from the butcher claiming the man was wandering around the market again. He watched the heads; wives, farmers, office workers, a glimpse of dark hair. A Mohawk.

Familiarity caught Frank in a blink of an eye, and then he was gone. He moved forward through the crowd, seeing if he could get confirmation of what he'd thought he'd seen. Was it him?

A glimpse again, making his way to the far exit. The head turned slightly to look around and Frank immediately saw it was the Russian or 'Kobra' as he had called himself. Frank quickened his pace, pushing through the faces that glared disapprovingly. This was a fine thread, a one chance throw of the dice.

Frank stepped out onto the street outside the east exit, glancing to the back of the Russian, who was walking fast, carrying a plastic bag of what Frank assumed to be meat just purchased. Kobra tossed a cigarette butt into the gutter and zipped his jacket against the cold.

Frank kept within a few metres, gambling there were enough bodies around to give him cover. At a crossing, the Russian stopped at the lights and Frank saw, just in time, a large dark glass frontage opposite, the reflection almost giving him away. Frank knew he looked different but it was not worth the risk. He stopped at a greengrocer and pretended to be interested in the fruit on display. Cobra moved across the road heading northwards, dodging vehicles, and Frank moved off again, determined not to lose him.

For around ten minutes, Frank kept close enough to the Russian before there was a sudden surge of people exiting a tube station that forced Frank to slow down, and he lost sight of him. Frank shoved people aside to get through quickly but on getting through the throng, he suddenly had no visual on his target.

Frantically scanning the line of shop entrances that ran along the high street looking for a glimpse, he saw nothing. Shit! Maybe he should have stuck closer and risked being seen?

As he checked the crowds on the opposite side, he saw a glimpse of the familiar rake of black hair, moving away from him down a side street.

Frank made up for lost ground and closed the gap, keeping ten metres back or so on the opposite side of the road. He noticed his target was on a mobile phone but Frank was too far away to hear anything. It was a residential street, with detached houses that looked more and more dilapidated the further they walked. Most of the houses had metal sheds or carports next to them, washing lines strung across fences, rusty caravans that had long since seen the freedom of a road.

The Russian swivelled around to glance behind himself briefly as he fished out a bunch of keys and stepped into the forecourt of an anonymous-looking house. Frank debated stopping, hiding, and watching but decided against it and moved casually down the road. Kobra disappeared through the front door. Frank clocked the number and took in as much information as he could with a brief glance. The windows at the front were boarded up and there was a driveway at the side that leads to the rear of the property.

Now he was convinced that this was Maria and Joe were being kept.

Frank did a circular appraisal of the surrounding roads around Prince Street, taking mental notes of anything that might prove useful. He walked down the street directly parallel to the road he was targeting, looking for a way around the rear of the house. There was a wall with a wooden door that Frank guessed led to the gardens and he checked that he wasn't being watched before jumping up and having a quick look.

Briefly, Frank could see a row of gardens that buffered back to back behind the houses. It was a potential route in except he would easily be seen by any curtain twitchers who chose to glance out the back unless it was at night. He couldn't risk any calls to the police; it could blow the whole fragile situation and potentially risk Maria and Joe's lives.

He jumped back down onto the ground and walked along the street, taking in anything that could be useful, assessing the situation. Then he came across a derelict house that had its windows boarded up with metal sheeting. He calculated it wouldn't be far off opposite the target house at the back. The front garden had an old sofa that had long since seen its sell-by date, its leather cover ripped open, spewing mounds of fibre filling. Around it lay piles of rubbish, black bags, and planks of wood that looked to have been ripped out of the house itself. There was a mound of worn burnt carpet that had been cut up and discarded.

Glancing up and down the street he could see it was still quiet and ducked down the pathway to check the front door. It had been secured by a sheet of metal and Frank could see it would be no easy task getting in that way. Alongside the exterior wall of the house was a narrow pathway that had a wooden doorway that had been bolted shut. Along the top of the door frame, a roll of barbed wire acted as the only deterrent. Frank barged the door with his shoulder to check how secure it was. It stood firm against his weight, without any hint of give. He took off his backpack and rummaged around for a few seconds before pulling out the wire clippers and putting them in his inside jacket pocket. Frank then replaced the bag on his back. Somewhere in the distance from a nearby open window, he heard the sound of clanking dinner plates and a slamming of cupboard doors.

After one more glance back to the road, Frank reached up and grabbed the top of the frame, hauling himself up using all his strength. Reaching up with his leg, he managed to get a foot on the round door handle for leverage. With his body leaning against the outside wall, he carefully untangled the barbed wire and took out the wire cutters. Carefully and methodically he clipped away at the wire, pushing sections down over the other side until he had enough space to get through. He replaced the Clippers in his pocket and pushed his body up on top of the frame and leapt down on the other side into the backyard.

At the rear there was another mountain of crap that had been ripped out of the house; an old olive green bathroom suite from a bygone era of style lay in a heap; mounds of plasterboard and more rubbish sacks.

The sun had disappeared behind the houses as evening drew in, casting the gardens in shadow. Fences either side that gave him privacy from the immediate neighbours and a low brick wall at the end backed onto other gardens for the houses on Prince Street. He had a good, clear view of the house where his family was being held. There wasn't time for a detailed reccy, he needed to make sure he would not be seen. There would be too much of a risk of police being called by nosey neighbours.

The rear windows and door of the old house were boarded up with metal sheeting in the same way the front was, except Frank noticed one of the ground floor windows had been forced open, revealing the smallest of gaps that would barely fit a child through. He had a quick look inside and listened carefully for any sounds and then eased back the loose section of metal sheeting to get a better look. It would make a perfect lookout to put eyes on the target house.

He peered into the darkness and just saw an empty room. There was a smell of damp, a few empty beer bottles strewn over the floor.

It would do just fine.

44

The black BMW 5 series headed south out of central London on the A24, past Morden and Wimbledon towards Epsom. Marcus Brady was at the wheel, looking smart in his dark cotton shirt and Matt Fulford, the *Liberatus News* journalist, slumped next to him in an old Ramones T-shirt and jeans as he flipped through the CDs from the glove box.

"What's this? Dire Straits?"

"This ain't my car, nothing to do with me," Brady replied curtly.

"Yeah, of course. Diana Ross, Whitney Houston...think I'll pass on the muzak then."

"Diana Ross is the soul queen, have some respect," said Brady.

Matt sighed and put the CDs back in their place and glanced out at the rows of semi-detached Tudor style houses, set back from the road.

"So, you think these precautions are needed?"

"Most definitely. This is a serious business we're in and it's only going to get a lot worse. They're almost certainly watching the office now."

Brady had taken as many measures as he could to make sure they weren't being followed or bugged. He had a bit of help from Frank Bowen after their meeting; just some pointers but it had really helped. They both dumped their phones for new ones and

Brady eventually persuaded Matt to let the business buy him a new laptop. No conversations of their plans to anyone, in the office or on any phone line.

They had taken separate tubes to Stockwell station and after both doing extended detours to shake off any tails, ended up in Brixton market, along the Atlantic road, to a section of fabric and carpet shops nestled in behind the rusting blue pillars, underneath the railway line. Brady arrived first, gripping the hand of the small stocky shop owner before giving him a bear hug.

"Still flogging these old rat rugs, Merv?" he jibbed, glancing around the cramped space that was filled to the brim with textiles and carpet rolls. Merv grinned and let out a low, staccato laugh. He was one of the early Jamaican immigrants to Britain in the 1950s and had been the 'go-to carpet king' ever since. The two men had known each other for a long time. As they chatted about the old days, Matt Fulford had no idea whether he was being followed or had succeeded in alluding any potential tails, he was virtually lost himself and just as he was silently cursing Marcus, he spotted the carpet shop. He strolled over, his large holdall bag containing his most essential needs slung over his shoulders.

Matt shook hands with Merv and then his eyes settled on Brady expectantly.

"We better be going, Merv. So, the wheels?"

Merv handed Marcus the keys to his beloved beemer and suddenly grabbed his arm, holding his stare for a moment, his eyes deadly serious. "Take care of my baby, won't you, Marcus?" he said. Both men suddenly burst out laughing and Brady slapped him on the shoulder. "Your baby gonna be alright, I drive safe, ya know."

"Alrigh'...I see you,"

Matt and Marcus slipped out the back of the shop, walked several paces up the street, and into the waiting car. When the doors slammed shut, Marcus asked, in a low voice, "You definitely weren't followed?"

Matt leaned his head back against the leather headrest, his eyes slid towards his boss.

"I have little or no idea. I did exactly like you said but...I have little or no idea."

"Come on, Matt. Tell me you weren't followed, please."

"I wasn't followed...," Matt said dryly.

Marcus sighed and pulled out, glancing in the rearview mirror. "Okay, well, we're gonna have to make sure."

"So you and the carpet man go back some?" asked Matt.

"He's a brother. I trust him more than my real brother," Marcus said.

"And this place we're going to...how do you know it's safe?"

"No one knows about this place, no one at the office. It's not owned by John...it's another one of my connections. They own it and usually rent it out. Just happens to be vacant at the moment. So you can focus on the story."

Marcus did another detour, heading west before doing a U-turn and heading back in the opposite direction the way Bowen had suggested. He checked his rearview mirror for tails and saw none.

As they approached Epsom and the houses became a lot smarter, all thatched roofed and barn style, surrounded by neat gardens. The car turned down along a narrow lane, slowed for a horse rider to go past and continued down the winding road that skirted scattered woodland.

The house was comfortable, cosy even, but sparsely furnished. A fireplace dominated the main room, which lay central in the cottage, off of which was a kitchen, bathroom, and a bedroom, and two rooms up above. A detailed painting of a crowded Epsom race day adorned the wall.

"I'll pick you up in a few days, just get the story done. There's a phone box back along the lane if you need anything but don't use it unless you have to and don't under any circumstances phone the office or me. Just the number I gave you. Merv will then contact me. There's plenty of food here so you shouldn't need anything."

Matt nodded, trying not to look bored. Marcus had gone through the spiel several times already. After his boss had left, Matt found himself a modest pasta meal, sipping a glass of water as he leafed through his notebook. Mopping up his plate with bread, he dumped the dishes in the sink and put the coffee on. It would be a long night and caffeine would be the cornerstone of his strategy.

Plugging in his Toshiba Satellite laptop to the mains, the young journalist navigated to the encrypted folder and keyed in the password to access the files.

Fulford read carefully, taking shorthand notes as he skimmed the classified files on the monitor. There were thousands of pages of information that outlined hundreds of secret covert operations. It would be impossible to cover everything, even within a series of news stories. He would need to find the gems to make the maximum impact. He was certain that after these went public, there would be a major shitstorm erupting that the mainstream media would find impossible to ignore.

Matt shook his head silently as he read some of the paragraphs with a mixture of shock at the lengths the intelligence apparatus had gone and were planning to go to increase their power but also a rising sense of excitement at the impact this story would surely have. GCHQ had been pushing ahead with a plan to listen in on every man, woman, and child in the United Kingdom. It felt good to him to fight back, to give the people some ammunition, and to blow this wide open.

He took out yellow post-it notes from his work bag and scribbled down main points and stuck them on the far side of the table in a sequence. When he had a first draft, it would need to be run past the company's legal advisors before publication to make sure no lives were inadvertently endangered.

The scale of the programme was planned to be ever increasing with a target of ten gigabytes per second of data for each cable that fed into the Bude GCHQ station in Cornwall, within the next ten years. In theory, the report claimed, this would give them a capacity of more than twenty-one petabytes a day, which was the equivalent of sending all the books in the British Library every twenty-four hours. It seemed astonishing. Matt doubted the Liberatus ADSL connection could even get six megabits per second, a drop in the ocean compared to what was proposed here.

Intercept probes attached to transatlantic fibre-optic cables would glean useful information from this data, which included phone calls, emails, or any electronic communications. The Internet surveillance involved planning a duplication of all the web data, hived off onto a separate network, stored, and ready to analyse with the co-operation of the phone companies.

There was plenty of crap to wade through: protocols, footnotes, and references to files that were not in the files.

After reading for around forty-five minutes, he decided to focus on the surveillance that affected people now rather than historical operations. The story would have more traction with the public if it affected them directly – their rights to privacy and the very core of civil liberties were threatened. Effectively, the British intelligence agencies were forming a system where they could spy on everyone, every day, without any kind of permission.

Matt wrote late into the night, only stopping to help himself to more coffee from the ever steaming cafeteria. He liked to hit a story head on, break the back of it over a few sleepless nights, and then mop up afterwards. The key, as Marcus Brady had explained, was to move fast and get the story out there. Once out, nothing and no one could reel it back into any dark corner from where it had come. They would be too busy denying and counter-claiming and although the storm would make it difficult for everyone involved, it was a lot less dangerous than it was now. This brief prelude was like crawling through the web of a spider as it waited to attack.

They had certainly weaved hard and fast these last few years, in the dark corners of central intelligence agencies. And he was under no illusion that lives were at stake, very likely his, for one. Matt leaned back in his chair, wondering what their reaction would be.

Brand him and the *Liberatus* as traitors? Almost certainly. Attempt to murder him like they tried with John Rhodes? The thought made him shudder; he was scared and not afraid to admit it to himself.

45

Carl drummed his fingers on the desk as he leafed through a series of papers on Frank Bowen. He was sitting in a corner communications room at Studio 31 on the Limehouse Cut Canal; his desk lamp seeming the dominant light in a sea of darkness. Several screens lit up his face, making him appear, if anyone were to look, like a sculpture deep set with heavy shadows. Whispers and crackles seeped from the audio feed on his computer, revealing that Frank was approaching Blackfriars Bridge.

Carl was certain that his friend, now black flagged by his superiors, was the figure in the covertly taken grainy black and white photos on his screen. The MI5 crew keeping tabs on the *Liberatus* offices in Soho square had reckoned it was Bowen and they were right. A worrying development. What the hell was he doing there? Surely not selling them the information they had been chasing? That would put Frank in traitor territory. Selling out the company was a big no-no.

Funny how things worked out. All that time and investment wasted. It had been a few years since Frank had joined the company. They'd had a good steady run within MI6 in the last few years. A few hairy moments, for sure. At times, Carl had thought he had lost him. Frank was good, he had talent, but why had he turned against his paymasters? Against him? Deep down, he knew where Frank was coming from. The blanket term, "in the interests of national security" had been taken to the limit and used to justify some eyebrow-raising actions, as Carl had seen for himself. These thoughts had to be cast from his mind. Well, they were bringing him in now. Questions needed to be asked.

Suddenly eager to shake that direction of thought from his mind, Carl focused on the other cogs in the wheel. Operation Whisper Hunt, the centre of his troubled mind. His first Ghost 13 op had turned into one big screw up; a major flapping turkey with bells on. One minute surveillance was on the target and everything was fine, then comms went dark and on the other side, Brull, Greene, and Piper all turn up dead! Killed by Russians apparently. It was an extremely hostile act by the FSB, to say the least. Acting like that could start hot wars. It didn't make much sense.

And now the whistleblower herself was holed up with Frank. To say it had gone tits up was an understatement.

Carl knew he shouldn't give himself a hard time. It was the business he was in. Things inevitably went wrong, despite the detailed planning. Greene and Piper were his men, good men who had been taken out purposely and expertly. He had worked with them for years. He would find out exactly what the hell happened over there, starting with his old friend, Frank Bowen.

46

Frank walked quickly down Black Friars Lane, high office blocks loomed either side as a milieu of suited workers stood outside one of the buildings, smoking and chatting. Blackfriars Bridge was just ahead and then he would head south of the river to East Dulwich, which was a hike that he really didn't want to make but he needed to get some stashed equipment.

Weapons were needed and luckily, he had the foresight to put a few tools away that no one else knew about. It had been way back in 1991 before he had set off travelling to Goa that he'd seen Carl's lock-up garage. On his return to the UK, he always thought it would be a good idea to get his own and so he had. Setting it up in secret, he had a backup stash site he was relieved to be able to count on now.

He quickened his pace, even more, wanting to get back as quickly as possible. The prospect of losing his family through one error of judgement loomed larger than ever. This operation had to kick off as soon as possible and Frank steeled himself to focus. He had no idea what Maria and Joe were going through, whether they were in immediate danger or what?

He turned onto the main carriageway of Queen Victoria Street and went under a railway bridge. The stream of traffic, the expanse of the Thames and the skyscrapers on the far side of the river beckoned just ahead. A man with a green hiking jacket and laptop bag over his shoulder weaved through the traffic across to Frank's side.

A young couple, taking in the sights, took photos of the Thames. A gust of wind broke across the bridge, causing a loose coke can to freewheel across the tarmac.

Frank suddenly felt exposed on the bridge; he should have found another way across the river. Why didn't he take the bloody tube? Soon, he was on the other side but the man in the green coat ahead of him had stopped and was looking in his bag for something. A black Mercedes with tinted windows travelling towards the bridge seemed to be driving the slowest possible speed. Frank's senses felt like a cascade of pins.

He suddenly turned right at the steps that led down to the riverbank and jumped down them as fast as he could. On the path he turned right again underneath the bridge, trying to be as unpredictable as possible. Racing past a couple who stepped out of his way, he quickly glanced back. A stocky man with a shaven head and squat-like features reached the bottom of the steps on the other side of the bridge and started to run after him. The path opened up into a wider walkway, the shimmering cityscape of central London across the water beyond and red brick office blocks on his immediate right. Another brief look and he saw his pursuer was keeping pace with him but hardly gaining.

Ahead, the man wearing the green hiking jacket who had been on the bridge stood directly in front of him, holding his hand inside his laptop bag. He shook his head at Frank as if to say the chase was over.

Frank came to a resigned stop after catching sight of his weapon in the bag. The thug came up behind him, his face all puckered skin and scars, red from the exercise as he pointed a handgun that was partially hidden by a suit jacket over his arm directly at Frank.

"Frank Bowen. You're to come with us," he said. He had a trace of a northern English accent.

Frank let out a sigh and levelled his gaze onto the man speaking. "I take it I can't speak to a lawyer?"

The thug waved his gun impatiently. "Just come with us to the car or there'll be consequences."

There was no point in playing games. It was bad timing but he knew who they were. His old employers had tracked him down. They took Frank back along the path in silence and then back up the steps where the parked Mercedes waited. He was ushered into the rear seat, followed by the thug and then the man wearing the green hiking jacket got in the other side, closing Frank in.

The bald thug pulled out a black hood. "I'm putting this on you."

"Is there really any need?" Frank started to protest but no discussion followed as he shoved the hood over Frank's head without a word and then jammed his pistol into his chest, to emphasise the situation.

After an hour's drive, he was bundled out of the car and through a series of doors, then down endless concrete steps before the hood came off. He was in a room with no windows. The walls were stark and grey; old concrete, some underground place, but still in London. Steel mesh surrounding him, tied into the walls. After an hour of being on his own in the room, a man entered and offered him a drink. Frank held up his cuffed wrists that bit savagely into his skin.

"Can you get these off me please?"

The young man shook his head.

"Sorry, but I can get you a drink?"

"Coffee."

Another hour. There must be a connection. He thought through everything in his mind trying to make sense of the broken pieces. Russians in Cuba, doing the bidding of whom? FSB or some other entity? They were desperate for the information Sarah had taken. The Russians would be interested in GCHQ secrets but something didn't fit.

The other pieces. The One Time Code evidence in the warehouse, the same paper his side used. And most of all, their safe houses in Havana blown. Not once but twice. Someone here at Ghost 13 must be feeding the Russians the info.

Someone.

The door clanked open again and a tall woman with dark hair tied back into a bun, and a shorter, gruff man stepped in and sat down opposite him.

The questioning began. Simple questions at first. His name. His role. School. Names of friends. But Frank knew they were just getting rolling.

"What is your given codename?"

"Auditor."

"What happened to Piper and Greene?"

"They were killed. We were ambushed at the safe house. Greene got hit and Piper died later from his wounds."

"Why did you communicate and then take off with Pandora when in Cuba?"

"A group of Russians turned up. There wasn't time to follow protocol. She might have been killed and then we'd all have lost."

"What happened to Piper and Greene?"

"I already told you."

"Tell us again in detail. Indulge us, Frank."

He told them. The chance meeting with Pandora and then the word that the Russians were in the hotel. There was no time except to grab her and take off. Then once again, he described the ambush, the shooting, and how Piper lost his fight to live.

Didn't Frank realise he was going against protocol by communicating with the surveillance target? Yes, he did. That they could lock him up and throw away the key?

"Where's my family?" Frank demanded. They didn't know. He explained the photograph, the Russians showing Maria and his boy bound and gagged and imprisoned somewhere.

They didn't know anything about it but they assured him that the police were working the case.

Frank wasn't convinced he could trust the police to carry out a safe rescue mission of his family but now he was incarcerated, he might not have much choice.

"I need to see Carl Paterson, my superior."

After another hour, they took a break and Frank was left in the room alone again. He just wanted Maria and Joe safe. Fuck what his employers would do to him, it didn't matter now.

Another few hours passed. Was it day or night? The cuffs were killing him. How the hell had he got into this mess? He wouldn't do this again, ever. No more bullshit from that bastard, Carl.

On that thought, Carl walked into the holding room and slammed a briefcase down next to the table. He took out a batch of keys and undid Frank's cuffs before sitting down opposite him.

"Thanks. So what the hell's going on? Maria and Joe...they've been kidnapped. You need to get me out of me, Carl!"

Carl sighed and swept imaginary dust off the top of the table with his hand.

"Frank, you're in serious shit. You had a job to do; put a target under surveillance. Instead, you approached that target and disappeared with her and then your team was seriously compromised. I need to know what happened."

"Compromised, Carl? We were ambushed, pure and simple. Piper, Greene, and Brull all died out there. The same group who have my partner and child, here in London. Thanks for looking out for them, by the way. Look, I know where they are. You could help me!" Frank was shouting now.

Carl ignored him and stuck to the subject.

"You took off with a traitor to the group. Where is she, Frank?"

"You mean you don't know? She's dead, Carl."

"Can you prove that?"

"What do you want, her head in a bag? Gruesome pictures? I just heard she was dead."

"How?"

"Shot by that Russian mob."

"Maria works for *Liberatus News*, whose owner, John Rhodes, also runs a sister activist group under the same name. Did you know that?"

"No, I didn't," he lied. "But whatever that's about, I'm sure she knew what she was doing. She's a smart woman. So is working for a cause illegal now?" he said, tightly.

"I'm sure she didn't have illegal intentions, Frank, but I'm telling you that Liberatus are showing up on intelligence radars. I know MI5 are taking a keen interest in the group."

Carl stared at him unblinkingly as if waiting for a response. Frank shrugged.

"They're nothing to do with me," he said, lowering his head and closing his eyes as if to rest them, if only for a second.

"Are you sure? Maybe you killed the team, took the information, and sold it to someone, like Liberatus?" Carl had lowered his voice to an accusing whisper and he stared down at him.

Frank looked up, a veneer of contempt on his face.

"You actually believe that?"

Carl pulled up his briefcase that was standing against the table leg and opened it up, bringing out a manilla folder before snapping the briefcase closed. He nonchalantly emptied out a batch of photographs onto the table. Frank glanced down at the pictures that showed him entering and leaving the *Liberatus* newspaper office in Soho square. Frank silently cursed his mistake, wondering whether he jeopardised his chance to find Maria and Joe but he breathed evenly, his facial expression giving nothing away.

"Their offices are under surveillance by a team from MI5. Our contacts there knew we were keeping an eye out for you, so they passed on the information."

"Why are you telling me all this shit, Carl? I thought the key to intelligence was to never let on anything you didn't have to?"

Carl grimaced for a moment and adjusted himself in his chair as if biding time.

"I want to help you, as a friend," he said.

"Help me get Maria and Joe back, that's all I want. Then you can throw me in prison or whatever you're going to do afterwards, I don't give a shit."

Carl closed his eyes for a second as if regretting something.

"I'm really sorry about them, I will look into it, see what I can find out. The police are on it. But this whole operation has been a screw up from beginning to end, as you know. And you were right in the middle of it."

"You have to help me," said Frank, quietly but determinedly. He was growing anxious. Time was ticking.

Carl paused and rummaged around in his pocket. He threw a packet of cigarettes onto the table.

"Go ahead," he offered.

"I gave up."

"Well, I never said this before but you have an addictive personality, Frank. Always have. So, given the circumstances, I thought I'd offer."

Frank shook his head and pushed the packet away.

Carl exhaled slowly and stood up to leave the room. After a minute, he returned with the shaven-headed thug who had been in the car on the bridge. Frank groaned inwardly and prepared himself for the beating that was surely coming. The thug had a black hood in his hand.

"Stand up, Frank."

"Friendship over then, is it, Carl?" Frank snorted in contempt.

"Shut up. You're going to be hooded and cuffed again, temporarily."

He did as Carl asked, getting to his feet slowly.

"I need to find Maria and Joe, Carl. They're in danger, do you understand me? One last favour?'

Before the hood went over his head, Frank caught Carl's eye. He nodded ever so subtly and then his world went black.

47

Frank had been in the back of a van travelling fast for around thirty minutes before it slowed down and traversed a few corners before pulling over. A hand grabbed his forearm and he heard the side door slide open before a shove in his back forced him out of the vehicle. A shock wave of pain shot through his body as he hit the hard pavement. A screech of tyres and the sound of the van engine receded.

Frank pulled off the hood and gasped in much needed fresh air. He rolled onto his side and groaned out loud, holding his shin that had taken the brunt of the fall.

No time to piss around, Frank.

He sat upright and looked around, discovering he was on a pavement that ran along a council estate car park. A boy around nine or ten years old, holding a skateboard, stared at him in awe, obviously having just witnessed the scene.

"Hey, where am I?" Frank asked. The kid seemed frozen, transfixed on the haggard figure pulling himself to his feet and then brushing himself down.

"It's okay, just tell me where I am."

"Camberwell," the boy spoke rapidly in a South London accent and then threw down his board and lunged his right foot on before skating off into the estate.

"Camberwell? That's good," Frank whispered to himself and

he began to hobble towards a main road to get his bearings. He kept his eyes peeled in case he was being watched but it didn't matter anymore. Maria and Joe, they were all that mattered. Did Carl know where he was heading? He had let him go. The friendship was possibly still on then. The past still mattered, it seemed, even in the murky grey world they lived in. Had Carl defied his bosses? If so, he had done him a huge favour.

A bus got him closer to Dulwich and then cutting through a park, he came to a maze of council house complexes, red-bricked and packed tightly like cubicles. Eventually, he turned a corner where a line of lock-up garages stood and pulled out a bunch of keys, unlocked the padlock, and the secondary locks on the doors.

Slipping into the darkness, he flipped a switch that sparked a flickering lone light bulb into life. Frank shut the doors behind him and carefully looked around his garage, looking for signs of entry. The dust was still on the floor as he remembered. He was sure it was safe. The garage had not been mentioned to anyone, including Maria. The paperwork for the rental had been done through a fake name with no connection with his employers, or ex-employers as was now the case.

After looking at surfaces on the wooden table, and the shelves and chairs, Frank immediately checked for the SIG Pro SP 2009 pistol in the sofa lining. He felt around for several seconds, unable to find it. Just as he was beginning to think that maybe the lock-up garage had been compromised, the tips of his fingers brushed the familiar steel of the weapon. His fingers clasped around the butt and he slowly ripped the masking tape that secured it to the inside back of the sofa and pulled it free.

Frank soon found the 9mm bullets case alongside it and placed both items on a table top. He painstakingly took the weapon apart, cleaning each piece before putting it back together and loading it. After finishing with his weapon check, Frank gathered up equipment into a haversack. Small binoculars that he had used in the woodland exercise so many years ago, a couple of listening devices that could easily be hidden or attached on the underside of any table or chair. They transmitted to a notepad device, similar to what he had used in Havana. A pen torch with a powerful battery life and a hunter's knife in a pouch.

Finally, he strapped a concealed knife holster to his ankle and secured the Gerber fixed blade in place. After triple checking everything and grabbing a wad of pound notes from a hiding hole under the floor, Frank slipped out of the garage, locking the door behind him and disappeared into the evening gloom, determined to save his family.

Or die trying.

48

The Golden Lion was one of those old forgotten London pubs that no one except local old men and traders from the market went to. The wallpaper had a flowery pattern that had faded over the decades and the upholstered seats seemed to melt into the walls in the dim light. Frank glanced around as he walked in. Three men touching 60 sat at the dark wooden bar nursing their ales, checking him out for a moment before continuing their chat about the football game on the television behind the bar. A few more solitary figures near the back, avidly read their newspapers.

Frank ordered a lime and soda and sat down in an alcove seat, facing the door.

After ten minutes, Griff walked in and after spotting Frank, made a beeline for his table. He slipped in and propped his laptop bag next to him.

"Hi, Frank. How're you doing? Nice place."

"Yeah, you can't beat a bit of spit and sawdust," he said grimly. There was sarcasm and no smile but he was genuinely glad to see the young techie again. He had always liked him, trusted his judgement, and admired the fact that he had a wise head on young shoulders.

"So what do you have for me, Griffy?"

Griff slipped a photograph to Frank and spoke low to him, relaying from memory while his eyes moved around the bar, settling on the 3 old guys watching the game.

"The man you thought might be the one? His name is Viktor Kozel, uses the codename Kobra. He entered the UK two months ago, we picked it up as he was on a Russian organised crime list. Usually, it would have been passed onto the Met crime unit but because he also had KGB connections, MI6 took an interest."

Frank looked over the clearer image of Viktor Kozel. Now that he had seen the Russian with his own eyes, it was merely confirmation of what he now already knew, but the background information finally answered some questions.

"So who's his sugar daddy?"

Griff shook his head and then pointed out other photos of associates in the folder.

Frank glanced over them, recognising the faces from Havana.

"Any idea who hired these charmers?"

"No idea."

"I think I found the house where they are but I might need you to help me with something," Frank said.

Griff shifted his gaze back to Frank again. "Help? As in what? Am I not helping already?"

"I don't want to go into the house without you nearby. I might need a distraction, an extra pair of eyes, someone to call it in if things go south."

Griff looked worried. "Frank, I'm a techie, not some kind of action man. Don't make me do something crazy!"

Frank smiled at his concern. "Relax, mate. I'm not going to ask you to go into the house. Just be nearby, keep an eye out. Watch my back."

Griff shook his head defiantly. "Fuck no!"

Frank continued in a low, calm voice. "Please, Griff. Just keep watch for me, just in case. You'll be well away from any action.

My kid, he's only eight years old and most likely terrified. I don't know how they're being treated, what they're being threatened with...Believe me, I just want to get up right now and go in all guns blazing. But that's hardly gonna save them..."

Griff held his hands over his forehead for a moment. "Ah, Jesus!"

Frank took a lug of his lime and soda, the ice cubes rattling in the glass.

"First thing is to get eyes on the place. I need to do a reccy. See what I can see. We may need to cause a distraction at the front of the house to help me sneak in the back."

Griff had taken off his glasses and was cleaning the lenses with his shirt.

"Do you have an RP?" Griff was referring to a reconnaissance point.

"I do. A derelict building looking across the gardens towards the back of the house."

"And who's in the target house exactly?"

"I don't know how many are holding Maria and Joe. There could be hundreds of those bastards all heavily armed and itching for a fight but I very much doubt it. I reckon three at the most."

Frank could almost sense the fear radiating from Griff.

"It's okay, bud. I won't put you in any danger. I promise you."

Griff looked unconvinced.

49

The Secret Mass Surveillance Plan

18th August 1999

by Matt Fulford.

Although the technology would take at least another decade to reach the levels capable of this amount of data surveillance, the intelligence seems to be a statement of intent by the powers in Government to create a state reminiscent of George Orwell's novel, *1984*.

GCHQ and MI6 are at the centre of a plan to put the UK population under mass surveillance. The story has been uncovered thanks to the covert efforts of an unnamed whistleblower named only as 'Pandora'.

Not since a seminal investigation into GCHQ in Time Out revealing its very existence in 1976 has there been a more shocking story focused on the intelligence community.

The top-secret documents received by Liberatus reveal a myriad of covert plots, the bulk of which relate directly to a plan to access streams of data including emails, phone calls, and information from the increasingly popular Internet. The plan, codenamed 'Oculus', involved tapping into the cables and the communications they carry that run from the Atlantic and through the Bude GCHQ station.

Full details inside...

50

Viktor Kozel took the call and heard the familiar rasping voice, altered by disguise software that made it sound like the man was speaking inside a tin bathtub.

"We're closing down 'Whisper Hunt' as there's been a leak. You know what you need to do. Please acknowledge."

There was a pause on the line before Viktor uttered a simple "Okay" and the Marquis disconnected. The kidnapper stood looking at his phone for a moment and swore to himself, before glancing at his watch. He would have to deal with this personally to ensure it was done right. It wasn't quite so much killing the woman, she knew what she was into, but having to pop the boy as well? That would be harder to wipe from his memory. He must be getting too old for this job.

It would have to be a couple of shots apiece, with a big fire to cover up the whole scene. Forensics could be paid off, pressure applied, and it would just be another tragedy in London hardly warranting a write up in the papers.

He ran through a mental checklist of the items needed as he climbed the stairs to the upper landing and then went up the spiral staircase that led to the secured room. After unlocking the door, he glanced in and saw them huddled in the corner of the sparse room wrapped in the duvet he had given them earlier. The heating had stopped working and the nights had been getting colder.

He felt bad having to kill them both but that was the order. Frank Bowen and the whistleblower had slipped through his fingers. That incident had been very unfortunate and Viktor surmised he would have to watch his back. The Marquis had expressed his dissatisfaction that he had lost them but that was all and the Russian was certain he'd want to punish him for that screw-up.

Now his gang had been wiped out and he was stuck with that paedophile, Yegor, who had to be brought in for the kidnapping.

No, he would finish the job, shoot the kid first and then Frank's bitch. After that, it would be a case of hunting down Frank Bowen for revenge, which was the least he could do for his fallen comrades. The second payments from the Marquis weren't going to happen now. At least he still had some of the money that should have gone to his men.

When this whole mess was over, he would go back to Mother Russia and work for the Chinese or his old employers. No more western intelligence agencies, they couldn't be trusted.

He took out his phone and began to type in a message to Bowen and then he pressed the send button. Was he already back in the UK? Most probably. And if he had any tradecraft skills left, he would be close to finding them. There wasn't much time.

Viktor studied the pathetic figures in the room and almost felt sorry for them. They were victims in a world they did not belong to. A world of spies, power-mad men, and covert plots. It was not his problem though, he had his orders. It was what he was been paid for. For now, though, he would give them one last meal. He had a heart after all.

"Do you want to eat? Food?" he asked gruffly.

Maria looked up at him with a fierce hatred Viktor had grown used to. If it had not been for Joe, she would probably have refused, but for his sake, she had been playing it calm and cool.

"Yes," she managed and the Russian closed the door behind him.

51

Frank and Griff arrived at the derelict house and scrambled over the door frame to the rear. Griff struggled and was not being particularly quiet about it but they were soon in the backyard. Frank took out a pair of pliers from his backpack and began unbolting the metal sheeting that he had peered through earlier. After removing all four bolts on one side, he was able to peel it back, opening up just enough space for them both to squeeze through.

Once inside, they checked the whole house to make sure they wouldn't get any nasty surprises. Apart from random debris and the smell of piss on the top floor, it wasn't in that bad a state. A few licks of paint, new windows, doors, kitchen, and bathroom and it would be perfectly habitable. It seemed such a waste.

They set up in the rear room that was probably once a dining area, making sure they were able to get a good view of the target house from their position. Some of the plasterboard had been ripped away from the walls and electrical wires hung from the ceiling.

Frank scanned the immediate area through his binoculars before focusing on the target house. As he had seen at the front door, most of the rear windows were all blanketed with curtains, pulled tightly closed.

On the ground floor, there was an extension that was probably the kitchen with a side rear door. Frank raised his night vision binoculars to the upper part of the house again and inspected a small skylight window built into the roof. It was shut tight and along the edge of the blackout blind, he noticed a faint light. Whether it was from a lamp or a stairs hallway light, Frank couldn't be sure. He took the glasses away from his eyes, passed them to Griff and assessed the gardens. It would only be a few metres to get across to the house. That wasn't the difficult part.

"Okay, you get a good view of the rear of the house from here. Just keep an eye out and text me if you see anything at all."

"No problem, Frank. That I can do!" Griff peered through the binoculars.

"Just like a real stake-out, huh? Bit of fieldwork beats staring at a screen all day, huh?"

"Hmm, I dunno. I like the comfort of the flickering screen. I'm in a warm place and there's all the Doritos and Cokes I could ever want. This place is dark, cold, and damp."

Frank felt the vibration of his Russian phone in his pocket. He whipped it out and saw it was a text message. The words on the screen chilled him to the bone.

"Seen the news, Frank? You fucked us and leaked the information...this little game is over for your family."

52

Frank had immediately tried to call the Russian back but only a disconnected, dead tone could be heard. Now he hung his head, taking shallow breathes as the danger hit home. They could be already dead...if not, then their time was very close. Brady had already published? It was too early! He couldn't believe what was happening.

"Frank?"

Griff was looking at him with concern. He was holding the night vision binoculars in his hand after looking over the target building.

"Give me those," he demanded and Griff quickly handed them over.

Frank scanned the terrace and once again stopped at the target house. It was quiet and most of the neighbours seemed to have gone to their beds.

"They're in immediate danger. I can't wait any longer," he said, rummaging around in his bag before pulling out the SIG Pro SP 2009 he had brought from the lock-up garage. He started to load up the chamber from the bullet case, his hand clearly shaking.

"Be careful. Just see if there's a way in there first. Don't make any stupid mistakes, Frank. You're angry now but that could cost you," reasoned Griff in a level voice. Frank nodded impatiently.

He knew the geek was right but there was no time anymore. He put the safety catch on the SIG Pro, tucked it into his belt, and checked his watch. 22:35 hours. Ideally, he needed to wait another few hours or so but that was never going to happen.

"Just keep your eyes on the house for me, could you, mate?"

"Sure, Frank. And if I see anything that you need to know about?"

"Text my phone."

He took the compact Nokia out of his pocket and double checked it was on silent. The last thing he wanted was some stupid ringtone blasting out as he crept up the stairs. Frank checked the hunter's knife in a pouch was securely attached to his belt on his rear and the ankle holster with the smaller knife was tightly fastened.

A minute later, Frank moved through the gardens in the darkness, pausing every few yards to check he hadn't been seen. Razor focused, nothing else in the world mattered now. He slipped over the last fence into the target's garden, checking every step before crouching against the wall.

As expected, the back door was well secured but Frank thought he could get the kitchen window open. He began working away at the handle, probing a piece of looped wire into the key lock to try to get some leverage. Suddenly a light went on behind the blind and Frank froze. He heard the noises of someone about to prepare food, the clanking of saucepans and then the low tone of voices. Two men speaking in Russian.

Frank lowered his hand from the lock and crouched back down with his back against the wall, his head turned to the kitchen window, listening carefully just to see if he could pick up any clues or information. His eyes rested on an old black bin that had been dumped in the garden. Across the gardens, he could see the dark shape of the derelict building set back in the row of houses. There was no sign that Griff was watching from the small gap in the bottom window. A light went off in one of the neighbouring rooms.

Suddenly, there was a clank of an unlocking back door and then a light squealing sound as it opened. Frank kept dead still but positioned himself to pounce up if needed. If they came out into the garden and looked directly to their left, he might well be seen, at which point, he would need to attack.

Instead, a bag of rubbish was thrown from the doorway towards the main collection of plastic bins in the garden. Whoever was doing the deed obviously didn't fancy coming out into the night. The bag clanked with the sound of glass and tins just several yards from where Frank was crouching. The door slammed shut again and he waited for the sound of the lock but it didn't come. Then he heard more clanking in the kitchen as if dinner was being served. There was a way in.

Frank took out his mobile and began texting Griff a simple message.

It was twenty minutes before the kitchen light dimmed and he chanced a quick look through the window. He could see through the kitchen doorway that led to a living room where the flicker of a television set lit the hallway in between. He checked his Nite MX10; it was just after 23:00. He had no idea if these guys would be going to bed, or whether one of them would be staying up to keep an eye out. He had to assume Maria and Joe were still alive, otherwise, they would surely have cleared out long ago? The thought also crossed his mind that it could be a trap. Lure him in, take him out. Perhaps they would be satisfied with his head only and let Joe and Maria go?

Move now or wait? There was no alternative. Was there another way? Something else he could have done?

Frank realised he was already losing his focus, the feeling of impatience overwhelming him now. Just to see their faces again; to know they were safe. It seemed right to go now; it was his instinct telling him.

He went through the plan in his head. Work out how many hostiles were in the house without detection and then find the room Maria and Joe were in as quickly as possible. Try to extract them without confrontation.

Without further hesitation, he moved around the corner towards the back door and slowly turned the handle, easing the door open by a few millimetres, listening hard for that squeak.

A sudden sound of rapid gunfire and an explosion burst from a television that spiked Frank's guard for a moment. He eased the door open further, taking full advantage of the noise cover, and slipped through the gap, closing the door behind himself. He moved slowly to the kitchen doorway, pausing for a moment. He moved a step to see if he could see more of the living room, which had an open door and clocked a pair of feet in socks crossed over each other. No shoes, obviously, they were not expecting any change in routine or surprises.

Frank moved carefully across the doorway and along a hallway that led to the stairs. Luckily, the floor was covered in thick carpet, which kept the sound down and he reached the steps and began climbing.

The television action scene suddenly came to a halt and there was a silence. Frank froze on the first few steps. The louder sound of an advert came on, blasting the advantage of a premium pet food. Voices of two men speaking in Russian began. Frank guessed they were discussing the film and then more worryingly, there was the sound of movement. Someone was hauling their ass out of the sofa and a shadow moved across the wall. A tall figure went into the hallway, obscured by shadow and went into the kitchen, flicking on the light.

Frank continued to move, slowly but surely until he was near the top. There was a door directly in front of him, which he had guessed from his earlier surveillance was the bathroom. A hallway ran back parallel to the stairs with several closed doors.

He was aware and ready in case anyone suddenly sprang out of one of the rooms, but his instinct told him there were only two in the house.

Behind the first door was indeed the bathroom. He assessed it for possible exit routes and checked the window. The drop outside was around thirty feet, probably okay for him but probably too far a drop for Maria and Joe.

Back in the hallway, moving back towards the front of the house, he spotted two doors and then spiral stairs leading to the top. Each room on the mid-level was empty. One had a distinct smell of tobacco with an unmade bed and a pile of unwashed clothes. The window was facing the rear with tightly closed curtains. He slowly moved the curtain open by about a centimetre but saw very little in the darkness.

In the second room, it appeared cleaner but still lived in and Frank crept across the carpet to check the window, again, slowly edging the curtain open. The window looked out onto the street and Frank decided he preferred getting out via the rear and left the room. The sound of the television receded as Frank crept up the spiral staircase leading to the attic level. When he reached the top, there was a single door, reinforced with a metal frame and panels that, even in the gloom, looked like it was a formidable obstacle. He pressed his ear against it and focused hard on any sign of movement. There was none that he could hear.

CHAPTER 52

A sound of footsteps arriving at the landing below made Frank hold his breath and then he heard them slowly climb the metal spiral staircase towards him. Frank moved back into the alcove and crouched, making himself still in the shadow opposite the door.

A figure appeared, easily six and a half feet tall with short black hair and carrying a tray with a metallic pot of what smelled like stew. He bent his considerable bulk down to place the pot on the ground as he searched for his keys.

Frank went through the options in his head, quickly assessing how to overcome this piece of shit. The knife was one but the guy was big and if he got it wrong, it would make him yell out. It had to be kept quiet, even with the television blaring on the ground floor. A clean cut on the vocal cords would be the only way but Frank would need to jump to get that high, could he really be that accurate?

Once the big man had his keys out, had unlocked and opened the door, Frank made his move. He pounced onto the man's back, his right arm gripping the kidnapper's throat in a rear naked strangle. Both men fell into the room, spilling the stew pot and Frank kept squeezing his bicep and forearm as hard as he could against the Russian's carotid arteries. He croaked like a frog, bucking and struggling, reaching for Frank and trying to pull him off. With the blood pressure dropping from his head, his body began to shut down from lack of oxygen. After ten long seconds, the bulk of the kidnapper suddenly relaxed as he fell unconscious, his chest rising and falling as he breathed heavily.

Frank rolled onto the floor and looked up to see the shocked faces of Maria and Joe staring back at him. He got to his feet and went over to them. For a moment, it seemed like they weren't going to acknowledge it was him as if he was an intruder and then their faces changed to relief.

"Frank?"

He leaned down and put his arms around them both.

"Is he dead?" Maria added.

"He'll live, but you have to do exactly as I say, okay? How many are in the house, do you know?"

"I think it was just two. All we've ever seen is this man and another with the mohawk."

"That'll be my friend, Viktor," said Frank. He wasn't smiling.

"What's the plan?" asked Maria. Frank noticed a calm but determined expression fall over her face, one that he hadn't seen since they were on the run from a Chinese assassin in Asia.

Frank looked at his Nite MX10 watch. "We get out of here, just wait."

Frank grabbed the man's keys and began to go through them, looking for the one to their door. He searched his pockets but there was no weapon.

"Right, okay. We need to get down a level and get out the back across the gardens. Be as quiet as you can. I'll check first."

Frank locked the big man in the room while Maria and Joe waited just outside it and then paused at the top of the landing, listening intently. He signalled them to stay put and descended the spiral stairwell, careful to be light-footed. There was still the faint drone of the television on the ground floor but no other sound.

Suddenly, a figure appeared in the hallway below. Where the hell had he come from? It was Kozel the Kobra.

"Yegor?" the Russian shouted upwards and immediately began to climb the spiral stairs. Frank reached for his gun but it was gone! There was no time. Frank had the height advantage and the fact he hadn't seen him yet.

He dived head first. The Russian, instinctively sensing the danger, curled up, bracing for the impact. Their bodies collided and fell heavily into the hallway, Frank's weight driving through the Russian before he rolled clear. Both men quickly jumped up, facing each other. Frank's eyes darted to his opponent's right hand and the blade he held within it.

"Why don't you have a go, Frank?" baited the Russian. "All that pent-up steam, waiting to be released."

Frank already with his right arm slightly behind him moved slowly, freeing the knife from the holster.

"Where are your friends, Viktor Kozel?"

The faintest hint of surprise flashed across his eyes at his real name being mentioned and then he smiled and nodded.

"Very good, Frank."

"Oh, yeah, they're just corpses in a Cuban warehouse now, already burning in hell, aren't they?" said Frank with as much bitter venom in his voice as possible. The knife eased slowly out of the pouch and Frank held it inversely in his palm. There was a rush of anger in the Russian's eyes before he moved forward suddenly, slashing out with his blade at Frank's chest. Jumping backwards, Frank kept clear of the attack and as the knife passed by, Frank drove his hidden blade across the Russian's forearm. The strike was deep. Victor looked surprised and stood backwards quickly. The blood was running freely from the wound, down his hand and dripping off his fingers, where it quickly pooled on the floor. He still held his weapon tight; these Russians were something else.

Kozel, enraged, struck out with his injured knife hand. Frank held up both hands instinctively, blocking with his own knife but the impact came from the Russian's shoulder in his chest as he level dropped and ran at him. Frank was thrown against the hard wall, the wind driven from his lungs. Dropping his knife onto the ground with a clang, he slumped to the floor, winded and gasping for breath.

Viktor grabbed his shoulders, thrusting a knee into Frank's chest. The impact felt like a cattle truck slamming against his lungs. He coughed and choked, hardly finding the air he so badly needed. Catching sight of the blade on the floor Frank grabbed it with his left hand but the Russian quickly stamped down, crushing his knuckles with his boot. Frank grimaced as the boot dragged the blade away from him and kicked it out of reach.

"Looks like I'll be getting sweet revenge for my comrades, Frank. Then I'll have the pleasure of blowing out the brains of your family. No one will ever avenge them, never."

Frank lifted his head up and glared at the kidnapper. His right hand slowly slipped out the blade he had packed on his ankle at the lockup. His eyes looked beyond the Russian at the spiral stairs behind him. "Maria," he whispered.

Viktor turned to the empty stairwell. It was just enough of a distraction. Frank lunged with the knife, stabbing the Russian just below the groin in his inside leg and with a violent twist, turned the blade before pulling it back out. Blood spewed from the injury; Frank had hit the femoral artery.

Instantly, Frank reached over and grabbed the Russian's knife hand. Lunging forward, Frank wrapped his arm around Viktor's calf and drove his weight into his leg. The blood streamed onto Frank as he brought him crashing to the floor. Kozel cried out in agony, his hands desperately trying to grab at Frank's head but the strength was draining out of him, second by second.

At that moment, Maria did actually appear, her face transfixed with horror as she saw the father of her child covered in blood.

Frank held his hand up as if to say he was okay. "It's all right, his blood!" he managed to gasp before standing up, stepping back from the Russian who was now attempting to hold his wound, breathing in short gasps, eyes wide with fear. Maria and Frank watched him, transfixed as his life ebbed away and then the gasping stopped, his eyes staring straight ahead.

Frank leaned over the body to check his pulse and nodded at Maria, confirming what he already knew.

"Better get a towel to cover him," he said and Maria came back from the hallway bathroom and threw it over the body as best she could. "It's all right, Joe," she shouted.

Soon, a light footfall came down the staircase and the boy stood looking at the Russian man in fascination.

"Everything's okay, Joe," Maria held out her hand for him but Joe stood as if fixed to the spot looking at the covered corpse.

"Yes, everything's okay – you're safe now," Frank added.

Joe nodded and went to his father. He held the SIG pistol in his hand and held it out for his father.

"It was on the floor. When you were fighting...," he said.

Frank took the weapon and put back in his belt. He ruffled Joe's hair and held him close against him.

"Good man. Jesus, thank God you're alright, Joe."

It hit him in that moment how close he came to losing him.

"I'm all good, Dad," Joe said. He leaned down and gave his son a hug and then he held his shoulders, facing him.

"You're the bravest kid I have ever known and I mean that. Now you have to do exactly as I say and we're going to get out of here, okay?"

Joe looked at his mother and back at his dad before nodding, his face fixed and calm, as if he had every confidence that he was now safe.

"I need to check the coast is clear and then let's get out of here." Maria and Joe nodded as they moved along to the top of the stairs as Frank descended to the ground floor.

Soon enough, he was ushering them across the gardens to safety where Griff waited for them.

53

Nigel Harrison had already made the decision, but he still tidied up around the flat, putting items back in place and tearing up old letters. The sink needed cleaning, it hadn't been done for a while and then once he had started spraying bleach cleaner and scrubbing, the cooker and the other kitchen surfaces beckoned. It took his churning mind off the inevitable and distracted him, if only for a while.

A gust of wind rattled the kitchen window and for a second, Nigel wondered if he should change his mind but then dismissed his own cowardice. Because that was what it was. *Looking for loopholes already, Nigel? Trying to find a way out?* No, he was determined to see it through now. No excuses.

It was the method that concerned him. Slitting his wrists didn't sound appealing – he couldn't imagine how anyone could do that? Although they say that you just drift away into the oblivion, don't they?

A bullet in the head? Quick, certainly. Probably the fastest method. It would be over before he knew it, just a squeeze of the trigger. But it could go wrong. A bullet in the wrong place might leave him alive but paralysed or a dribbling vegetable. There would be no control after that. He'd be strapped to a wheelchair, fed by a nurse for the rest of his life. Besides, getting a gun would not be straightforward.

Hanging by rope? It would be easier to arrange, but he couldn't stand the idea of the strangulation. The gripping, tight squeeze on the throat made him feel uneasy.

No, it would be an overdose of pills, already purchased over the previous few weeks from separate pharmacies to avoid any suspicion and then squirrelled away until he was sure he had enough to do the job.

He thought about how he had let down John Rhodes, a man who had given him an opportunity that no one else would ever have given him. And the prospect of being framed for the child porn still hung over him like a guillotine – that was not something he was willing to live with, never in a million years. They would never stop, he knew that now. He was owned by them and he believed every single word when they told him that they would find him, no matter where he ran.

The faces of Maria and her son, Joe, appeared in his mind. He had helped seal their fate, leading the wolves to their door. What a creep. Now they were almost certainly rotting in a hole somewhere if they were still alive.

And Mother.

He wanted to join her in death, escaping the blanketing remorse, guilt, and hopelessness that had been smothering him since this whole bloody episode had begun.

Nigel switched off the electricity at the mains and went into the dark bedroom.

54

Frank was sitting down at the dining table in the house at Barnes Bridge as a gentle patter of light rain mottled the window that faced the narrow stretch of the Thames. He put down the mug of tea he was cradling and cracked his knuckles; still brooding after reeling from anger at the timing of the *Liberatus* revelations. He had told Marcus to hold off for three days, hadn't he? It had very nearly put Maria and Joe on a collision course with death and he hadn't brought himself to tell Maria about that.

He needed to speak to Marcus Brady.

Laughter from the children running around the house echoed through the corridor as Maria finished a phone call on her Nokia mobile and turned to the breakfast bar to finish the sandwiches she was making. Rosie was somewhere in another part of the house, giving Frank and Maria some space.

The radio was on in the background and they both heard the familiar pips of the news.

"Can you turn it up a bit?" Frank asked. Maria turned up the volume and they both listened.

A parliamentary investigative enquiry has been announced, to be headed by Leo Smith, M.P. for Braintree, into the 'Pandora revelations' on the recent GCHQ spying scandal. Smith promised a thorough investigation into the matter but would not comment on whether GCHQ Director, David Devlin, should resign.

This follows several mainstream newspapers picking up the story amid calls for the resignation of the top brass at GCHQ and MI6 by privacy campaigners. Public demonstrations have also been adding to the pressure and Smith added that it "threw open the question whether GCHQ had violated human rights legislation."

In other news...

Frank nodded and Maria switched off the radio.

"So, John Rhodes nearly died in a car accident. He's at St. Thomas' Hospital in intensive care and I'd really like to go and see him, Frank."

"It's not safe," he said, almost monotone.

"The Russians who kidnapped us are all dead, aren't they?"

"I just think we should be careful." He softened his voice, appreciating that she was alive and with him, pottering around the kitchen. It could have been so different.

"And while we're over there, I want to check on Nigel Harrison. He was used by them but I don't believe for a second he was overtly on their side," she continued.

"For God's sake!" Frank was exasperated. "We can't go hairing around London right now."

Maria turned to him.

"When is it ever going to be over? We need to take control. The story. This Pandora thing is going to press right now. The heat will be too much. They can't act once it's out."

"You don't know that!"

Maria was determined. Frank knew she wouldn't back down and exhaled slowly with exasperation. He was turning events over in his mind, trying to make sense out of it all. He had to admit to himself that it would be good to hear exactly what had happened from Rhodes.

"How is Rhodes? Is he conscious?" he asked, more calmly now.

"I spoke to Marcus. He's in and out of consciousness. Many broken bones but he'll survive." she said quietly. "He is very lucky to be alive apparently."

Frank thought for a moment, his eyes wandering back out at the rain.

"I'd like to speak with Marcus. And Nigel Harrison, the guy who you worked with who turned up with one of the Russians. You think he was forced into it?"

Maria came and placed the plate of finished sandwiches on the dining table and sat down opposite Frank, who grabbed one and began to wolf it down hungrily.

"Yes, he was scared, I could tell. They had something on him. He even said John was dead to get access to our flat. An odd man, but really completely harmless. He..." She stopped and shook her head, unable to fathom what had happened. She looked at Frank, her eyes telling him she wanted to do this.

"If we go, is it safe here? Leaving the kids?" he asked.

"You took care of the Russians, Frank, remember?"

It wasn't them he was worried about. It was whoever had hired them and lay waiting behind the curtain.

A woman, looking harassed with life in general, opened the main door of the flats just as Frank and Maria were looking for Nigel's name on the buzzers without success.

"Nigel Harrison? Do you know which flat he's in?" Maria asked quickly before she walked on. The woman, in her 50s with tightly permed hair, glanced at them and jolted her head.

"Top floor, luv. Number nine. He's a bit of a funny one. Go see for yourself." She held the door for them and they nodded their thanks and climbed the stairs to the top floor, their footfalls silent on the thick carpet. It was a well-maintained house that still held the faint smell of paint. They stopped at the dark pine door of Flat nine and Maria rapped it with her knuckles and then pressed her ear against it, listening carefully. She looked concerned.

"Can you kick it down?"

Frank looked puzzled and glanced around. "Kick it down? He's obviously out, Maria."

She knocked again. "Nigel? It's Maria. Are you in there?"

She took out her mobile and pressed it to her ear. Within a few seconds, they both heard the gentle chirping of a ring tone from inside the flat.

No answer.

Then they heard footsteps slowly coming up the stairs and an Indian man in his 50s appeared, ashen faced with swept back grey hair. He was fumbling through a huge bunch of keys before looking up to see the couple standing on the landing.

"Can I help you? I'm the landlord."

"Yes. We're looking for Nigel Harrison, a bit worried about him. I'm a work colleague," said Maria. "He hasn't been seen for a quite a while."

The landlord knocked on the door and continued to rummage through his keys.

"We've been knocking for a minute or so," said Frank.

The landlord unlocked the door and they entered the flat. "Hello?" their voices asked.

No answer.

Frank checked the bathroom, which was the first off the hallway and the others went into the main living room that had a kitchenette partition inside. He then went through the door opposite and saw what looked like a body lying on the bed in the gloomy room.

"Nigel?"

He went over to the window and pulled up the blind, flooding the room with much needed light. A vomit trail came from the mouth and a dried pool of it had conjuled onto the bed sheet.

"In here!" he shouted to the others before checking on Harrison but Frank already knew he was dead. He checked his pulse, two fingers on his wrist, and could feel nothing. The skin was cold.

Maria and the landlord came into the bedroom, concern etched on their faces. Frank caught Maria's eye and shook his head. He double-checked the pulse and then stepped back.

"I'm really sorry but he's passed on."

55

Maria was shocked but remained calm as Frank drove to the hospital. They had waited for an ambulance to confirm what they already knew and then slipped away before there were any awkward questions. Frank was still feeling exposed and concerned about what lay ahead.

They walked into the busy reception at St. Thomas' Hospital and asked a stressed looking young woman behind the desk where John Rhodes was. She tapped on the keyboard and narrowed her eyes at the screen. She looked up at them. "Are you relatives?"

"Work colleague."

She smiled thinly and gestured towards a row of red plastic seats. "Could you wait and I'll get the doctor."

"Is something wrong?"

"The doctor will explain further," she replied quickly and then looked back down at her monitor.

"That doesn't sound good," Maria said quietly to Frank.

They sat down, Maria holding onto Frank's hand tightly. The day was taking a very unreal turn for her. Then a petite nurse in her mid-30s with her hair tied into a bun appeared before them.

"Mr. Bowen and Ms. Chapman. You're associates of John Rhodes, I believe?"

"Er, yes, that is correct," said Maria.

"Please come with me," she said and began to walk along a corridor, towards the back of the hospital. They followed her through double doors and into another stark walkway bleached by light from florescent tubes on the ceiling until they were at a fire exit, which she pushed open.

Frank and Maria looked at her quizzically.

"What's going on?" asked Frank, clearly wary.

"It's okay, Marcus is out here," the nurse said.

They walked along an enclosed path and then turned into a car park where they immediately saw Marcus, standing in front of a dark BMW.

"Marcus, what the hell is going on?" asked Maria.

"I'm taking you to see John. We'll come back and get your car later if that's alright?"

They weren't really in a position to argue and the thought of getting some answers prevented them asking anymore. Frank glared at him, another thought at the forefront of his mind.

They all got into the vehicle, Frank in the front passenger seat and Maria behind as the nurse returned to the hospital.

Frank turned to Marcus.

"So what the fuck happened to our agreement?" he said, his voice low and menacing.

"Frank?" Maria said in surprise from behind them.

Frank ignored her and continued staring hard at Marcus. "Three days! Not two. Fucking three!"

Marcus shook his head in realisation. "Oh, shit...I'm sorry. There were complications...a lot of pressure. We got raided..."

Maria grabbed at Frank's shoulder and shook it.

"Frank! Explain what's going on."

Frank turned his head slightly.

"They published before I was ready to get you out. We agreed to wait three days. It's a miracle everything turned out okay but the Russians were going to kill you and Joe after your crowd..." He threw a hand up toward Marcus. "...was so hell-bent on publishing!"

Marcus turned back to face Maria.

"Maria, I'm so sorry. The police raided our offices, tearing the place apart, looking for the information. Our staff were harassed and followed. We had to get to get it out there."

Maria shook her head as if to dismiss the apology.

"Maria? They were going to kill you and Joe, because of this bloody story!" Frank shouted, turning fully to face her.

"I think they were going to kill us anyway, Frank."

Frank, fighting himself to keep his temper from exploding, turned to look out of the window. *They were safe, that was all that mattered,* he kept telling himself, over and over. *They were safe.*

"Can we fucking go?" he said.

Thirty minutes later, after a silent journey, Marcus, Frank, and Maria were standing next to a bed upstairs at the Epsom cottage where Marcus explained, Fulford had hidden himself during the writing of the GCHQ revelations for the Liberatus news outlets.

She had been taken aback by John Rhode's appearance. He looked thinner, a dark purple and yellow bruise covered his cheekbone and eye, and a bandage was wrapped around his forehead. His eyes were closed and he was perfectly still, the gentle rise of his chest, monitored by a heart rate machine next to his bed, the only clue that he was still alive.

"So they let him out? Has he been conscious?"

Another nurse with short blonde hair and an officious manner came into the room, looking at the visitors with slight disapproval.

"Yes, he has been awake a few times. Karen here says it's just a case of careful nursing, nutrition, and plenty of time, isn't that right, Karen?"

The nurse nodded and pushed past Frank to check on the monitor and drip.

"It's one step at a time at this stage. He needs complete rest and no distractions," she said, making space around the bed so the visitors had to step back as she began to replace the drip.

Marcus looked at Frank and Maria and gestured silently with a nod of the head to leave and they climbed down the creaky stairs to the living room.

There was a copy of *Liberatus News* on the dining table and Maria picked it up. The headline of the small tabloid-sized newspaper read: 'The Secret Spy Programme Revealed.' Maria started reading the cover and then opened it up and spread it out on the tabletop. It was extensive coverage that dominated the paper's contents.

"You and Matt did a great job," Maria said, attempting to disperse the tension between Frank and Marcus.

Marcus nodded but he was looking at Frank. "It's just the tip of the iceberg. It'll run for some time. There's a lot more to come out yet though," He paused before adding, "Thanks to Sarah."

Maria looked up from the paper at Marcus and then turned to Frank questioningly. "Sarah?" There was a pause as both men realised she had not yet been privy to Sarah Edwards' involvement.

"She was the whistleblower who started all this trouble," Frank gestured once again with his hand at the spread out newspaper. "She revealed the secrets and was the one I had to track in Cuba." Maria glared at him for a moment before Marcus slowly sat down with them at the table, picking up the thread.

"Sarah Edwards is the unnamed source for the stories we're

running. She was part of our group, Liberatus. She has been with us from the beginning and John was supposed to meet her in Cuba but..."

"...he had an accident." Frank finished the sentence.

"Where is she now then?"

"Safe...," Frank said. "But she wanted the authorities and anyone else to think she was dead. It was her request."

Marcus looked at Frank in surprise and then his face changed to realisation.

"Ahh, you didn't trust me," he said.

"I did," said Frank. "But not your offices. Anyone could have been listening."

56

It was early evening when they heard the noise from upstairs, like a thud. The nurse had driven to Epsom to get some supplies as Frank, Maria, and Marcus drank tea in the room below.

"He's awake?" asked Maria to no one in particular. Frank and Marcus were already standing up. When they reached the room, John was reaching from his bed as he tried to stretch for a mug that had fallen off his table and onto the floor.

"Hey," said Maria. "How are you doing, John?" She instantly leaned over and picked up the mug with one hand and gently pushed back his arm. He slumped back onto the bed in relief and gave Maria a faint smile.

The others came in and gathered around the bed, pulling up chairs, Marcus nearest to him on the far side of the bed and Frank at the end.

"How are you feeling, John?" asked Marcus.

"Could be better," he wheezed. The voice was faint but it was obvious he was mentally intact and still his old self.

"Do you want anything?" asked Maria, who cast an eye over his drip.

John flapped a hand in dismissal, a mask of tiredness falling across his face.

"Tell me what is going on?" he asked, his voice so low, the others leaned in slightly to make out his words.

Marcus cleared his throat.

"They tried to kill you, John. You were in the car, driving back from Braintree in Essex. Do you remember?"

Rhodes shook his head.

"We got the information from your contact inside GCHQ. There's gold in those files and we've been flat out publishing as quickly as we can. Operation Oculus...a massive surveillance programme. There's other damaging revelations in there, too. We're causing big waves in the establishment. I'll give you the full details later but it's big." Marcus paused as if to reign in his enthusiasm.

John leaned his head and looked at Marcus, a grin appearing on his pale face.

"That's fantastic. Good work, Marcus. The girl?"

"She decided to stay in Cuba...for the time being. It's probably safer for now."

Rhodes turned to the window, to the view of a tree in the dusk light. "I hope we can help her one day," he said weakly.

57

Liberatus News. 12th September

Shocking Oculus Files Reveal Covert Assassination Programme

Recent documents have revealed a secret assassination programme led by a group, as yet unnamed, associated with MI6. The documents, unrelated to the Oculus surveillance programme, detail how a small Cabal within the intelligence community unleashed what can only be described as a murder policy on deemed enemies and threats to their interests.

More inside...

13th September

Intel Chiefs Resign

Braithwaite and Devlin resign as agencies look to clean up acts amid mass political fallout following the breaking of the story, led by Liberatus.

Following the Oculus revelations, both heads of MI6 and GCHQ resigned yesterday as the political fallout intensified and further revelations also indicated that the planned data fishing was to be shared with America's National Security Agency, who is also thought to have a similar surveillance programme at an advanced stage.

More inside...

58

Frank arrived at Hyde Park and speaker's corner and walked towards the gathered crowd as a young woman was getting into full swing with her speech. From what he could hear, she was on the topic of the recent revelations concerning surveillance and the intelligence services role in it. There were murmurs of approval from the listeners as anger poured through her words.

Frank spotted the familiar reddish hair in the crowd and eased towards Carl.

"Enjoying the speech?"

"It's very topical and no one's talking about anything else at the moment," Carl replied.

Both men started to walk along the pathway towards Tyburn Brook and the Serpentine Lake in the centre of the Park, the pronounced voice fading behind them until only gusts of wind carried the odd word of the woman's speech.

"Everyone is safe then?" asked Carl.

"My family, you mean? Yes, they're safe."

"That's great, a relief."

Carl nodded and took out a stick of gum, offering one to Frank, who shook his head, before rolling one up and popping it into his mouth.

"Bad for your digestion," said Frank almost as an afterthought. "So why did you release me?" he asked.

"Believe me, I'm in a world of trouble for doing so but thanks to your friends at Liberatus breaking this story it's turning into a huge political scandal. There's enough firefighting going on for them not to be focused on me right now. Devlin stood down and was then arrested, Braithwaite is probably next..." He paused. A group of children were shouting and laughing, running through the grass past them.

"I wanted you to have a chance of getting Maria and Joe back. Why do you think I had you dropped off in Camberwell? I knew you had a lock-up around there somewhere but I wasn't in a position to help you directly and I'm sorry about that. We're still friends after all."

"Are we? There isn't really such a thing in this business, is there?"

Carl thought about that for a second. "Maybe not."

"So, this is what I have discovered. Devlin used information that I gave to him to target your team. He was directing the mercenary Russians as a clean-up operation. He wanted the stolen information and Edwards destroyed."

It confirmed what Frank had long suspected although he had not realised the extent of Devlin's involvement.

Carl continued. "Devlin ordered them to leave Russian made equipment in the warehouse in Havana, just to throw up false scents. It would confuse the Cuban authorities, who would wonder what the hell their allies were up to. Devlin could then claim that their team had been intercepted by the Russians or an unknown entity. It wouldn't make him look very good, of course, but he didn't care. His main objective was to silence Edwards and get the data she took...or just destroy both."

"So the safe houses were comprised because you passed on the details directly to Devlin?" Frank interjected.

Carl avoided Frank's glaring stare and nodded slowly.

"There was no way I could know the top level of the company was compromised."

Frank shook his head in disbelief.

"Unbelievable! Unbelievable. Bloody hell, Carl."

Carl ploughed on. "To make it seem like a genuine Russian FSB mission, he had them wipe out your team and then kidnap Maria and your kid to bring you out of the woodwork."

"A big fucking mess," Frank spat.

They had reached a snack hut that stood next to the brook, water rushing by, and beyond in the haze stood the grey jutting buildings of London. They ordered a couple of coffees and strolled along the bank.

"The Rhodes crash, it was a warning," said Carl.

"A murder attempt, you mean."

"You know how this all works, Frank."

"Like Nigel Harrison."

Carl gave Frank a sideways glance. "Nigel Harrison?"

"He sold out Rhodes or gave some information about his movement. But he had been pressured, blackmailed. Do you know anything about that, Carl? I assume you know he committed suicide."

"No, I...didn't know that."

Frank had a feeling that Carl was lying, he had known him too long. At that moment, Frank wasn't sure if Carl was friend or foe.

"Did your people get to Harrison, did they try to kill Rhodes?"

Carl stopped walking and Frank turned to face him.

"My people? Frank, you need to choose which side of the line you're on because you're way over it right now. This is your ex-employers we're talking about; your allegiance to the government and the crown. Leaking those state secrets is treason!"

Frank jerked a finger at Carl's chest as he made a face of disgust. "Our employer sent in a mercenary gang of Russians who ambushed and killed my colleagues. Our bloody employer then kidnapped my family. Why are you defending that? By the way, I think I have a case for a lawsuit, Carl."

Carl sniggered and shook his head.

"Look, I understand the shit you went through. You've forgotten that your contract forbids any legal action. But the treason...well, maybe they'll let it slide."

"An apology, then?"

Carl shook his head and pushed past him. Frank turned to follow. A couple passed them by and they stayed silent for a while. A family of ducks made their way past them towards an old man throwing bread in the water.

"Piper and Greene were my people, too, mate. I never met Brull but he was a major asset, a good operator."

Frank nodded. "I know, he was a legend. I liked him. We could've been friends."

"Now tell me honestly what happened out there and I'll tell you about Rhodes and Harrison but it has to stay between us, Frank."

Frank held out his arms in a defensive manner. "Sure, it can stay between us, but don't forget I saw Greene killed in front of my eyes and I tried to save Piper's life. I was the one who was there, Carl."

They continued to walk along the edge of the Serpentine Lake.

"We're getting nowhere. I answered all the questions about Cuba in your charming little basement room. Yes, I took off with Sarah; the circumstances changed slightly with the Russian mercenary team bouncing in. They wanted to kill me and Edwards. I was doing my best to save her," said Frank.

"And she's definitely dead?"

"What else do you want me to say? Like I told you at your interview, I heard from reliable sources that she was dead." Frank re-affirmed the lie. He didn't feel guilty about it at all. He was protecting her.

Carl seemed to accept it and blew on the stream from his black coffee for a moment, took a sip, and stared off across the park.

"It's ironic. At any other time, I'd be the one getting the boot but as Liberatus named Devlin, he had to step down. Prison is around the corner for him but I get to keep my job...for now."

Frank began to walk away, discarding his coffee cup. "I'm so glad for you. Goodbye, Carl."

"I helped you, Frank, remember? I released you and gave you a chance to save Maria and Joe. Don't forget that."

Frank Bowen kept walking past the trees, the milling crowd at speaker's corner, and disappeared into the thronging city.

It felt like the world was changing, darker elements taking an increasing hold and Frank wasn't sure if he could be a part of it any longer. He had a family that he nearly lost – he had to keep them safe. The question that hung over him as he walked through the city streets towards home: should he actually be on the other side of the line? Should he fight for those who railed against freedom, disguising themselves as the establishment?

Or should he join Liberatus?

Authors Note

Pandora Red, the Frank Bowen follow up to False Flag, has been a long time coming. It started life in July 2013 and has been a difficult book to write. Why? I'm not so sure but it was research intensive and along with a few personal life interruptions, Pandora just took a lot longer than I hoped it would.

Firstly there were major changes in the plot, characters dropped (goodbye Sergio) and others re-aligned. As the story developed and after really useful feedback from the editor, Cate Hogan I had to strengthen the difference between the official G13 mission and the mercenaries hired by Devlin who had more sinister plans for the whistleblower, Sarah Edwards (Codenamed: Pandora) than extradition.

After discussions between myself and collaborative partner, Jay Newton we looked at working in some changes. We made Frank and his associates work a lot harder to find the location of Pandora, whereas originally they were handed the info on a platter. That involved writing a whole new sequence of scenes and re-jigging a lot of other sections which in turn pushed the release date back two months but has resulted in a much stronger book. It's amazing what fresh eyes will do and that's precisely why we are looking to build up our beta reader core group.

So, as you've read the story takes place eight years after the False Flag. Bowen has joined MI6 and has been through several years of training in surveillance and combat as well as having live mission experience. The intermittent Frank Bowen years between False Flag (1991) and Pandora Red (1999) will probably be covered by a short story or novella series which is shaping up as I write this.

Will there be a full third Frank Bowen book? Yes, I'm on it! Look out for 'Ghost Order' in 2018/19. The Frank Bowen series are prequel books to what is coming: a pretty ambitious project set in the same world called Dark Paradigm.

I very much hope you enjoyed the read and please do leave a review on the platform where you purchased this. It means so much to receive feedback. Thanks!

Jay Tinsiano

Also Available

False Flag by Jay Tinsiano. (Frank Bowen #1)

ISBN: 978-1-9997232-2-4

1991: A plan to destabilise Hong Kong is emerging; the key players are being put into place, the wheels are in motion and innocent people will die.

Frank Bowen is a Londoner on holiday in tropical Thailand. Half drunk and strapped for cash, he's the perfect bait for a political plot that will leave him running for his life, with nowhere to turn.

An international conspiracy thriller by Jay Tinsiano, False Flag spans South-east Asia, with twists and turns that leave every character in question.

White Horse by Jay Tinsiano and Jay Newton. (Dark Paradigm #1)

ISBN: 978-1-9997232-1-7

Half a world away in Spain and running from his past, a Los Angeles gangster unwittingly takes a train that's headed straight into a terrorist attack. He survives only to face an even deadlier threat.

On that same train: a virologist with clues to a deadly epidemic. Did his secrets die with him in the strike?

Raging in the aftermath, a foul-tempered police chief with a daughter caught in the attack thirsts for revenge. But against whom?

An orphan child without a name disappears down a dark, illegal CIA mind-control programme. Now trained in the ways of death, he prepares to do his master's twisted bidding.

From its first pages, the relentless techno-thriller White Horse drops you with a thunderclap in the middle of these colliding worlds. This tale of global conspiracy that threatens humanity itself will keep you guessing whether anyone can survive.

Red Horse by Jay Tinsiano and Jay Newton. (Dark Paradigm #2)

ISBN: 978-1-9997232-4-8

Haleema Sheraz, a cyber hacker for the Iranian government, discovers her father has gone missing. Frustrated at the lack of urgency from the police, she investigates and soon reveals a kidnapping network that spans back to Operation Paperclip in World War II.

Meanwhile, her brothers join an ISIS-inspired uprising that is wreaking havoc inside Iran, and finding her father quickly becomes a mission to save her family.

Joe Bowen and Hugo Reese continue to prepare Liberatus for a wider global struggle and find themselves called to help one of their own secret assets; Sirus aka Haleema Sheraz.

Soon they will all be thrust into the battle zone and their lives will change irreversibly in this epic story of bitter struggle against the backdrop of total war.

For more information on the full catalogue visit: ***www.jaytinsiano.com***

www.ingramcontent.com/pod-product-compliance
Lightning Source LLC
Chambersburg PA
CBHW061613190726
48288CB00007B/2307

* 9 7 8 1 9 9 9 7 2 3 2 3 1 *